D0935423

OVER MY DEAD BODY

Recent Titles by Claire Lorrimer from Severn House

BENEATH THE SUN
CONNIE'S DAUGHTER
THE FAITHFUL HEART
FOR ALWAYS
NEVER SAY GOODBYE
AN OPEN DOOR
THE RECKONING
THE RELENTLESS STORM
THE REUNION
THE SEARCH FOR LOVE
SECOND CHANCE
SECRET OF QUARRY HOUSE
THE SHADOW FALLS
A VOICE IN THE DARK
THE WOVEN THREAD

OVER MY DEAD BODY

Claire Lorrimer

This first world edition published in Great Britain 2003 by
SEVERN HOUSE PUBLISHERS LTD of
9–15 High Street, Sutton, Surrey SM1 1DF.
This first world edition published in the USA 2003 by
SEVERN HOUSE PUBLISHERS INC of
595 Madison Avenue, New York, N.Y. 10022.

Copyright © 2003 by Claire Lorrimer.
All rights reserved.
The moral right of the author has been asserted.

British Library Cataloguing in Publication Data

Lorrimer, Claire, 1921-
    Over my dead body
    1.   Detective and mystery stories
    I.   Title
    823.9'14 [F]

ISBN 0-7278-5985-4

Except where actual historical events and characters are being
described for the storyline of this novel, all situations in this
publication are fictitious and any resemblance to living persons
is purely coincidental.

Typeset by Palimpsest Book Production Ltd.,
Polmont, Stirlingshire, Scotland.
Printed and bound in Great Britain by
MPG Books Ltd., Bodmin, Cornwall.

For Emily, Jemma and Polly
with love

Acknowledgements

Most of all I would like to thank my secretary, friend and neighbour, Pennie Scott for her continued back-up, enthusiasm and many helpful suggestions. I would also like to thank Mel Hack for his editorial comments; Bruce Chater for advice on legal matters; Mary Robinson for so many useful bits of information, and by no means least, Edwin Buckhalter for his continued support and encouragement to attempt this new genre.

Finally, I want to thank my neighbours for not objecting to the use of our private lane as a skeleton for this story; and to reassure them before our next Lane Meeting that the characters are entirely imaginary.

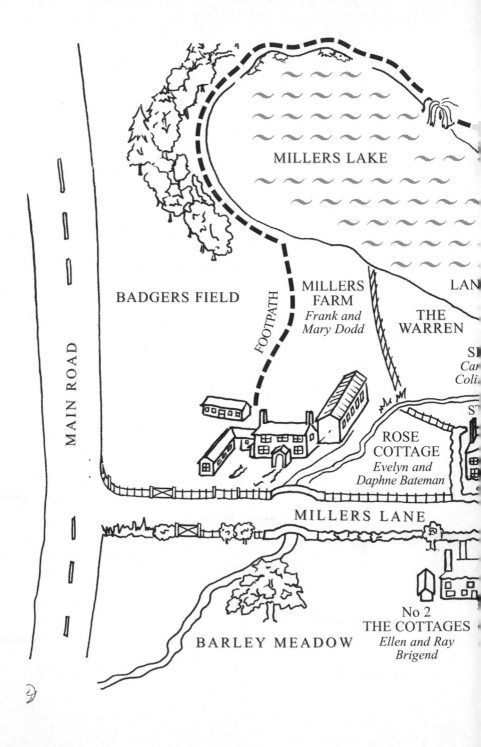

MILLERS LAKE

BADGERS FIELD

FOOTPATH

MILLERS
FARM
*Frank and
Mary Dodd*

LAN

THE
WARREN

S
Car
Coli

S

ROSE
COTTAGE
*Evelyn and
Daphne Bateman*

MAIN ROAD

MILLERS LANE

No 2
THE COTTAGES
*Ellen and Ray
Brigend*

BARLEY MEADOW

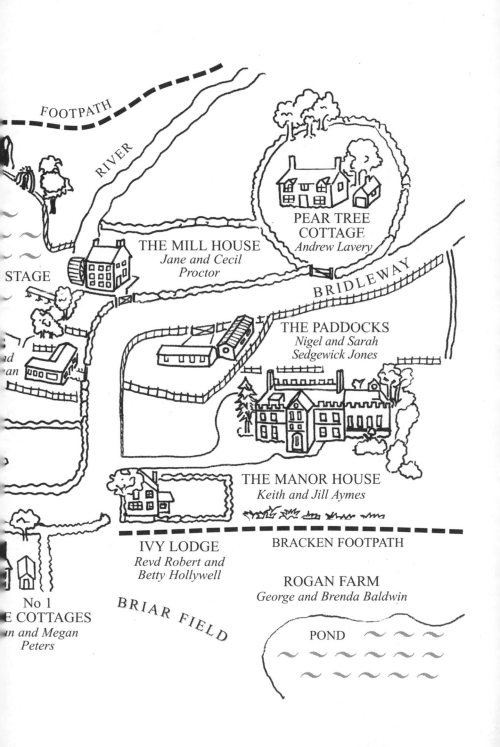

FOOTPATH

RIVER

STAGE

PEAR TREE
COTTAGE
Andrew Lavery

THE MILL HOUSE
*Jane and Cecil
Proctor*

BRIDLEWAY

THE PADDOCKS
*Nigel and Sarah
Sedgewick Jones*

THE MANOR HOUSE
Keith and Jill Aymes

IVY LODGE
*Revd Robert and
Betty Hollywell*

BRACKEN FOOTPATH

ROGAN FARM
George and Brenda Baldwin

No 1
E COTTAGES
*n and Megan
Peters*

BRIAR FIELD

POND

Prologue

'**B**est get off now, Shirl, while the coast's clear!'
Reluctantly, the girl unwound her arms from about the boy's neck and rolled over on to her back leaving her bare breasts exposed both to his gaze and to the hot, dusty air of the barn.

'In a hurry to get rid of me now I've let you do it?' she said, her tone both reproachful and provocative.

Jack Dodd looked quickly away from the sight of the girl's naked body, aware of the temptation it evoked but equally aware that he'd taken a big enough risk as it was allowing her here on the farm in broad daylight. But at seventeen, he was still discovering the intoxication of sexual gratification; and although he wasn't particularly attracted in other ways to Shirley, she was not only available but made no bones about the fact that she fancied him. He had only just discovered that his strong, muscular body, tanned to a deep golden brown by hours in the open air, had a special appeal to the girls in the village which overrode the disadvantage of his having no money to spend on them.

'Go on, Shirl, get dressed!' he said. 'You know Mum and Dad could be back any time; and if we was caught . . .'

'OK, OK!' she said petulantly but at the same time, reaching for her miniskirt and suntop. She had a certain respect for Jack's elderly father, Frank – a brusque man with old-fashioned ideas – the opposite of her own dad who'd said with a wink, 'If you can't be good, girl, then for God's sake, be careful!' That was when her mum had put her on the pill, so now they didn't bother if she was back home late after a disco.

Jack was like his father. It had taken her the best part of a

1

month to persuade Jack to use the barn. Even then they could only do so when he was certain his parents wouldn't be around, and it irked her that he wouldn't ever risk them being caught. There were plenty of other boys who would give their right arm to be in Jack's place – she was undoubtedly the best looking of all the girls in their crowd.

Jack could tell now by the expression on Shirley's face that she was angry; she could sulk for days if she didn't get her own way and then she wouldn't let him have his way and he'd become more and more frustrated.

'We'll fix another time soon!' he said, trying to put an arm round her shoulders. She shrugged him off.

'Ain't hardly worth it, Jack!' she said coldly.

'Aw, don't be like that, Shirl!' he pleaded. 'Look, I'll meet you up the King's Head this evening, eh?'

Her large blue eyes narrowed.

'So's someone else can treat me to a drink? Only time you treat me is on a Saturday when your dad gives you your pocket money!' She laughed derisively.

Jack's face flushed an angry red. This was not the first time Shirl had taunted him about the fact that he never had any cash in his pocket. Even the lads on social security had more to spend than he did. The fact that Shirl was right in that he wasn't ever paid proper wages by his father but given a few quid on a Saturday as if he was still a kid, did nothing to ease his discomfort at her jibe. He'd tried to explain to his father who refused to understand his need for money. 'Never had aught to spend when I were your age, boy!' If he said it once more, Jack often told himself, he'd kill him! Even his mother hadn't be able to talk the old man round.

'You don't understand, Jack!' she kept repeating. 'Your dad's having a job to make ends meet. Things are in a bad way . . . the milk money . . . the harvest . . . the recession . . . You've got to be patient, dear. Look, here's a couple of quid from my egg money. Will that help?'

Not much, with Shirl able to put away three vodka and tonics in the time it took him to get through a pint. Then there were her fags; she smoked like a chimney and the price of a packet of cigarettes was more than the cost of hiring a video – not that his family had a video recorder but Shirl's parents had one and let them use it if they weren't watching telly themselves.

Jack had searched his mind for ways he might make a bit of extra money; but his father kept him too busy on the farm to allow him enough time to take on odd jobs elsewhere. It wasn't even as if there was anything he could sell, other than his bike and he needed that for getting up to the village to see Shirl.

The worst of it was he knew he couldn't justify his resentment at his situation. Again and again, he'd heard his parents talking – Dad going through the accounts at the end of the month, trying to work out which bills would have to be paid and which could be left to run on a bit longer. There'd even been talk about having to chuck it all up and go on social security, and he'd not needed his mum to tell him that would kill his father, break his heart. One of the few times he'd ever heard his parents come close to a serious row was over money. Dad had said he'd have to give up paying the insurance premiums and Mum had said over her dead body. Just suppose one of the barns went on fire – it could happen . . . had happened not a year past over on the far side of Ferrybridge. Several thousand pounds' worth of hay up in smoke and no money in the bank to replace it. What would the cows eat then over winter? Whatever other economy they made, it mustn't be the insurance.

'Well, are you going to see me off or what?'

Shirl's voice jolted Jack on to his feet.

'I'll wait here a bit and watch you from the granary!' he said. 'Someone might come into the yard and . . . well, go like you always do over to the dairy as if you'd come for eggs.' His voice softened, became pleading. 'Shirl, you know I don't like it this way no more than you do. You agreed it was the only way we could be together . . . and well, you know how I feel about you. You . . .'

'Oh, stuff it!' Shirl said, pushing his hand away and turning her face to avoid his attempt to kiss her. 'If you really loved me . . .'

She tossed her head and holding her heeled sandals in one hand, made her way down the ladder leaning against the bales of hay which were piled one upon the other almost to the granary floor. She paused, wondering if Jack would follow her down, wanting him to do so. She'd give him a minute or two – have a fag whilst she waited. She reached in her shoulder bag and pulled out a packet of Silk Cut. Her face creased in a smile. If Jack saw her smoking in here, he'd have a fit! Well, let him. Maybe the smoke from her fag would waft upstairs to the granary. That would bring him down quick enough if anything did! Then, maybe, she'd let him kiss her. She didn't want him to change his mind about meeting her up the pub tonight. She was only just beginning to find out that 'doing it' once wasn't nearly often enough for her.

On the other hand, if he caught her smoking after all his cautions, he might be so angry he'd dump her and take up again with that fat cow Lynn, who he'd used to snog before he met her.

She was momentarily distracted by the Dodds' collie barking furiously in the yard.

Jack glanced at his watch. Several minutes had passed since Shirl had gone off in a huff and still he hadn't seen her go into the dairy across the yard. Maybe she'd decided to go straight out of the farm gate which he couldn't see from here – just to annoy him. That was one of the things about Shirl – she liked taking risks, egging him to go faster on his bike when she rode pillion and grumbling because he wouldn't take a chance losing his licence by breaking the speed limit. In some ways, Shirl was a headache! But then he remembered how hot and eager and loving she'd been not a half hour since; how urgently he'd wanted her; how she'd let him do anything he wished and think of things to do to him, too. Maybe she had slept around a bit, but he didn't care. She'd wanted him for all he hadn't any money to spend on her.

Time he went back to work, he told himself. There was still plenty to do, but the air up here in the granary was soporific and it would be as well, if anyone were about, for him not to emerge too quickly after Shirl. The neighbours – particularly Mrs Brigend – were hopeless gossips and if word got back to his father . . .

Jack left the granary window, lay back against the sweet

smelling hay and watched a large brown spider weaving a web between two beams. It worked methodically without pause until the noise of a sudden clatter from below disturbed the stillness of the room. Frowning, Jack rose to his feet and looked down the hatchway. There was no beam of sunlight coming through the barn doors and it was dark enough for him to have to feel his way down the rungs of the ladder. Halfway down he stopped, his breath catching in his throat. The air was filled with the acrid smell of smoke. There was a sudden whoosh and a bright tongue of flame leapt upward from between two hay bales. Beneath Jack's horrified gaze, the flame became a sheet of fire as the dried grass erupted in ever growing circles.

Recovering from the initial shock, Jack could now see that if he was quick, he might yet make the safety of the barn doors and let himself out into the yard. He slid down the last half of the ladder and, coughing violently as the smoke attacked his lungs, he stumbled to the doors. That they might be shut from the outside had not crossed his mind and as he beat against them with his fists, panicking now, he realized that somehow the wooden bar had fallen into its heavy oak slots, effectively imprisoning him.

My God, Shirl! he thought as he stamped on the flames now licking his feet and edged his way back to the ladder. She must have closed the door when she left. But why? And how had the fire started?

His mind raced with thoughts as he groped his way up to the granary. It was now fogged with smoke, stinging his eyes and throat even further. He could see the outline of the granary window where once, long ago, the sacks of corn had been hauled up on a pulley for storage. The rope had long since gone and there was no escape but to jump the five metres to the concrete yard below. No sane person would risk a broken neck by jumping but one glance at the flames now creeping through the gaps in the floorboards made the prospect of the leap less frightening than death by fire.

Gasping, he tried to draw fresh air into his lungs as he leaned out of the window. The ladder to the granary was bolted and he knew without trying that it would be useless to attempt to loosen

5

it. There was nothing beneath the granary window which would soften his fall. The boards beneath his feet were now unbearably hot and at any moment, the tinder dry floor would burst into flames. He must jump now – now before the lack of oxygen rendered him unconscious. For a moment or two, Jack clung to the wooden frame of the aperture and then, closing his eyes, he forced his fingers to unclench themselves.

Driving into the yard in their battered old Ford, Mary and Frank Dodd were just in time to see their son's body hit the concrete. He lay there motionless as with a roar, the roof of the barn collapsed inward and a shower of golden sparks shot up into the sky and fell, gently covering his body with a myriad specks of soft, black ash.

One

I an Peters poured himself a whisky and added a measure of soda before settling himself in the armchair opposite his wife. Megan – Migs to her friends – was curled up on the sofa giving their firstborn his going-to-bed feed. The sight added to his feeling of contentment as his glance slowly circled the room.

'It looks great, sweetheart! How d'you manage to get so much done?'

This morning when he had left to catch his commuter train to London, the tiny room had been a clutter of unopened packing cases, odd pieces of furniture covered with unhung curtains and sundry bulging dustbin bags tied with string.

Migs sat the nine-month-old child on her lap. Smiling, she brushed back the sweep of blonde hair from her forehead. Her hyacinth-blue eyes sparkled with pleasure at her husband's comment.

'For a moment, I thought you hadn't noticed!' she said. 'As a matter of fact, I'm feeling pretty pleased with myself. It's beginning to look nice, isn't it?'

The tiny semi-detached cottage – one of a pair of farm labourers' dwellings – had taken all their capital and when Ian had learned Migs was pregnant only three months after their wedding, he'd been worried. There simply wasn't going to be enough left in the bank to add on a larger kitchen and garage as they'd planned with the expense of all the gear a new baby seemed to need.

'We'll manage!' Migs had said. 'The windows in the cottage are tiny, so I can cut down those long curtains; and we've got

7

those two Persian rugs Aunt Joan gave us as a wedding present to put on the sitting-room floor. Don't worry, darling. Anyway, think how much better it will be for the infant breathing fresh Kentish air instead of the horrible London fumes! We must have had a premonition of things to come when we bought No. 1.'

Ian had been far too much in love with his young wife to reveal his own feeling that the purchase of this tiny cottage, tucked away down a bridleway in the heart of the Kent countryside, was going to prove a big mistake. They'd moved in on Saturday and as he'd taken his annual holiday to coincide with the birth of the baby, he'd had to go back to work this Monday morning. Yet despite the obvious handicap of their small son, Migs had already transformed the place into a home.

'I met the two inhabitants of Rose Cottage today – that's the one opposite!' Migs was saying. 'Miss Evelyn Bateman – she's in her eighties, I think – is the elder of the two old girls. She brought me over that bowl of pansies, heartsease, she called them, as a welcome-in gift. She said if we were going to make a garden, she could give us lots of cuttings. It's her passion, I gather – growing things. She asked me over to see her garden and it's really lovely, Ian – a real olde worlde outfit full of lupins, old-fashioned roses, and things like that.'

'What about the other old biddy – the one we saw picking those yellow things in the front who waved to us when we moved in?'

'Well, Miss Daphne, as I was asked to call her, is rather odd – not quite all there, I gather. Seems she was in a loony bin until last year when the government shut them all down and her sister took her in.'

'Didn't that charitable act come a bit late in the day?'

'Not at all, Ian. Miss Bateman was a legal secretary all her life until she retired – and that wasn't until she was seventy as they kept her on because she was so ultra efficient, so you see, she couldn't have been responsible for a dotty sister, could she?'

Ian grinned as he rose to pour himself another whisky.

'How dotty? She looked like a witch to me in that long black dress.'

'Stop it, Ian! She's actually rather sweet – sort of childlike. As soon as she saw Dougal she came scurrying up the path to the gate all smiles. I told her who we were but she wasn't much interested and started telling Dougal nursery rhymes in a sing-song voice, "Rock-a-bye Baby", "Bye Baby Bunting", etcetera, and she knew all the words. Dougie was intrigued. She was starting on "Georgie Porgie" when Miss Evelyn came along, grabbed hold of her and invited me in to see their garden. That didn't stop our Daphne – she trotted along beside Dougal's buggy giving him a nice rendering of "Mary, Mary, quite contrary, How does your Garden Grow". Miss Bateman couldn't hear herself speak, so she packed Daphne off to put the kettle on and that started the poor old girl on—'

'Don't tell me – "Polly, Put the Kettle On"!' Ian said laughing. 'Here, give me The Monster and I'll take him up to bed. You must be tired. No little drink first?'

'Not whilst I'm feeding him, Ian. Anyway, I honestly don't miss it. The only thing I missed today was you!'

'And I missed you!' Ian answered, kissing her warmly before taking the sleeping baby up to his cot.

When they had first viewed No. 1 The Cottages, Millers Lane, they had driven to the end of the road where it became a footpath. It was a roughish surface, potholed, with grass verges filled with wild flowers. Migs had been delighted – it would be somewhere to walk Dougal. He'd love looking at the sheep and cows in the adjoining fields. There were ducks, too, on the lake which lay to the left of the bridleway just beyond the big manor house.

The estate agent had told them there were actually ten dwellings other than the old manor house but, for the most part, the houses lay back off the road in secluded gardens, which was why Ian and Migs had not noticed all of them. They had exchanged a private smile over the agent's assurance that the residents were 'all very respectable', whatever that might mean.

'Tell me more, darling!' Ian said when he came back into the room and settled himself beside his wife. He put his arm round her shoulders. 'Have you met any other of our neighbours?'

Migs nodded.

'Ellen Brigend from next door popped in to see how I was getting on. Needless to say she had a good old look round but why shouldn't she be curious? She's a real gossip, of course, but kind as they come – said I must have a mountain of washing with the baby and to use her washing machine until we got ours going. Which I did! So I got to meet Mr Brigend who I was told to call Ray. From what I gather, Ellen "does" for most of the houses up the lane and Ray does the gardening. He used to work on the farm down the road but it seems Mr Dodd, the farmer, has been having a job to make ends meet and couldn't afford his wages so Ray was forced to find other work. Ellen said he would cut our hedge for us one weekend if you hadn't time.'

'Sounds like we've landed on our feet!' Ian said laughing. 'Will this Ellen of yours babysit if I want to take you out for a meal?'

'Couldn't have anyone better – she's had six of her own; and she adores babies!'

'Just as well if The Monster starts yelling in the middle of the night. The dividing wall is pretty thin, you know.'

Migs drew a deep sigh.

'I'm not complaining about anything. I think it's wonderful that we've got our own home, a mortgage we can manage and no other debts. We're very lucky, Ian. I don't even mind being semi-detached. If you have to go away on business, I won't be nervous with the Brigends next door.'

Ian nodded.

'Shouldn't think there's much to be nervous about in this neck of the woods. Can't see Millers Lane crawling with rapists, muggers, drug dealers and the like, can you?'

Migs pretty face creased suddenly in a frown.

'Well, no,' she said slowly. 'But it's not all rural bliss. You know that burnt out old barn we noticed in the farmyard? Well, Mrs Brigend – Ellen – was telling me that although the insurance investigators accepted that the fire last autumn was an accident, she and Ray don't think so. The farmer's son Jack was in the barn when it caught fire, and the investigators were convinced he must have used matches or a lighter because the straw bales had ignited from the inside.'

'So the boy was having a quiet smoke!' Ian said with a shrug. 'A stupid thing to do, but the fire would still be accidental, so why the doubts?'

'Because, according to Ray and Ellen, Jack doesn't smoke – never has done! Moreover, he'd know better than to use a naked flame where there was straw or hay about. Ellen is convinced somebody deliberately set fire to the place.'

'You must be joking!' Ian said. 'Did she give a reason? And what happened to Jack?'

'He jumped out of the granary window breaking a leg in the process. The interesting thing is, he swore that the barn doors were locked when the fire started and he'd tried to escape that way. Obviously he couldn't have locked himself in, which is why he was exonerated. The insurance company accepted that the fire must have been started by a shaft of sunlight reflecting off the glass of an old storm lantern that was stored in the barn, on to the hay which was tinder dry. But Ray, who fancies himself as Inspector Morse, is convinced someone started the fire deliberately.'

'Too much telly if you ask me!' Ian said grinning. 'Murders don't happen without motives and so what motive has your Inspector Morse come up with? Who does he think might have wanted to bump off a lad like the Dodds' boy? Next thing you'll be telling me Jack had got some local girl into trouble and her irate father wanted revenge! More likely he was screwing a married woman – always supposing the murderer knew he was in the barn!'

Despite her uncertainty, Migs laughed.

'Trust you to think on those lines!' she said reprovingly. 'You have sex on the brain!'

'Who wouldn't, married to you!' he rejoined kissing her.

When Migs managed to extricate herself from his embrace, she said, 'Ellen thinks it was arson. Everyone knew the Dodds were up against it financially. Dougal was yelling for his lunch so I didn't really grasp what it was all about, but Ellen thinks it was done to get the insurance money – unless a tramp or an immigrant had been hiding there and managed to escape before the fire took hold.'

'Immigrant, for heaven's sake!' Ian said. 'As Jack was in the barn, he'd have seen an intruder!'

Migs smiled.

'I expect you're right. Anyway, silly as it sounds, that idea is more plausible than Ellen's other conjecture – that the curse of the Horsboroughs has now been extended to the farm. She insisted that the farm was part of the manor estate when she saw me looking somewhat sceptical.'

'Am I hearing you right?' Ian asked quizzically. 'What curse and who are the Horsboroughs?'

Migs shook her head.

'You know, darling, Brigadier Vaughan Horsborough who used to live in the Manor House before the Aymes bought it. The original part of the house is apparently Elizabethan and was the family seat of the Horsboroughs. The story goes that way back in the nineteenth century Viscount Cecil Horsborough's eldest son, Lord Hugo Horsborough, shot himself when his son and heir, Eric, I think Ellen called him, disappeared and was never seen again. According to the locals, Lord Hugo haunts the grounds, calling for his son from midnight to dawn.'

'I don't believe this!' Ian said grinning. 'What other horrors had Ellen to relate?'

'Well, a distant cousin inherited when Lord Hugo died but *his* eldest son was killed in the Boer war and his surviving son drowned in a storm at sea. The uncle who then inherited lost his wife and two daughters who were on the *Titanic*. The heir survived but was killed in World War II and *his* son, the Brigadier, lost all his money in the Lloyds disaster. He sold off bits of the estate until finally, two years ago, when he went into a nursing home with Parkinson's disease, he sold the Manor to the Aymes.'

'So the family is cursed!' Ian commented. 'Some story! If you can believe it.'

'Well, I do!' Migs said. 'You've only to go along the lane and look at the Manor and you can believe anything. It's a huge stone-built edifice covered in ivy and Virginia creeper, and has lots of turrets and chimneys and little attic windows. Quite creepy!'

Ian looked surprised.

'I thought you said the Aymes were extremely rich and were spending a fortune on the place.'

'Yes, I did, and they are. As far as I can gather they got planning permission to do almost anything they wanted and I think they have had builders *inside* modernizing everything.'

'They must be hand in glove with someone on the council if they really are allowed free rein.'

'They don't seem so fussed about outside, although they have had several big trees cut down.'

'Presumably the Aymes aren't superstitious,' Ian stated. 'Anyway, even if there was a ghost, it would hardly commit arson at Millers Farm.'

They both laughed and, linking her arm through Ian's, Migs said, 'Well according to Ellen, the Dodds got their insurance money for the barn, and before I forget, she also said to tell you there is a Road Meeting tomorrow and she'd mind Dougal for us if we wanted to go.'

'A Road Meeting? What's that all about?'

'The estate agent told us, don't you remember? Millers Lane is a private road and so the council don't pay for its upkeep. All the residents chip in a small amount each year to pay for filling in potholes – that sort of thing. The meetings take place once or twice a year to decide what needs to be done with whatever cash is in the kitty.'

'Very democratic!' Ian said wryly.

'Ellen doesn't seem to think so. She says everyone living up the road is rich and from here on down to the main road, they're poor. She calls them the "One Pound End" and us the "Fifty P End". According to her, the "pound end" call the tune where the road is concerned.'

'Can't see it makes much odds to us, darling. Still, if we go to the meeting, it might be a good way to meet our neighbours if they're all going to be there – and where's "there"?'

'"There" is Ivy Lodge, the Reverend Hollywell's house, that's the one just round the corner. It used to be part of the Manor House estate – the Aymes own the lake and quite a bit of land around them.'

'Definitely the one pound end!' Ian laughed. 'Let's go, darling. It could be fun. Besides, I'm dying to meet Mr Aymes – he's the owner of the Rolls, isn't he? He drives behind me down the lane every morning with his chauffeur beside him and passes me as soon as we get on the main road. Funny chap! We both catch the ten past eight so passing me won't get him to town any earlier. It's good old one-upmanship!'

'Takes all sorts!' Migs said as she rose to go to the kitchen where a casserole was gently simmering in the ancient electric cooker. Ian watched her figure – more rounded now than it had been before the baby – with a hunger that was in part for his supper but also for her.

On the opposite side of the lane, from where she was sitting in her chair by the window, Miss Evelyn Bateman saw the lights go on in the newcomers' kitchen. Laying down her crochet work, she turned her attention to her sister. Neat as a pin herself, it never failed to irritate her to see how quickly Daphne's hair and clothes managed to become disarrayed. Although washed and changed from her gardening clothes in time for their high tea, Daphne's grey hair had already escaped in strands from the neat bun she, Evelyn, had arranged; whereas her own was perfectly intact. She sighed. Doubtless Daphne's clothes would have been left in an untidy heap on the bedroom floor had she herself not stood commanding her sister to put them away.

Daphne was sitting – or rather sprawling – on the red velvet pouffe playing cards. They were spread out on the carpet in small piles which were supposed to represent a game of patience. Try as Evelyn had, Daphne seemed incapable of mastering the basic principles of the game. She could barely manage snap which was a game Evelyn herself disliked intensely.

She felt the familiar wave of dismay that had clouded her life ever since the authorities had more or less insisted that when her sister's psychiatric hospital had closed, Daphne should come to live with her. For all Evelyn's adult life, she had lived on her own and she deeply resented this invasion of her precious privacy. However, she'd had no real grounds for refusal, and a year ago Daphne had been deposited on her together with little more than a bag full of pills required to counteract her depression, the rag doll she had kept since her childhood, a few clothes and a faded scarlet dressing gown which was practically threadbare.

It had not been an easy year. Evelyn liked to think her brain was as sharp as it had ever been. She could still do *The Times* crossword without having to resort to a dictionary or encyclopaedia. Daphne, poor soul, had the mental age of a five-year-old – if that! No wonder the police had thought she might somehow have wandered down the road with a box of matches and set fire to Millers Farm barn just for the fun of it! Fortunately, Daphne's social worker had called that morning and given her a lift to the day care centre where she was off Evelyn's hands for one treasured Thursday every week, so they'd had to wipe Daphne off their list of suspects.

Evelyn had demanded an apology although privately she hadn't blamed the policeman for suspecting Daphne. He'd done his best to be tactful and had been charmingly apologetic. Daphne, to Evelyn's own acute embarrassment, had taken a fancy to him, called him 'Daddy' and had wanted to kiss him goodbye. There were moments, Evelyn thought now, when she could happily strangle her unfortunate sister. When the inspector had called to ask all those tiresome questions, Daphne had been aimlessly shuffling a pack of cards and singing to herself in endless repetition: '*London's burning, London's burning, Fire, Fire, Fire Fire!*' Talk of the fire in the barn which at the time Evelyn had plainly seen from her sitting-room window, had clearly triggered in Daphne's brain a long-forgotten memory of this particular nursery rhyme which was not one of her usual infuriating repertoire.

Evelyn picked up her book and tried to concentrate on the words; but tonight she felt particularly concerned. Daphne's reactions today when the young mother who'd just moved in had come over with her baby, had opened a train of thought which would not go away. Was her sister still quite as badly retarded as had been previously supposed? If, as so often happened, Daphne's choice of nursery rhyme matched the current circumstance, there had to be some kind of mental association going on in her brain. Was it simply an association of words: her own invitation to young Mrs Peters to see the garden, triggering 'How Does Your Garden Grow?', the Peters' infant waving as his mother said goodbye, triggering 'Bye Baby Bunting'? Or was there more to it – an association of events, such as the barn fire? Was this a new development – Daphne getting better now she was out of that awful institution? After all, she'd not been retarded as a child. Her regression had not taken place until she was in her late teens. The doctors said she had suffered a minor stroke since they could find no other explanation for her sudden regression.

Evelyn had little time for doctors. Even in her old age – and she was nudging eighty-two – she had no illnesses to speak of and she retained all her mental faculties. But for the doctor's objections, she would have tipped Daphne's drugs down the lavatory where they belonged. Daphne was medically depressed, Dr Grainger insisted, and became suicidal without them. She, Evelyn, must trust them to know best.

Well, nothing had changed her view that these modern drugs did more harm than good, in just the same way as the chemicals the farmers were using to grow better crops were poisoning the planet. Thank goodness that some people were beginning at last to realize what dreadful harm they were doing: plants, butterflies, animal species slowly but surely becoming extinct! She'd been warning them for years but no one listened to her. Her letters to *The Times* were either not printed or ignored; the local Women's Institute – one of the few platforms she had for speaking after her retirement – had declined a second talk by her on the subject of ecology. As for her MP – she had a drawer full of polite replies from him promising to do what he could to alert people's consciences and then he had refused to vote against the Dungeness Nuclear Power Station.

'Daphne, put the cards away now. It'll soon be your bedtime. You can go and make a cup of cocoa!'

Her voice, sharp and incisive, was the voice of a schoolmistress who had never had any trouble with discipline in her school. The younger of the two women scrambled to her feet obediently. Her face – not unlike that of her elder sister – was more rounded, gentler, the mouth flaccid but the forget-me-not blue eyes astonishingly youthful, especially as now, when she smiled, saying, ' "*Polly, put the kettle on . . .*".'

16

'No, *Daphne* put the kettle on!' Evelyn said sharply. 'And by the way, Daphne, I saw you trying to lift that baby out of his pushchair. You are not to touch the child without permission, do you understand? Mrs Peters will have quite enough to worry her without bothering about you. I mean it!'

Daphne's smile faded and her round blue eyes filled with tears which spilled slowly down her cheeks.

'For heaven's sake, Daphne, there's nothing to cry about!' Evelyn said crossly. She handed her sister an immaculately clean handkerchief. 'It's time for your pill, I dare say. You can have it with your cocoa. And don't forget to do your teeth.'

She would forget the instruction, Evelyn thought, as Daphne shuffled out of the room. Even as a child, long before she became ill, she was hopelessly forgetful. It was partly their parents' fault. They had always spoilt her – the pretty, blue-eyed, golden-haired baby everyone admired who had totally usurped Evelyn's own place in the family. Daphne could get away with any misdemeanour simply by smiling, whereas she, Evelyn, with her ugly spectacles and straight black hair, was always expected to 'know better'. When she excelled at school, it had done little to alter the status quo: Daphne had remained the undisputed favourite, the adored, spoilt little girl who could do no wrong. From a very early age, Evelyn had known that she was too plain – and probably too clever – ever to find a husband. Daphne, of course, had only to look at a boy for him to be enslaved. But of course, marriage was out of the question after she lost her wits.

Life was very unfair, she thought, closing her book and putting away her crochet work. But then she had always known that. It was better not to think about the past – better just to tackle each day as it came and make the best of whatever fate had in store; which thought reminded her that the Road Meeting was scheduled for tomorrow and whatever happened, she must go. There was too much at stake for her voice to go unheard. At least the meeting was at the Reverend Hollywell's house and Betty Hollywell would keep Daphne out of the way in the kitchen once she had served the sherry.

The sound of a china cup smashing on the quarry tiles brought her thoughts back to the present. Evelyn rose hurriedly to her feet and, fearing the worst, went out to the kitchen to see what Daphne had broken this time.

Two

June

'I 've polished the tables, Mrs Hollywell, and there's still twenty minutes left. Shall I do some ironing?'

Betty put the last sprig of gypsophila into the vase on the draining board and smiled at the dumpy little figure of her daily help.

'Thank you, Ellen. Really, I don't know how I'd manage these Road Meeting evenings without you. I do wish my husband had consulted me first – Friday's such a busy day!'

'I der say as how the Reverend forgot the church jumble was tomorrow!' Ellen said cheerfully as she plugged in the iron and set up the board.

'And I do the library trolley for the hospital. He's so forgetful these days!'

Her beloved Robert was only in his early seventies, Betty thought, yet he seemed to be ageing alarmingly rapidly. It wasn't just his memory that was failing. Physically he was far too thin and Dr Grainger was having to give him regular medication for chronic bronchitis. Robert had worn himself out serving the parish tirelessly until health had forced his semi-retirement. The village had been amalgamated with the neighbouring village and St Joseph's had been sold and converted into an ordinary house – a state of affairs with which Robert had never been able to come to terms, poor darling!

The vicarage, too, had been sold, and it was only by God's grace that when the impoverished Brigadier, Lord Horsborough, the former owner of the Manor House, had sold his house to the Aymes, he'd also sold the lodge to Robert. Fortunately, the price had been ridiculously low, due in part to the fact that it was an ugly Victorian ivy-clad building that was always damp, situated as it was below Rogan Farm's pond and the stream running past Siskins to Millers Lake. Not only was it unattractive to look at but the local rumours persisted that the ghost of the suicidal Horsborough haunted all parts of the estate. Unable to afford anything better in the district and disbelieving the 'haunted' theory, Robert had been delighted that they were able to stay in the neighbourhood and take occasional services for the vicar of Hunnington when he was on holiday. Nowadays her husband's main enjoyment was walking the length of Millers Lane, stopping for a chat with any resident who happened to be about, and visiting some of his old parishoners in the nearby village of Delhurst. He did so love feeling that he could offer comfort and, occasionally, spiritual advice to those in need. Sadly, not many people these days had time for religion and of all the residents in the lane, only Miss Bateman and her poor sister, and Mrs Proctor, the church organist, went regularly to church.

With a sigh, Betty picked up the finished flower decoration and carried it into the sitting room. Evelyn would be up later with flowers for the hospital chapel – beautiful bunches of blooms from her lovely garden – and she, Betty, would not have time after that to prepare for the meeting this evening.

If only Robert would resign his chairmanship of the Road Committee, she thought for the hundredth time. Granted the meetings were only twice yearly but they were no longer the friendly gathering of neighbours they'd been in the past. New people with new ideas had moved in and there was now quite a lot of controversy about how Millers Lane should be run. The arguments could become quite heated and at the last meeting, Andrew Lavery, the author who lived in Pear Tree Cottage at the very end of the lane, had walked out in a huff saying he was wasting his time! Poor Robert had been quite distressed.

Then there was the difficulty about taking minutes of the meeting – something they'd never done in the past, it being left to the Brigadier to act on a verbal agreement as to what needed doing. Their next-door neighbours, the Sedgewick-Jones, had written quite a stiff letter to Robert complaining that his memory had been at fault when recalling the numbers after a show of hands. Privately, she, Betty, feared the Sedgewick-Jones were right and Robert's memory had failed him; but try though she had in the most tactful of ways to suggest he relinquish the position, he still refused to do so.

For the past week, he had been preparing the opening speech he liked to make as soon as everyone had arrived and been given a glass of sherry. Betty knew how much he looked forward to giving his 'little talk', as he called it. It was a reminder of the days of his sermons, which he sorely missed. Poor Robert! Old age was not very pleasant when the time came to face up to it. Take Evelyn Bateman for example – such a good woman who'd worked hard all her life. She'd really looked forward to a peaceful retirement with time at last to devote to her beautiful little garden – and then she'd been landed with her retarded sister who was quite a responsibility. With Evelyn's still sharp brain, she must be driven quite mad at times listening to the unfortunate Daphne's endless repertoire of nursery rhymes. They were the only form of conversation, if you could call it that, the poor woman could muster. Otherwise, of course, Daphne was physically quite sturdy, but with her mental retardation she had to be cared for by Evelyn as a child of five or less.

Betty took a last look round the sitting room which was spotless, she decided with approval, thanks to the hard-working Ellen. It would do. Now, after she had paid Ellen, she could give Robert his lunch and get down to making some scones for tomorrow's jumble sale. Perhaps, if she had time, she could nip down and introduce herself to the new tenants in No. 1 The Cottages – a young couple called Peters, according to that fount of information, Ellen! It was nice to think there were younger people in the lane. Mr Peters was an insurance salesman so they sounded respectable.

'I'm off now, Mrs Hollywell. See you next Friday, same as usual.'

'Won't I see you tonight at the Road Meeting?'

Ellen shook her head.

'I'm sitting in for Mrs Peters' baby, but my Ray will be here. Quite worked up about the road, he is. Come to that, we all are down our end.'

Not that Ray would vote one way or another, she thought, he being gardener to Mr Aymes and paid double what everyone else in the lane gave him. 'Be cutting off my nose to spite my face,' he'd said, and Ellen agreed with him.

Betty Hollywell sighed. She hated controversy, and the Aymes' proposal to have Millers Lane widened, which would cut off the corner of Rose Cottage garden, and then resurfaced, had turned out to be extremely controversial. Half the residents were keen on the idea and the other half opposed to it. Of course, the issue was still very much in the preliminary stages.

The Aymes had asked Robert to notify each household of their proposal. Water from the pond in Briar Field fed Millers Lake, the water course running under the lane and resurfacing at the bottom of Siskins' garden. The trouble was, in winter the corner of the lane and its surrounds were often flooded, at times several inches deep, as was their garden. The Aymes – who were very particular about the state of their cars – were prepared to pay for a culvert to be dug and pipes laid beneath Rose Cottage garden so that the excess water rejoined the stream just beyond the boundary of Siskins. They were prepared to fund the work and pay for the lane to be resurfaced with a small contribution from the other residents and an insignificant one from George Baldwin, the farmer who owned Rogan Farm. Although his house and farmland was approached from a different lane, the end of his field adjoining Millers Lane was too wet for cultivation and he was agreeable with Aymes' suggestion that it should have new land drains leading into the proposed culvert.

Robert was keen on the idea. Quite apart from the flooding, the lane was badly potholed. A smooth, tarmacadam surface would make it far easier for him to ride his bicycle the half mile to the village where he still paid regular visits to some of his former, elderly parishioners. Since his operation two years ago, he'd not been able to drive their old Morris and although she, herself, still drove the car, he liked whenever possible to be independent. For his own sake, therefore, he supported the Aymes' proposal and it did have other merits – namely that these relatively new but well-to-do occupants of the Manor House were funding nearly all of it.

Betty was far from sure that she liked Jill and Keith Aymes who were without doubt not from the aristocracy as the former resident, the elderly Brigadier, Lord Horsborough, had been. Robert, of course, would have chided her for being so class-conscious. As it happened, he had not got along too well with the Brigadier, who had tended to patronize him and irritated Robert profoundly by always calling him 'Parson'. 'Morning to you, Parson. Saved any souls today?' was invariably his greeting and Robert had resented it.

As far as she was concerned, Betty considered that the Brigadier, Lord Horsborough, being a member of the aristocracy, could not be expected to treat Robert and herself as equals. Moreover, she had felt sorry for him living alone in that huge decrepid manor house with its dozens of empty rooms, draughty passages and general air of decay. She pitied not only his extreme poverty but for being yet another link in the chain of family tragedies. On winter nights when the wind howled and strange shadows swayed across the Manor House lawns, she could even believe the place was haunted. She'd wanted Robert to carry out an exorcism, but he'd been fiercely reluctant even to put such a suggestion to the Brigadier.

Despite Robert's refusal to believe the place really was haunted, on the few occasions she went up there to sell flags for Christian Aid or the Retired Gentlewomen's Association, the stuffed animals and forbidding faces of Horsborough ancestors were scary enough without the old man appearing suddenly from a dark passageway, bent double by arthritis and looking like a deformed gnome. He'd been polite enough in his abrupt manner and very much the gentleman, and she'd felt deeply sorry for him when he'd been obliged to sell off bits of the estate and finally his ancestral home – the Manor itself – to the Aymes.

The Aymes had turned out to be as gregarious as the Brigadier had been reticent. They invited Robert and herself up to the house for drinks soon after they had settled in and several times since. Within a year, a swimming pool, tennis court and billiard room had all been built, and the interior of the house, which had fallen into total decay, had been completely gutted and refurbished. The drawing room looked like one of the showrooms of

Harrods – luxurious without any doubt – and was much approved of by Robert, but not by her. She preferred her own beautifully polished antique furniture and even the shabbiness of her curtains and chair coverings to the festoon blinds, reproduction Queen Anne furniture and Poggenpohl kitchen units Jill Aymes had proudly shown her.

Most important to Robert, however, was Keith Aymes' friendliness. A huge sturdy six foot seven, the middle-aged man slightly resembled a St Bernard despite his beautifully tailored clothes and carefully blow-dried mane of hair. He would clap an arm round Robert's shoulders, call him by his Christian name and keep his glass liberally topped up with champagne. Jill, his wife, had been equally charming to her, promising a trunk full of clothes for her summer jumble sale and offering the use of the swimming pool whenever she wanted! Yes, she was kind and attractive, too, a tiny blonde young woman with lots of dangling bracelets and designer clothes and a high, bell-like voice which could be heard above everyone else's.

Whilst having opposite views of the new Master and Mistress of the Manor, she and Robert were in complete agreement in their antipathy to the Aymes' chauffeur, Stewart Parker. He lived in the flat over the garage block and was on call as a handyman as well as a chauffeur. Although he was scrupulously polite to both Betty and her husband, there was something shifty – indefinable, but there – about the way he avoided contact with them, cutting short any attempts at conversation or polite enquiries about where in Australia he came from, what had brought him to England, or where he had been employed prior to his job with the Aymes. He'd avoided answering such enquiries saying he'd got to dash off, or he'd be late meeting a train, or finishing a task that was overdue. A dark-haired, well-built fellow, his bushy eyebrows tended to meet across the bridge of his nose, which was pugilistic. Ellen, who'd met the man on several occasions, was convinced he'd once been a boxer who had killed an opponent and was therefore unwilling to disclose his past! Betty did not encourage such wildly dramatic outpourings from her cleaner but secretly wondered if perhaps Ellen was not that far from the truth.

However, attired in the grey uniform with which Keith Aymes had supplied him, he did look quite smart driving Jill's BMW sports car which she preferred to her husband's Rolls. In the winter, the Aymes used one or other of their two Range Rovers. It was not to be wondered at that they wanted the lane 'improved' as both seemed permanently in a hurry: he to keep a business appointment, she to get to the hairdresser, a party, a big social event in London.

Sometimes Betty wondered why they had bought the Manor House, since they were so rarely in it. Weekends, of course, they entertained and the lane was often blocked with their visitors' cars. Widening it would mean that two cars going in opposite directions could pass each other without one or other having to back into the nearest drive or lay-by. Cutting off the corner would quicken it, too, as well as getting rid of the flood water.

Seeing Ellen's broad figure disappearing down the drive, Betty was reminded that it was time for Robert's lunch. He did like to eat punctually. She hurried into the kitchen and retrieved the shepherd's pie from the oven, carrying it through to the dining room where her husband was already seated at the table. He glanced at his watch.

'A little late, my dear!' he reproached her mildly.

'I know! I'm sorry, Robert. I've been busy preparing for the meeting.'

Robert dug the serving spoon into the dish, sniffing appreciatively as he ladled a helping on to his wife's plate.

'Ah, yes, of course! I've been rehearsing my ser– my little speech,' he corrected himself. 'I suppose you realize that Aymes is relying on me to carry the vote this evening, so I have to take extra care if we're going to convince the objectors this plan is best for all of us.'

Betty nodded.

'I know you think so, dear, but we do have to see the others' point of view. I mean, up this end of the lane, we aren't really bothered much by the traffic; but Ellen, for example, and the Batemans – well, the noise of passing cars and the dust must be very inconvenient right outside their front windows. There's the danger, too, with the cars going by their gates so quickly. Mary

25

Dodd was nearly knocked over as she came out of the farm gate last week, and poor Frank has quite a problem taking the cows across the lane to Barley Meadow.'

The Reverend Hollywell looked over his knife and fork at his wife.

'I don't wish to be uncharitable, my dear, but Mary Dodd never looks where she's going. As for that ne'er-do-well son of hers, he'll kill himself one of these days on that motorbike of his. Frankly, I'm not the least surprised their barn went up in smoke. The boy's totally irresponsible. I can't imagine what Frank thinks he's doing allowing Jack to go round looking like . . . like a girl with that dreadful ring in his ear and that horse tail hanging down his back.'

'It's called a ponytail, dear, and lots of young men wear their hair long these days. As a matter of fact, I think Frank and Mary have brought the boy up very well indeed. He's always polite when I call at the farm for eggs and I can't count the times he's helped me load and unload the jumble and won't take a penny piece for it.'

'Yes, well that's as may be; but someone started the fire in the Dodds' barn and there wasn't anyone else near the farm that day. If you remember, Miss Bateman said there wasn't a soul to be seen when she went to fetch her milk from the dairy. Doubtless they'd be a lot more in favour of the Aymes' proposal if they had to bicycle through the flood water like I do.' He drew a deep sigh as he remembered his calling and that he was not being quite as charitable as he should. 'However, you're quite right, Betty,' he admitted, adding unctuously, 'It's not for me to judge my fellow man. God will do that in His own good time. Now, a second helping, my dear?'

Realizing that the topic was closed, Betty passed her plate.

'Ellen said the new people are coming to the meeting – she's babysitting for them. I wonder if they will vote for the Aymes' proposal?'

Her husband shook his head.

'From what I have been able to gauge from the replies I received to my letter, we have a majority of two in favour, so it won't make much difference which way Mr and Mrs Peters vote.

As to their opinions, I doubt if they will carry much influence since they've only just moved into our little community. No, it's the Sedgewick-Jones I'm a bit worried about. Nigel rang me up, you know, and was . . . well, quite abusive. I don't wish to be unduly critical of my fellow men but the fact of the matter is, these horsey people are all the same – can't see any other viewpoint but the needs of their animals!'

Betty removed the empty dishes and returned with a bowl of trifle, a pudding she always made when there was a Road Meeting because that – and Christmas – were the only times Robert decanted one of his carefully hoarded bottles of sherry, given to him by his old parishioners at Christmas time.

'Sarah and Nigel do have a point!' she resumed the conversation. 'Millers Lane is a designated bridleway, Robert. It's not meant to be a proper road, or it would have had foundations and a concrete culvert, wouldn't it?' Nigel had recently voiced this snippet of information to Robert and said he would repeat it at the Road Meeting. 'In the old days, only horses and carts used it, going to and from the Manor.'

Robert said, frowning, 'That's as may be, but as Keith Aymes pointed out, these are modern times and there are now seven cars – eleven counting their four, as well as those of the tradespeople and visitors – who use Millers Lane.'

But that was exactly the problem, Betty thought but refrained from saying since she disliked on principle arguing with Robert. Those against the Aymes' proposal were complaining that the road was rapidly turning into a motorway and that hadn't been their intention when they'd chosen to live in a private, dead-end country lane. If only Robert would not be aware of how she was casting her vote this evening, she really thought she might herself have voted against the Aymes' proposal; but it would upset Robert dreadfully were she to oppose him. Had it not been for the extraordinary influence Keith Aymes exerted over her husband, she might perhaps have been able to talk him round. But in Robert's eyes, the man could do no wrong and Mr Aymes' recent substantial cheque to Robert's favoured charity had elevated the man to almost saintly proportions.

Betty felt it preferable, therefore, not to reveal to Robert the fact that of all the people in Millers Lane, she very much concurred with the views of Andrew Lavery, who, like the Sedgewick-Jones, was all for leaving Millers Lane as it now was. Mr Lavery was not only a well-known author of murder mystery books, but he was the image of Clark Gable, the actor she had idolized ever since as a young girl she'd first seen him in *Gone With The Wind.* Often to be seen out walking his three Irish wolfhounds, he was a most romantic figure, and when she slowed her car to pass him in the lane and he nodded his thanks and smiled at her, it made her feel like a girl again!

More often than not, he was on his own with the dogs but occasionally, he had a young, red-haired woman with him. Ellen, being the gossip she was, insisted the woman was married and the pair were carrying on an illicit affair, but Betty preferred to believe Robert's report that Andrew Lavery had introduced his companion as his secretary. Betty could well understand the author's wish to keep the lane as it was since the traffic was at present obliged to go slowly and it was therefore safer for his three beautiful dogs.

At least this evening she would have the pleasure of serving him sherry, Betty thought with an inner glow, even if for the rest of the time she had offered to keep poor Daphne Bateman occupied in the kitchen. At the last meeting, when people had begun to drift off home, Mr Lavery had come out to the kitchen and helped himself to one of the jam tarts she'd been teaching Daphne to make. He'd perched on the edge of the kitchen table and laughed and chatted to them both until Evelyn had come to collect her sister. Perhaps this evening she would cook something similar since he had lavished such praise on her pastry.

'That's the Batemans' car just arrived!' Robert broke into her thoughts. 'I'll leave you to it as I have a little more work to do on my speech.'

Betty hurriedly cleared the table and went out to help Evelyn unload the flowers from her car.

Three

Frank Dodd removed his boots, put on the waiting pair of carpet slippers and sat down at the kitchen table, his hands reaching behind him to rub his aching back. The afternoon milking was done at last and he'd left Jack behind in the dairy swilling the floor down before taking the pails of milk over to the calves' shed. He was tired – not just physically but tired of his whole way of life.

With a nod to his wife, he took the mug of tea from her and drank it slowly, his mind still on the herd. Daisy wasn't yielding too well – hadn't been for a week now. If he'd had any sense, he'd have let her go when the new Common Market regulations had obliged him to reduce the amount of milk he was producing. Bungling lot of bureaucrats! he thought angrily. Wasn't one of them knew the first thing about dairy farming as far as he could see. Maybe he was being a bit soft about old Daisy. Mary had had to hand rear her as a calf, and now the old girl was in her dotage she was something of a pet to them both; as a consequence, although they'd never discussed it at the time, Daisy's name had never been on the list of those to be driven off to market.

His wife came and sat down beside him. A farmer's daughter herself, she was a strong, healthy woman who'd more than pulled her weight on the farm. A few years back, it had seemed as if after years of struggling to make a go of it, they were beginning to see daylight; making enough profit to take on extra help. He'd employed Ray Brigend, who had moved in across the road and who easily earned his wages. It was a bitter day when he'd had to pay Ray off. Fortunately, Ray had managed to get gardening work from the new people at the Manor and for

29

his own part, with Jack leaving school, he'd had the boy to help with the haymaking and ploughing and mucking out.

But nothing had stemmed the slow, steady fall in profits. A small dairy farm was simply not economical any more, not even with grants and all the other new-fangled ideas that had cropped up since European policy had interfered with the old ways. If there was one thing which Frank felt really bitter about, it was the way politicians had surreptitiously allowed Europe to dictate their lives!

'You haven't forgotten it's the Road Meeting tonight, dear?'

Mary's voice with its soft, Kentish accent, broke in on his reverie.

'No, I've not forgot!' he said wearily. 'I've half a mind not to go! Doesn't seem much point, really.'

Mary's brown eyes narrowed anxiously.

'But suppose the voting goes against Mr Aymes' proposal?'

'Reverend doesn't think there's much chance of that.'

'Yes, but suppose it did? Then Mr Aymes wouldn't want to buy that bit of land from you.'

Frank put down his mug and scratched his head.

'Wouldn't want that to happen!'

There was five thousand pounds at stake and that was a lot of money if you'd come as near bankruptcy as he had last year. Granted the insurance money for the barn, which he had not yet rebuilt, had paid off his immediate debts; but another year had gone past and, by the end it, he could see they would be in trouble again. The five thousand the Aymes' had offered him would keep the bank quiet for a bit.

'Better go then!' he said. 'Lose the sale and we'd have to set fire to the cowshed or summat!'

'Frank!' Mary's voice was as reproachful as her expression. 'That isn't something to joke about and you know it. Our Jack might have died!'

Frank sighed.

'I know! I know!' he said patting her arm. 'All the same, that insurance came in the nick of time, didn't it? I'd have given up paying the premiums if you hadn't been so against it – so it's thanks to you we did get paid, and I'll not forget it.'

The day of the barn fire was one Mary preferred not to think about. It was still a mystery who had started it. She didn't blame the insurance investigators for suspecting that Frank or Jack had done it deliberately. They'd soon found out about the debts and the bank threatening to foreclose. For a while, the dreadful word 'arson' hung over them all. Fortunately, Frank had been away at a farm auction hoping to buy a couple of metal gates which he'd not been able to afford new, so they knew it wasn't him; and she'd gone with him to Ferrybridge, it being market day, to do the weekly shop. So that only left Jack who could have done it.

Mary's chest swelled with indignation at the memory. Her Jack was a good boy and just because he wore his hair long and went on a Friday night to the disco in the town with the other lads, the insurance man seemed to think he was a yobbo. It would have suited them to label him the culprit and maybe they'd have done so except for the fact that when they'd made enquiries about the boy, everyone had spoken well of him: the Reverend Hollywell, Dr Grainger, and his old schoolmaster, not to mention George Baldwin, the sheep farmer whose land bordered the farm at the southeast end of Millers Lane. Ever since Jack had been old enough, he'd helped George out at lambing time to earn himself some pocket money and George wouldn't have it that Jack could be so daft as to light a match in a barn full of hay with himself trapped inside. Rather suspect his wife Brenda, he'd told them.

So what with her son's good reputation and the fact that he didn't smoke, Jack ceased to be a suspect – or so they said, which only left poor Miss Daphne daft enough to drop a lighted match, and it couldn't have been her, poor soul, since she happened to be at the day care centre.

It had taken six months, but the insurance company had finally paid up and she and Frank had been able to sleep in peace again – or more or less without worry. The trouble was, neither the police nor the investigators had found out who had done it. At least none of their neighbours had ever considered that she and Frank were the guilty ones. For one thing, none of them knew their desperate financial state; and for another, Jack had been in the barn and broken his leg, poor lad, trying to get out, and if he'd meant to set fire to the barn, he would have made sure the barn doors were open before he did so. Like everyone said, it had to have been an accident. Lots of people were in and out of the farmyard in the course of a day: the milk tanker, the postman, the residents in the lane who came round for milk or eggs to name but a few. Any one of them could have tossed a cigarette end into the barn where it had smouldered and finally ignited – except that the barn doors were shut.

'Ellen said the new young couple in No. 1 The Cottages would be at the meeting,' Mary said now to Frank. 'Ellen said the wife was a very nice, friendly young lady and the baby was really bonny.'

She sighed. It was good to have a baby in the lane. She loved children and it was a very long time – seventeen years – since she'd cradled her only child, Jack, in her arms. She and Frank had all but given up hope of conceiving a baby when in her mid forties, like a miracle, Jack had arrived. Now he had turned eighteen and there'd be a few more years yet before she could expect grandchildren. God willing, they'd still have the farm by then. Kiddies loved collecting eggs from the hen house and watching the calves being fed. Milking wasn't the interest it used to be in the old days when they milked by hand – she sitting in the next byre to Frank, head tucked against a warm flank and the milk splashing into the pail.

Oh, it had been tiring all right! And she wouldn't want to be doing it now she was over sixty, nor staying up all night to help Frank with a difficult calving; but the hardship had somehow welded her and Frank together in their marriage; made them closer than other couples they knew of their age. Neither of them were given to words – expressing how they felt about each other – but they were close enough for her to know that she mattered more to Frank even than the farm! And he was heart and soul devoted to that. Others mightn't understand their closeness – like the time Frank had to sell off some of the cows and she'd never once had to ask him not to part with Daisy! It was stupid to let yourself get so attached to a cow but Frank had understood.

Sometimes she wished Jack was more like his father, but with close on two generations between them, the gap in their ages was too big for them to see eye to eye. Jack had no patience with what he called Frank's old-fashioned ways. He wanted his father to borrow from the bank to mechanize the farm; give up the dairy herd and go over to cereals; take advantage of the grants for growing rape or maize or whatever it was the European Market was encouraging.

It wasn't easy for her trying to keep the peace between them. Frank could be stubborn and Jack had a quick temper. Understandably, he wanted a better standard of living than she and Frank had: a computer, a car, holidays abroad which his young friends in the town enjoyed. On the wage Frank paid him, he hadn't a hope of having any of these things. He'd taken a part-time job at the local golf club to earn a bit extra. The pay wasn't bad and he would have gone full time, he'd confided in her, were it not for the fact he could see his father couldn't possibly manage the farm without him; and he resented the obligation this knowledge imposed.

'I just wish Dad would make up his mind to sell up and retire!' he'd said over and over again, but Frank couldn't afford to retire. Their savings had long gone to pay their debts and the farmhouse was heavily mortgaged. They'd have to go on the housing list if they sold up and it could be years before the council came up with accommodation. When they did, it would probably be an old people's flat and Frank would hate that. A farmer's son, he couldn't stand being cooped up indoors all day. If nothing else, he'd need a garden; space to keep a few chickens; grow some vegetables. Years ago, when times had been better, they'd talked about a smallholding where they could keep a cow, ducks and perhaps a pig.

As her son came into the kitchen, Mary looked at him with a rush of love accompanied by pity. At eighteen, he was a fine looking boy – a man, really. With his fair hair and brown eyes, he'd have no difficulty winning himself a nice girl so he could marry and settle down. If Frank could only afford to let him go – take on Ray again if only for a few hours a week – Jack could get a grant to go to agricultural college. With qualifications, he could get himself a good job, well paid, and make a life for himself.

'Cup of tea, dear?' she asked as her son kicked his wellingtons into a corner. He shook his head.

'No thanks, Mum. I'm meeting the lads down the King's Head.'

Frank frowned but said nothing as his son disappeared upstairs to wash and change. He disliked the gang of youths Jack called his friends. They hung around the street after closing time, smoking – and it could be drugs for all he knew – shouting and generally making a nuisance of themselves. The girls they picked up were little better – skirts too short and too tight, flaunting themselves and doing heaven knew what with the lads.

When he'd been Jack's age, he'd been courting Mary and saving hard for the day he could ask her to marry him, not wasting his money on drink and girls who were little better than tarts. When Jack had had his leg in plaster after the fire, there were words scribbled on the plaster that he wouldn't have let Jack use, let alone a girl: 'You can still get it over, Jackie-boy, love Tina!', 'Can't wait six weeks to have it off!', 'Any time, luvver boy, Helen', 'Keeps it stiff, just the job, Shirl!'. Fortunately Mary had never seen the plaster because Jack took care to cover it by wearing his tracksuit trousers. But it made Frank hot with embarrassment to imagine what the nurses in the hospital must have thought when they'd cut the plaster off. Granted a lad raised on a farm wouldn't be ignorant about sex, no more than he was at Jack's age. What shocked him was that young girls could be so crude.

When Jack left the house, Frank rose stiffly from his chair and followed his wife upstairs to change into his one and only suit. He didn't like wearing it and he didn't want to go to this dratted meeting, but he knew Mary was right and that he had to go. If Aymes didn't buy his piece of land, he'd have no alternative but to let the farm go.

Four

S arah Sedgewick-Jones wrinkled her nose in a barely concealed gesture of distaste and replaced her glass hurriedly on the table beside her.

'Ugh! Cooking sherry!' she whispered with a mischievous grimace at Migs. 'Can't stand the stuff. I'm Sarah, by the way. That big oaf talking to the Rev is my husband, Nigel. We live at The Paddocks. You must be the newcomer down the lane. Ellen told me you'd moved in at the weekend.'

Migs held out her hand.

'Yes, I'm Megan, known as Migs, and the guy by the door talking to Ellen's husband, Ray, is Ian, my husband.'

Sarah grinned. 'My, my, he's rather dishy! You must introduce me. No, better still why don't you both come and have a decent drink with us when this ghastly meeting is over? It's such a bore and the Rev does go on and on until I could scream. God knows how his wife stands it, but she doesn't seem to notice – married too long, I dare say!'

She paused to smile apologetically at Migs.

'Honestly, I'm the one to talk. I'm getting as bad as Ellen – she's our local grapevine and tells each of us what the others in the lane are up to. I wonder what she has told you about us?'

Migs smiled.

'Not much, as a matter of fact. I know your husband works in the city and that you're both mad about horses.'

'Oh, absolutely! You must come and see them. They're so much more intelligent than people, don't you think? And far less trouble than children. How on earth do you cope with yours?'

Migs smiled again. It was impossible not to like this outspoken but essentially friendly girl who, she judged, must be about her own age. Slim, dark-haired and hazel-eyed, she was quite attractive in a boyish way. It was easy to imagine how well she'd look in riding gear. Her high-pitched voice was an educated one – what Ian would call 'frightfully-frightfully' – but Migs had lived next door to a horsey family as a child and knew that most of them adopted this manner of speech, perhaps to make themselves heard on the hunting field! Ian, she noticed, had moved away from Ray Brigend and had seated himself beside the petite blonde woman on the sofa.

Following Migs' glance, Sarah said, 'Your better half is true to form – all the chaps make a beeline for our Jill. Funny how that girlish "silly little me" act gets to them. Nigel, bless him, falls over himself to attend to her needs. Well –' she giggled wickedly – 'not *all* of them, although he'd probably like to!'

'Like to what?'

Nigel Sedgewick-Jones had crossed the room and from a height well over six feet he smiled down at the two young women. 'Has the old girl been blackening my good name?'

Sarah made the introductions and, with the same easy friendliness of his wife, Nigel addressed Migs as if he'd known her for ages.

'We're absolutely counting on you to support us this evening!' he said. 'Sarah says you're bound to vote with us, you having a youngster and a gate opening on to the road.'

'Ellen gave us her copy of the Reverend Hollywell's letter,' Migs replied, 'but Ian and I still haven't quite fathomed what it's all about . . . I mean, I know some of the residents want to put drains in by the corner, widen the lane and resurface it, but I don't see why. It's lovely as it is. We haven't had time yet to explore properly but we drove to the end of the lane when we first came to look at the cottage and thought how nice it would be to live in a real country environment.'

Nigel looked pleased.

'Hit the nail on the head. We've been here nearly five years. Chose The Paddocks because we'd have somewhere to keep and exercise the nags without the traffic haring past. I've told Keith Aymes we don't object to the drainage idea as the road does get flooded in winter, but it's a crazy scheme turning a bridleway into a runway, and the sooner he drops it the better!'

'But I don't understand why he wants it changed,' Migs said.

'Because he's a speed merchant, duckie!' Sarah answered. 'He thinks if that nasty corner is straightened out and the potholes are smoothed over with nice, shiny tarmacadam, he'll be able to get his bloody Rolls out of bottom gear! And his chauffeur, Stewart Parker, will stop complaining that all their cars get spattered in muddy water in the winter if he puts this culvert thing in to stop the flooding.'

'Steady on, old girl!' Nigel cautioned his wife. 'Can't have that sort of language in the Rev's house.'

'Well, he hit Misty's saddle with his effing wing mirror last week!' Sarah said indignantly but lowering her voice. 'Doesn't seem to have a clue about animals.'

'No reason why he should, old girl!' Nigel said pacifically. 'Cars are his thing – and let's be honest, they've done him proud. He must be worth a bomb now.' He turned to Migs. 'Started in haulage – collecting scrap iron – and worked his way up. Got to admire the chap.'

Sarah shrugged.

'So OK, he's done jolly well for himself and I don't dislike him. He's extremely generous. The trouble is, money's his be-all and end-all. He thinks it can buy any damn thing he wants. My bet is, if the vote goes against him this evening, he'll fork out the lot and do it himself.'

'Well, he can't!' Nigel said matter-of-factly. 'This is a private road and that means we each own the land alongside our boundaries as far as the middle of the lane. Aymes can only muck about with his bit unless he has our agreement, and . . . hang on, the Reverend Hollywell's about to make his speech!'

The room quietened and Robert Hollywell's sepulchral voice rose above the clink of empty glasses. For a moment, Migs attention wandered and her glance circled the room. The round tubby middle-aged man sitting on the far side of his wife, Jill, was obviously Keith Aymes. Unlike Nigel, he was kitted out in immaculately tailored yellow linen trousers and a yellow and white striped co-ordinating shirt. Had he been slimmer, she thought with an inward smile, he could have been a model for Lillywhite's 'Casual Summer Clothes', or 'On The Cruise'.

The image was a little spoilt by the gold chain round his neck and chunky gold bracelet.

I'm being catty! Migs reproached herself, her glance moving on to the other middle-aged man in the room. He, she supposed, must be the author, Andrew Lavery. As if in deliberate contrast to Keith Aymes, he wore a crumpled pair of navy trousers and a pink T-shirt with 'Geriatric Gardener' stamped over it. His jet black hair was sleeked back and he sported a 1930s clipped moustache. Was the Clark Gable look deliberate, she wondered, but doubted it. He was well enough known for his thrillers not to need to look the part of a film star or an impoverished writer!

Beside him, Miss Evelyn Bateman sat perched on the edge of a high-backed chair, her spectacles on the edge of her nose as she lent forward to catch the Reverend Hollywell's words. With an effort, Migs turned her concentration to the steady drone of his voice.

'. . . the estimates we have received. I do realize that this imposes quite a heavy financial burden on . . . er . . . on those of us who are . . . er . . . pensioners. However, Keith Aymes . . .' – the voice now became unctuous – '. . . has more than kindly offered to subsidize those who cannot afford to contribute the whole amount at once – an interest free loan, I hasten to add – so I think you will all agree that this removes the last of the . . . er, hurdles.'

'Just a moment, Vicar. I thought I had made it quite clear in my reply to your letter that I object very strongly to the whole idea – and in particular to cutting off the corner of Rose Cottage garden. Apart from the potholes, that corner is about the only remaining effective way to stop people speeding. I see no real necessity for it or for the expenditure envisaged.'

Everyone turned to look at Andrew Lavery. He was leaning back in his chair, his legs crossed, his face impassive, seemingly quite relaxed; but there had been a determined note to his voice.

Robert Hollywell gazed at him anxiously.

'I'm sure everyone would agree to put up a speed restriction sign at both ends of the lane!' he said.

'In the hope that it will be observed, I suppose. Well, I'm sorry to say this, but I don't share your faith in my fellow man – and even if everyone living in the road slowed down, it won't stop the trades people. Some idiot in a blue van knocked over one of my dogs last Christmas – damn nearly died, too – as well you all know. No, I'm very much against this road improvement proposal and frankly, I'm surprised any of you go along with it.'

The ensuing silence was broken by Evelyn Bateman.

'I have to say I agree most emphatically with Mr Lavery. It isn't just the speed of all these cars, or, indeed, the noise. It's the question of the ecology. Turning a bridleway into a road will inevitably lead to the destruction of the flora and fauna we currently enjoy.'

'My dear Evelyn, we have no plans to destroy either, I do assure you,' the Reverend Hollywell added.

Evelyn's mouth tightened.

'Yet by cutting the corner you will be doing both. I have permitted that part of my garden where you propose to build the culvert to revert to nature for the express purpose of restoring a natural habitat for the birds, butterflies, wild flowers. There also happens to be a quince and a sloe tree growing there – quite rare fruits these days as I'm sure you all know. I object most strongly to them being removed for so unnecessary a purpose.'

'We all know how concerned you are about the countryside, Evelyn.' Robert Hollywell's voice was placating. 'Your quince jelly—'

'Is beside the point, Robert!' Keith Aymes broke in. 'Frank has agreed to sell that bit of land to me and it really is of no concern now to you, Miss Bateman, with the greatest respect.'

There was an awkward silence whilst those present remembered the dispute between Evelyn Bateman and Frank Dodd when Keith had first offered to buy the quarter of an acre, Evelyn protesting quite violently that it was part of her garden they were discussing. But Frank, who'd inherited Millers Farm from his father, had recalled that Rose Cottage had been given in perpetuity to Miss Bateman's aunt, who had been companion to the wife of Lord Hugo Horsborough. Looking at the deeds he had seen that the delineated boundary of the farm included the quarter-acre corner of The Warren – which had since been integrated into Rose Cottage garden. When he'd passed this information on to Mary, she had recalled an entry in the family bible in which Frank's grandfather had noted that he'd allowed Miss Bateman's aunt to make use of that part of his field for the excavation of a well, the water diviner having established it as the best siting for the purpose.

Neither Frank nor the Reverend Hollywell had imagined that the old lady would be so put out. The area in question, unlike her meticulously neat garden, was a mass of brambles and weeds – the well having long since gone into disuse. The quince tree lay at forty-five degrees, blown over in the hurricane, and ivy covered the trunk of the sloe. As far as Frank had been aware, Miss Bateman never went near the tangled undergrowth. Jack, to help the old girl out, was the only one to do so and that only once a year to gather the fruit. Although Frank disliked upsetting Miss Bateman – he considered her slightly paranoid about nature – there was too much at stake to allow her to retain the piece of land. The discovery that it belonged to him, coming as it did just when he was in such dire need of cash, was a godsend. Mr Aymes' offer was an exceedingly generous one, and neither quinces nor sloes would alter his decision to sell.

'. . . consider ourselves as er . . . a little democracy, and for the benefit of those newcomers to our small community –' the Reverend Hollywell's round face was beaming in the direction of Ian and Migs as he spoke '– I should point out that we put all matters of controversy to the vote.'

'That's all very well!' Andrew Lavery's voice was as decisive as Robert Hollywell's was hesitant. 'But we don't happen to have all interested parties present. Neither the Colemans nor the Proctors are here.'

'Ah, yes, the Proctors. They are on holiday, I believe.' The Reverend Hollywell shuffled through some papers on the table beside him. 'Yes, indeed—'

'Well, are they for or against? Presumably you told them we'd be voting at the meeting?'

Robert Hollywell shot an anxious glance at Keith.

'I rather think they er . . . well favour the scheme. That's to say, they gave me their proxy vote and—'

'Jane Proctor, wouldn't go against the Rev for the world!' Sarah muttered low key to Migs. 'She's church organist!'

'However, the Colemans . . . um, they did say they would be here!' Robert Hollywell glanced at his watch and looked somewhat helplessly at the sea of upturned faces. 'Er, perhaps in the circumstances, we should take it that they abstain?'

'No way!' Keith said forcefully. 'Caroline told me quite clearly that she was all for the improvements.'

'Well, I should have thought that Colin, being an ornothologist, was dead against it.' Nigel's voice had a quiet authority to it. He paused, suddenly remembering Sarah saying that Caroline wore the trousers in that household. She held the purse strings and poor old Colin did as he was told. Be that as it may, he saw no reason to withhold his views about the whole situation. 'Frankly, I don't much care for the way this road scheme is creating a kind of "us" and "them" atmosphere in Millers Lane,' he said. 'We've all rubbed along jolly well in the past – good neighbours . . . that sort of thing. If some of us don't want the road altered, shouldn't we just drop the whole idea of changing it and go back to doing necessary repairs only?'

The room erupted into a clamour of voices loud enough to dim the sound of the telephone ringing. A few minutes later, Betty Hollywell came into the room. Her face was very pale and it was clear to everyone as she faced her husband that she was deeply disturbed.

'That was Colin Coleman, dear!' she said. 'Something terrible has happened. His wife collapsed an hour ago. Doctor Grainger went straight there but . . . I'm afraid it was too late. Caroline Coleman has just died and I think you'd best go round to their house at once. Mr Coleman's beside himself and I said you'd go.'

Shocked into silence, no one spoke. Someone coughed nervously and Sarah leaned towards Migs and whispered, 'Frightfully nice couple . . . live opposite the Aymes. Wonder what happened to Caroline. She's . . . I mean was . . . only my age. Heart, I suppose!' She broke off as Daphne Bateman wandered into the room. Her face was covered in flour and she was waving a rolling pin in front of her face. Her voice, clear and precise, filled the room.

41

Queen, Queen Caroline
Washed her hair in turpentine,
Turpentine to make it shine,
Queen, Queen Caroline!

Evelyn sprang to her feet and hurried to take her sister's arm.

'Daphne slipped out when my back was turned!' Betty said apologetically to Evelyn. 'Come along, dear, we'll go and make a nice pot of tea, shall we?'

' *"Tea for two and two for tea!"* ' sang Daphne cheerfully with a smirk at Evelyn as if to say 'I put one over on you then, didn't I?'. She followed Betty back to the kitchen, preceded by the Reverend Hollywell muttering apologies for abandoning the meeting.

'I think our Daphne gets fed up with Evelyn's nagging!' Sarah whispered to Migs as they rose to leave. 'I suppose you have to feel sorry for poor Evelyn having to mind her sister morning, noon and night. If you ask me, she's overprotective!'

'Well, no one has asked you, my loved one!' Sarah's husband said, taking a firm hold of her arm. He smiled at Migs. 'I do assure you, our precious Road Meetings aren't nearly so dramatic as this one as a rule. Poor old Caroline. Bit young to pop her clogs, isn't she?'

'She was thirty-four!' Evelyn said as she came back into the room. 'I think the postman had told her Daphne was having a birthday and Caroline kindly dropped by and gave Daphne a little musical box. She said it was a wedding present neither she nor Colin wanted. She told us her birthday was the next day so we sent her a birthday card which is how I come to know her age.'

'That was nice of her,' Sarah said. 'We've known the Colemans for ages but don't socialize much. Nigel rather likes Colin, don't you, my loved one?'

Her husband nodded.

'But Caroline and I weren't on the same wavelength regarding this road idea. We had a chat about it last week and needless to say, our views didn't coincide. Sarah and I think it's because she came from Potters Bar? Only natural she'd hanker after that charming suburb: tidy roads, pavements, street lights, that sort of thing. She said she had only agreed to come here to the country because Colin is so mad on ornithology and dear old Potters Bar provided little other than starlings and pigeons to bird watch!'

'Nigel, a little more respect, please. Poor Caroline is, well, no longer with us.'

'One less vote for our good friends, the Aymes!' Nigel chortled, unabashed by his wife's admonitions. 'We haven't had a head count yet, but even without Caroline's vote for the road improvement, I have a nasty feeling the Aymes would have won the day.' He turned back to Evelyn as they followed the rest of the residents towards the door. 'None of us were close enough to Caroline to put some pressure on her to vote against the proposal, but you knew her very well, Miss Bateman, couldn't you have talked her round?'

Evelyn's pale cheeks coloured slightly as she shook her head, loosening one of the many hairpins securing the bun in the nape of her neck.

'If you want to know, Mr Sedgewick-Jones, I went to her house yesterday expressly for the purpose you are suggesting. She was quite adamant that she feels the improvements would benefit everyone and most certainly increase the value of their properties.'

As Evelyn turned towards the kitchen door to retrieve her sister, Sarah said, 'Was Caroline all right when you saw her, Miss Bateman? I mean, it's been terribly sudden, hasn't it – her death, I mean?'

'Perfectly all right! Now, if you'll excuse me, I will bid you goodnight. You, too, Mrs Peters!'

'Well, that wasn't very enlightening!' Nigel commented with a grin. 'However, sudden death means a post mortem so we'll hear all the facts in due course. Sorry for the wretched Colin, though. Must be a ghastly shock.'

'Nigel misses the Armstrongs who used to own Siskins,' Sarah said to Migs as they joined the queue in the hall waiting to say goodnight and thank you to the flustered Betty Hollywell. 'John Armstrong was a buddy he went jogging with every morning and played tennis with in the afternoons. As you may or may not

43

know, Colin Coleman isn't a sporting man – spends his spare time lying behind hedges staring at some species of bird life through his binoculars!'

With Nigel still grinning, Sarah was left to say their thank yous before extracting an invitation from Migs to pop in for coffee the following morning since Migs had to get back now to relieve the babysitter. There was little doubt, Migs told Ian as they walked home, that shocked though she was by the news of their neighbour's sudden death, she was happy to know that in Sarah Sedgewick-Jones she had found a very compatable friend.

Five

July

As Migs piled a second load of laundry into her washing machine and sat down at the kitchen table, Sarah pushed the cooling mug of coffee towards her with a wry smile.

'Better you than me!' she said. 'Thank God Nigel doesn't want kids any more than I do!' Her glance shifted to Dougal playing contentedly with a pile of bricks in one corner of the room. 'Mind you, your brat is so adorable I just could be tempted! My sister has three and they're absolutely ghastly!'

Migs returned her visitor's smile. Busy as she always was, she loved these now regular coffee mornings when Sarah dropped in.

'Dougie is good most of the time. We've been lucky!' she said.

Sarah stretched out her long legs – for once not clad in jodhpurs but in fashionable jeans – and regarded Migs thoughtfully.

'Is it luck, or is it the way you cope? It's the same with horses, you know. You've a way with them or you haven't. You don't ride, do you?'

Migs shook her head.

'Never had a chance to learn. I can ride a bike!'

Both girls laughed, then Sarah's face became serious.

'You know Nigel went to the inquest yesterday. He and Colin are quite chummy now. They have the odd drink together at the King's Head, so Colin wanted him as a sort of character witness.'

Migs put down her coffee mug.

'It *was* accidental death, wasn't it? Ellen said so.'

Sarah gave a deep sigh.

'So the coroner said, but Nigel thinks the police still suspect

45

murder. It's mad, of course, but . . . well, quarter of a million quid *is* one hell of a motive!'

Ellen, the inveterate gossip, had already passed on to Migs the rumour that the unfortunate Colin Coleman was suspected of killing his wife because he was penniless, whereas Caroline Coleman had been 'rolling in it'! According to Ellen, Caroline had always held the purse strings.

Glad to have Sarah here for company, Migs decided to leave the ironing for a while longer.

'Surely Colin wouldn't have needed to kill his wife. Why couldn't he just ask her for money when he was short?'

Sarah shrugged.

'You're new here so you probably don't know all the facts. Those two were always rowing. Caroline came from a filthy rich family and, being an only child, was terribly spoilt. Colin, as you've probably gathered, has one passion in life: birds – of the feathered variety!' Sarah grinned disarmingly. 'He spends most of his time at those wildlife sanctuaries or "twitching", I think it's called – staying out all night in the hope of seeing some strange bird or other.' Seeing Migs grin, she broke off, nevertheless smiling herself. She began again.

'OK, *species* of bird! Nigel thinks it was probably Colin's disinterest in Caroline which sparked off her interest in him – accustomed as she was to attracting most men at will. Can you believe he told Nigel he was late for his own wedding because he'd seen some rare bird or other on his roof! What with those bottle glasses and the binoculars always dangling round his neck, you can't exactly call him very attractive, but the funny thing is, you can't help liking him. Poor old sod looked pretty ghastly when I saw him yesterday after the inquest. I think in his way he was fond of Caroline. Besides, it was a rather horrible way for her to go! Colin told Nigel she was in absolute agony, poor thing!'

'I've never had food poisoning, but Ian did once after eating oysters and he said at the time, he wished he was dead!'

Sarah grimaced.

'Well, so much for the poison mushroom or toadstool or whatever it was that Caroline ate. The pathologist at the inquest gave it a Latin name I can't remember. Ask old Evelyn – she's the whizz kid on nature. Whatever, it must have acted horribly quickly. Evelyn had seen her earlier that morning and said she was perfectly OK. Caroline had dropped by on her way back from Delhurst to return Daphne's knitting which she'd left behind the day before when they went up to tea. Caroline was always very nice about Daphne – reckoned she wasn't half as loopy as everyone thought.'

'It doesn't sound as if she is that retarded if she can knit!' Migs said.

'Caroline maintained that Daphne was simply institutional-ized after sixty years in the loony bin, but Evelyn wouldn't have it. The old girl can be quite bitchy at times and once told me that Caroline suffered from delusions of medical grandeur, thought she knew all the answers because her father was a Harley Street psychologist! And to be honest, Caroline was a bit that way inclined – you only had to tell her you had a headache and she'd have some far-fetched reason for it even when you knew you'd simply got a hangover! Still, she meant well, poor thing. I wonder how long it will be before Colin gets through the money! Nigel said he was thinking of going on some sort of ornithological safari, something he's been wanting to do for ages but Caroline objected. She's lost control of him now!'

'Poor old Colin! It can't have been much fun being suspected of murdering your wife for her money!'

Sarah stretched her arms above her head and stood up.

'Can't blame the police, though, can you? Not with her holding the purse strings and he having to ask her for every penny. Ah, well! Thanks for the coffee, Migs. I'll leave you to your chores –' she bent down to tickle the baby who beamed at her angelically – 'although I must say, this particular chore is a real poppet. Bring him to lunch tomorrow, Migs, and don't say you can't spare the time, you've got to eat!'

'All right, and thanks!' Migs said, picking Dougal up and carrying him to the door of the cottage to see her visitor on her way. Sarah's bay gelding was tethered to the garden gate post and was happily grazing the grass verge of the road.

As Sarah swung herself into the saddle with an easy grace, she waved at the baby and said to Migs, 'Don't forget the new date for the Road Meeting: 15th August. Nigel said it's likely to be quite contentious because Colin told him that now Caroline has departed this world, he can vote as he wanted to in the first place. You know he's always been paranoid about the birds in the hedgerows and so on. So that makes one vote more for the "against" contingent and we could have a deadlock. Should be fun!'

With a friendly smile, she waved once more to the baby and rode off down the lane. Sorry to see her go but with plenty to do, Migs went back indoors to collect the first load of washing to hang out on the line.

She must remember to book Ellen to babysit, she told herself as she pegged up a pair of Dougal's dungarees. And to tell Ian. He was becoming quite vociferous regarding the road improvement scheme. The lane should stay as it was, he maintained, and Keith Aymes was a nasty piece of work who thought he could ride roughshod over his neighbours just because he had more money than they did!

Since their move into No. 1 a month ago, Ian had become as friendly with Nigel Sedgewick-Jones as she had with Sarah – odd friendships, really, since the two couples had little in common other than their ages. Nevertheless, both Sarah and Nigel, despite their rather loud, county voices and obsession with horses, were good fun and Ian was as pleased to have found a male friend as she was happy to exchange girl's talk with Sarah.

As she went into the kitchen to collect Dougal's lunch, pouring the chicken and potato purée into his dish brought to her mind the horrible description Sarah had given her of the poisonous soup which had killed poor Caroline Coleman. From what Ian had deduced from all the lane gossip in the King's Head, it seemed the unfortunate woman had gathered some roots of a plant growing on the edge of the stream which ran through the bottom of her garden. Believing them to be parsnips she had made soup and within no time at all she was dying. A friend from Delhurst had dropped in to have coffee with her and found her having violent convulsions and promptly telephoned for Dr Grainger. Caroline was unable to speak but was clearly in agony so he rushed her to hospital in Hunnington in his car. By the time they got there and had used a stomach pump on her, it was too late to save her. There'd been a post mortem which had identified the poisonous root: Hemlock Water Dropwort. The unfortunate Colin hadn't become a suspect until details of Caroline's wealth and the high insurance on her life came to light.

'The detective looking into the matter realized Colin had a strong motive for despatching his wife to the hereafter,' Ian had commented. 'That was when the finger of suspicion was first pointed at the poor chap.'

Spooning the baby food into Dougal's waiting mouth, Migs' uneasy thoughts gave way to a sigh of relief. It was all very well for Ian and Nigel to treat Caroline's death in so cavalier a fashion, but murder so near home – even if it had only been suspected – was unsettling.

Fortunately, old Miss Bateman – Evelyn as she insisted Migs should call her – was reassuring. There was little she didn't know about plants and herbs, she told Migs. She had made a study of Culpeper, the seventeenth-century physician whose works on the subject were invaluable. She was familiar with Hemlock Water Dropwort, the poison found by the pathologist. According to her, it was well known to be lethal and had been the cause of many fatal accidents – the pale yellow roots and leaves, too – not only to humans but to cattle. Only two days before the accident, Evelyn said, Caroline had asked her for her special recipe for parsnip soup. The poor woman had obviously mistaken the hemlock in her garden for parsnips and decided to try out Evelyn's recipe – hence the residue found in Caroline's saucepan in her kitchen. Evelyn had been quite upset, blaming herself for not warning Caroline about the lethal effects of the hemlock growing on the banks of the stream in Siskins' garden.

'Mrs Coleman was a Londoner – she grew up in Potters Bar – and had never lived in the country before they bought Siskins,' Evelyn told Migs. 'I expect you know, dear, that her husband, Mr Coleman, is an ornithologist, so not surprisingly, he renamed the bungalow after some birds he'd seen: siskins. Birds are his passion, she told me.'

At that moment in Evelyn's revelations, the dotty sister had started singing, '*"Two little dickie birds sitting on a wall. One named Peter, one named Paul . . ."*' Migs had thought it quite funny and not inappropriate, but Evelyn had been annoyed at the interruption and sent Daphne into the garden to see Dougal, who was busy with his toys within the safe confines of his playpen.

As the days went by following Caroline Coleman's inquest and funeral, the gossip died down and life in the lane went back to its customary *modus vivendi*. By the time the next scheduled Road Meeting came round on the calendar, Migs had become much more familiar with the other lane residents. Jack, the Dodds' son, had been round twice, once to clear the brambles at the bottom of the garden, and once to mend the door of the coal shed. A third visit occurred on a weekend when Ian was home and Jack came to help him repair the garden fence. To Migs' surprise, when Ian came in for lunch and Jack went back to the farm, Ian was unusually quiet.

'Cat got your tongue, darling?' she asked. 'How did you both get on?'

Ian looked up from his plate and the thoughtful expression on his face gave way to a smile.

'Very well. Jack's a good lad – works hard despite the ponytail and earring. We've just about finished the fence. No way young Dougal will get out of this garden, no matter how far he can crawl.' He ruffled the curls on his young son's head. Since they had moved into No. 1, as they now called their cottage, Dougal's mobility had increased considerably, as had his sociability. He'd taken a great shine to Jack, who used to whistle through his teeth at him which Dougal found fascinating.

'I was asking Jack about that fire in their barn,' Ian told Migs. 'You remember Ellen telling us he'd nearly killed himself jumping out of the granary window? He says no one ever did get to the bottom of the mystery; how the barn doors were closed from the outside the way they were. Seems the insurance company paid up in the end, despite knowing Frank Dodd needed the money so badly, because they couldn't prove it was other than an accident.

But Jack said his dad wouldn't do such a thing in a thousand years – righteous, God-fearing, honest man if ever there was one – according to Jack who, I rather gathered, wished his father was a bit less rigid with his scruples.'

Ian paused briefly whilst Migs removed his empty plate and replaced it with a bowl of home-grown plums and custard.

'Jack's having it off with one of the nearby farmers' daughter who, it would seem, wears too much make-up and too short skirts ever to meet his parents' approval,' he related between mouthfuls. ' "You'd fancy her and all, Mr Peters!" Jack said, ' "cepting you've got a right smasher of yer own!" Reckon I have, too, Mrs Peters,' Ian said bending over to kiss Migs. 'And remember, my girl,' he added laughing, 'you've got a perfectly good bloke of your own to keep you satisfied so no encouraging your admirer, young Jack.'

Migs put down the oven cloth she was holding and ruffled Ian's hair.

'If I was going to fancy anyone – and I mean if – it wouldn't be a boy like Jack. I'd go for Andrew Lavery. Now he's really cool!'

'So you fancy Mr Scarlet Pimpernel Lavery, do you?' Ian commented, pulling his wife down on his lap.

'He's very good-looking – six foot two, a physique to die for, stunning green eyes, and legs . . . well . . .'

'Well, what about his legs? How come you know what they're like, Madam?'

Migs laughed.

'Because he was out walking in shorts and stopped by the front gate to say hello, why hadn't we got to know each other better and what a pity I had another half – you.'

'To which you heartily agreed, you unfaithful besom.'

'What's a "besom"?' Migs asked when he stopped kissing her.

'It's a Scottish word. It can mean a broom or it can mean a low woman.'

'I love you!' Megan said laughing. 'Though goodness knows why. Anyway, our glamorous Mr Lavery had two of his wolf-hounds with him – they are just gorgeous, Ian. Dougal was fascinated by them. Anyway, we started talking about the lane and he's as much against improving it as we are. Andrew, Mr Lavery, told me one of his dogs had been run into by the Aymes' chauffeur. He said the man denied it was his fault although he was doing at least 40 miles an hour, despite the potholes. I told Andrew we were against changes too, and he wants us to be sure to go to the meeting next Saturday to cast our votes.'

'Football night!' Ian said, then seeing Migs' face, he sighed. 'Oh, well, if it's a matter of "every vote counts", I'll penalize myself.'

Migs planted another kiss on the top of his head and stood up.

'Andrew said since they are allowing a vote for each husband and wife, yours and my vote against will be quite critical – especially as Ellen and Ray Brigend have abstained so far. Andrew said Keith and Jill Aymes have been working on them and may very well bribe, cajole or bully them into a "for" vote.'

Ian, too, stood up and glanced out of the window.

'What a to-do!' he said. Then he added more seriously, 'We came here to raise a family, Migs, because here it was away from the traffic and our kids could ride bikes or pick blackberries or whatever in the lane. It is only a bridleway, for heaven's sake, not a proper road. Next thing, the Aymes will be wanting street lights and pavements.'

Migs nodded, her eyes thoughtful.

'They are already wanting all the hedgerows cut and the verges mown. As Andrew said, there won't be a dandelion left for Dougal's rabbit!'

'Think I might get on well with that chap after all,' Ian said as he headed towards the garden door. 'But don't you get on too well with him, Migs, my adored one, just because he's a glamorous successful author.'

'Don't worry!' Migs said smiling. 'He apologized for not having invited us up for a drink but said he badly needs to get on with his writing without interruptions, so we mustn't expect him to frat. But he will be at the Road Meeting.'

'So will I!' said Ian. 'Can't wait to have a word with the fellow.' He closed the door behind him then almost immediately opened it again and put his head round it. 'It'll give me the chance to tell him to keep his hands off my wife.'

'Ian, you wouldn't . . .' Migs began, and seeing the expression on her husband's face, she threw the dishcloth at him. 'Love you!' she called out as he closed the door a second time.

Six

' S hall I put your rod together for you, dear?'
      Jane Proctor's question was voiced tentatively, knowing
as she well did that her husband would almost certainly tell her
he was quite capable of assembling his rod himself; that he was
not totally incapacitated.

Linen sunhat pulled down over his bald head, Wing Commander Cecil Proctor, D.S.O., D.F.C., and bars, glanced irri-
tably at his wife before saying, 'I would have thought you'd know
by now that I'm perfectly capable of assembling my rod by
myself, Jane, thank you very much.'

He took the sleeve from her, not without some difficulty,
seated as he was in his wheelchair. He'd had a safety belt fitted
especially so that when casting, he could lean forward without
falling into the water. With an ill-concealed sigh of irritation, he
pulled the sections of rod out of their canvas sleeve. His wife's
red, perspiring face was only a few inches from his own as she
placed the box of flies, the spare reel, hooks and weights within
his easy reach.

Jane Proctor was both hot and tired, having wheeled her
husband – no light weight – in his chair from the house, across
the lane and down to the landing stage from which he fished.
Although he owned an expensive electric chair supplied by the
RAF Benevolent Fund for one of their few remaining Battle of
Britain pilots, he refused to allow it to be used on the pathway
leading to the landing stage at the south end of the lake.
Consequently, despite the fact that his wife was now, like
him, in her eighties, she was obliged on the carer's day off to

manoeuvre him plus his fishing gear to the one place where he could still manage to enjoy himself. Paralysed in a flying accident in the war, he had lived ever since on that one period of glory. Jane could have repeated word perfect Cecil's account of how he had outwitted the German Messerschmidt pilots. Fortunately there were few people left alive who the Proctors knew who might question the Wing Commander's assertion that he had shot down more enemy planes than any other Battle of Britain pilot.

Jane did not doubt her husband's former bravery but she did very often wish that he would exhibit a little of his courage within their four walls. He maintained his bravado in front of the district nurse, the doctor, friends, visitors, relatives – in fact everyone but herself.

It was probably her own fault, she often told herself, for allowing him to browbeat her the way he did, shouting at her, telling her she was stupid, ordering her to attend to his needs or his wishes as if she were a paid servant. But it was not in her nature to be a fighter, and in those early years when he'd first been allowed out of hospital and they'd been married, she had felt so deeply sorry for him she would have given him her own legs if they could have helped him to walk again. After Peter – a honeymoon baby – was born, the loving affection Cecil had hitherto shown her ceased to exist and was replaced by an ill-concealed irritation. It was due in part to frustration, their doctor had informed her, frustration not only because he couldn't walk but because he was frequently unable to achieve an erection.

'But I don't mind, Doctor, honestly I don't!' she had insisted. 'I love him and the bed side of it . . .' – she couldn't bring herself actually to say the word 'sex' – '. . . is immaterial . . . at least, so long as he goes on loving me. Sometimes it seems as if . . . well, I do have my little boy to love and who loves and needs me, so I don't need to . . . well, to *do it* the way Cecil seems to think I should. It's so confusing, Doctor. When I tell him it's for him I mind, not for myself, he gets so angry with me.'

The doctor had prescribed sedatives – not for Cecil who undoubtedly needed them – but for her.

'For heaven's sake, Jane, do stop messing about down there,' her husband interrupted her thoughts. 'I can manage perfectly well without you tipping my box of flies all over the place. Go home, Jane. I don't need you.'

Which was just about the truth of the matter, Jane thought as she straightened her back, put the unfurled umbrella a little nearer to him and moved off in the direction of The Mill House. At least she would have the next two hours to herself before she took down his mid-morning thermos of coffee. She glanced back once more to the chair-bound figure on the landing stage. He'd been so much better tempered ever since Keith Aymes had decided to stock his lake with trout and allowed Cecil to fish it; and not least, to have had the landing stage widened to accommodate Cecil's wheelchair. These past two years since the Aymes had moved into the Manor House had been the saviours of her sanity.

Despite the fact that it was Cecil who had wanted to move out of London ten years ago, imagining he would be less bored in surroundings familiar to his childhood, he seldom lost an opportunity to tell her he found life in the country excrutiatingly tedious, monotonous – until Keith Aymes had made it possible for him to enjoy once more his youthful hobby of fishing. He had complained even so, because he was unable to fish in the closed season. Now, despite his present enjoyment of his favourite sport, he still found something to complain about. Only the other week it was 'a pretty poor show when the highlight of our lives is a bloody road meeting!' Only he hadn't said 'bloody' but used the 'f' word and if there was one thing Jane really couldn't stand it was Cecil's bad language. At moments like that she could very easily have picked up a cushion and smothered him.

Not a day passed when Jane had not wished her beloved only child, Peter, had not married an American girl and gone to live so far away. She only saw him once a year at Christmas when Cecil put on his 'bravado' act and was exaggeratedly affectionate towards her. In fact there were so many 'dearests' and 'darlings' that Peter referred to his parents as the most devoted couple he'd ever met, and his father as the bravest person he knew. Peter and Ginny, his wife, were no sooner out of the house than Cecil reverted. Tormented by the knowledge that it would be eleven long months before she could hope to see her son again, although she would never have admitted it, for twenty-four hours after Peter had gone, she was so highly stressed that it only needed one more criticism from Cecil for her to have seriously wanted to kill him. But for her life of servitude to him, she would have been free to join her son and daughter-in-law in America. The young couple had said many times they would love to have Peter's parents to live with them but Cecil, of course, would not even consider it.

'You don't think the bloody Yanks would give a wreck like me a visa, do you?' he'd said the only time it had been discussed. 'And even if they did, we couldn't afford the medical fees. Let the effing NHS pay – the country owes me, doesn't it? But for chaps like me, Hitler would have invaded. It was us, not the Yanks, who won the bloody war!'

Jane had known better than to argue.

Down by the lake, Jack Dodd watched from behind the trees the carry-on of the Wing Commander's arrival across the water. Glancing at his watch, he saw that it was only just nine o'clock. When he'd started fishing it had been six o'clock and there had been a slight mist hanging over the surface of the water. Now, the sun was shining and a soft breeze gently swayed the leaves of the water lilies out by the island. Jack really loved the solitude, and especially when he was standing on the bank watching the moorhens scuttling on the leaf pads, and once in a while a fish leaping and falling back with a splash as the water made circles around it. High above his head, he could hear the willow warblers, tits, blackcaps flying to and from the birch and willows beneath whose branches he was concealed.

It was a beautiful place to be, Jack thought, and only people who really appreciated it should be here. Sometimes, the owner of the lake, Mr Aymes, had friends down for the weekend and they were not only very bad fishermen but were indifferent to their surroundings, their loud voices frightening the ducks, scaring away the kingfishers who were nesting on the far side of the island. Most of all, the Wing Commander should not be allowed here on what Jack half considered to be 'his' lake. Not only had the silly old codger twice caught him fishing – well, poaching really and told Mr Aymes, who had fined him a week's pay for the trout he'd had out of the lake – but the old turtle swore at him if he drove past him in his wheelchair, shouting that motorbikes shouldn't be allowed in the lane and he'd see they were banned by the Road Committee if it was the last thing he did.

Pity it wouldn't be the last, Jack thought as he lifted his rod for one last cast. It wasn't safe for him to go on fishing now the old man was there, even though he was pretty well concealed. But he needed one more fish. He could only get £1 each for them from the fishmonger over at Hunnington and he needed the money.

He had a new girl now, Sandra, who had succeeded Shirl. Like her predecessor, she was generous enough with her favours but expected more tangible favours from him: fags, booze, tickets for gigs, bracelets or bangles and such for birthdays and Christmas. He didn't earn much at his morning job as assistant to the greenkeeper at Delhurst golf course: £4.75 which was minimum wage these days anyway. He could pick up a bit more pocketing golf balls lost by the players but they only fetched £10.00 for fifty and that amount took some finding. Ever since the barn fire last year, his father had been unable to give him more than a few quid for the work he did round the farm. It wasn't even as if he liked farming. If he'd gone into the Navy as he'd wanted, he'd be earning a decent wage. No wonder Shirl had packed him up.

Indignation at his situation now doubled Jack's mood of irritation as he realized his hook was snagged on an overhanging branch.

Serve you right, you stupid git! he told himself. Weren't thinking what you were doing!

Dare he reach out to retrieve it, he wondered? Could he afford being seen by the Wing Co? Better buy a new hook and float, by the look of it. Carefully he took a step sideways so once again he could look down the length of the lake. A grin spread across his face. As near as he could see his fellow fisherman had nodded off. His rod was propped securely to the side of his chair, the float some distance out bobbing slightly in the water – at least Jack supposed it was for he was too far away to see such detail. Still grinning, he imagined a six pounder on the line and the old man unaware of it.

But the grin left his face as he glimpsed movement behind the trees at the back of the landing stage – movement which could only mean someone was about and might well see him. Forget the hook, he told himself as he took a cautious step backwards. And yes, there was someone there – Mrs Proctor, perhaps, to see if her husband wanted anything. Whoever it was, was not going along the lane as he'd supposed but was approaching the landing stage. As far as Jack could ascertain, the old boy hadn't heard the newcomer for he never stirred.

Once again, Jack's sense of humour got the better of him as he remained quietly in his hiding place. Judging by the way the Wing Co was sleeping, you'd think his long-suffering wife had put sleeping pills in his coffee, he told himself. Good job, too. Mrs Proctor had been extremely nice to him when he'd been up at The Mill House last summer with his chainsaw when one of their apple trees had blown down; given him hot drinks and one of her home-made current buns. And when the job was finished, she'd invited him into the kitchen to warm up as it had been a bitter day. Next thing the old man had come bumbling in in his wheelchair and sworn at his wife – in front of him, too – telling her she should effing well know better than to have strangers in the house with filthy boots and dirty hands and pansy hairdos. It wasn't until he'd got home and asked his dad, that he'd found out that 'pansy' was what they called gays in the old days.

Jack's thoughts ceased abruptly as the shadowy figure now moved on to the landing stage. For a moment, he thought he must be dreaming. Whoever it was – and through the leaf-covered branch directly in front of him he couldn't identify the person – was bending down behind the chair . . . clasping the handrail as if . . . It flashed through Jack's mind that the person might be intending to push the chair forward, over the edge; but reason told him that couldn't happen. He'd often seen Mrs Proctor putting a brick in front of the front wheel, doubtless as an added precaution lest the brake failed. No, that wasn't the intention at all; the person was tipping the chair sideways and it was falling . . . falling. . . . God Almighty! Jack gasped. They had actually tipped the chair over and it was sinking, sinking quickly moreover, with the Wing Commander still in it . . .

There was an almighty splash as the chair hit the water but now, as the ripples of the wake subsided, there was a gentle lapping of water against the bank. The silence was almost as shocking as the scene he had just observed. A full minute passed before the shock faded and Jack came to his senses. This was no place for him to be. For one thing he was fishing illegally, and the lake would surely soon be alive with people; but although one part of him wanted to run as fast as he possibly could from the scene, the other part urged him to race round the lake to see if he could get the unfortunate man out of the water before he drowned.

He paused as a further thought arrested him. Not only would he have insufficient strength to pull out the man, belted to the chair as he'd clearly been, but whoever had pushed him in wasn't going to hang about. If he, Jack, were found round that side of the lake, someone might think he'd done it. Everyone in the lane knew the Wing Commander had it in for him; knew the man had got him into trouble and was responsible for him being fined. They'd all think he'd done it – that the Wing Co had seen him fishing, threatened to report him again and Jack had tipped his chair in so he couldn't do it.

He'd done quite enough speculating, Jack decided as quickly he gathered up his gear and made off along the back path through the woods and across Badgers Field towards the farm. No one but he and the occasional walker ever used this path so he'd be very unlucky to be seen. He'd planned to have the morning off from work, to tell the greenkeeper next day that he'd been ill – got sunstroke or something! – but now he decided he would go to work after all. It was only ten o'clock. If he got on to the golf course by the ninth hole, he could say he'd been busy resetting the mole traps. They'd been plagued by moles recently and because Jack's father had taught him how to catch them, Jack had been given the job of getting rid of them. Fred, the greenkeeper, wouldn't know for sure how long it took just to check and set a few traps. Then, if anyone did ask if he'd been near the lake, he'd have a good alibi.

'Bugger me!' Jack said as he reached home and went to hide his fishing gear in one of the old pig styes. 'The way I'm going on, anyone would think I done the old boy in.' His frown deepened as it finally hit him that he had just witnessed a murder – not an accident, but a deliberate murder. Who could have carried out such an act – and in broad daylight, too?

Unbidden, his mother's description of the Manor House ghost, told to him in his childhood, caused his skin to prickle. The story of old Lord Horsborough calling for his lost son had caused him many a nightmare as a child – not least because Ray Brigend steadfastly maintained he'd seen him.

With a conscious effort, Jack shook himself as if to shrug away such nonsense. He was eighteen years old now – not a stupid little kid. He didn't believe in ghosts. But who had been moving among the trees by the lake? Jack shut his eyes and tried not to see the wheelchair with the man strapped inside it, tipping, as if in slow motion, into the water. But he could not silence the memory of the screech of a moorhen as, frightened by the commotion, it skittered away over the water lily leaves.

Seven

'What are all those bollards doing at the entrance to our lane?' Ian asked as he kissed Migs and dumped his briefcase on the sitting-room floor. 'And that official-looking sign saying "No Entry except for Residents"?'

'I'll tell you all about it later,' Migs said. 'You're awfully late back, darling, and we're due at the Sedgewick-Jones' in quarter of an hour.'

'Oh, Lord, I'd clean forgotten!' Ian replied. 'I'll have a quick shower and change. It was hot as hell in town. By the by, you look lovely, darling. New dress?'

Migs grinned.

'It was my going-away dress, stupid!' She lent over the bundle of ironing she was carrying to kiss his proffered cheek. But her humour was fleeting as she recalled the horrible events of the day. Fortunately, as she told Ian on the way to The Paddocks, she had taken Dougal to Crawley to see his godmother so they'd missed the whole gruesome business of Wing Commander Proctor's death. But there was no time to give Ian further information about the ghastly tragedy at the lake.

Half an hour later, Sarah filled in the details for both Ian and Nigel, who had also been in London the whole day.

'The two of you are going to be questioned tomorrow morning,' she told them as she handed the men glasses of ice-cold Pimms.

They were sitting on the pretty flagstone terrace outside The Paddocks – a rambling, whitewashed stone building which had once been part of a block of stables for the Manor House. The previous owner of the manor, Sarah had informed Migs, had been in need of money and had sold off some of the land, including the stables for which there was planning permission. Nigel and Sarah, who were badly in need of a country house with stables for the horses which were their passion, had converted a number of the buildings into a very attractive house.

'Two years ago the Brigadier sold the Manor House to the Aymes. Keith and Jill were livid when I told them how we'd come by our house,' Nigel had told Ian soon after Migs and Ian had come to live in Millers Lane. 'Keith was, and still is, desperate to buy more land round the manor to enlarge his estate, as he calls it. You'd think he had enough land what with that big garden, the lake, the wood and three large fields.'

But neither the manor nor their own home, The Paddocks, was the subject of conversation as Sarah started to relate the day's events. The Wing Commander, she told them, had been enjoying one of his fishing days in his usual place parked on the landing stage. There were no other fishermen there – or none that Jane Proctor had seen when she'd settled him down there. Soon after doing so, she'd left him to enjoy his fishing and gone back home to The Mill House. No one else was at home because Ellen only worked for the Proctors on Mondays and Thursdays.

Sarah paused while Nigel got up to replenish their glasses. No one spoke until she resumed her account.

'Jane said it was exactly eleven o'clock when she took a thermos of coffee down to the lake and saw the old boy had vanished. There was no one about so she assumed someone had been there earlier and he'd asked them to move him to a more advantageous position. That had happened once before, but only once, as the landing stage was preferable being quite far out from the bank and clear of trees, which made casting easier for her husband. In retrospect, she realized, she should have known he wouldn't have changed sites without taking his gear with him – the bait box, flies, that kind of thing – but you know how vague poor Jill is. Anyway, she went round the far side of the lake to look for him and it was only then, when she couldn't find him or anyone else, that she began to panic.'

Sarah frowned as she took a large gulp of Pimms before resuming her story.

'When she got back to the landing stage and saw all his

paraphernalia still there, she looked down and saw the dark shadow of the upturned wheelchair deep under water. Murky as it was, she could discern the shape of the Wing Co still in the chair. By this time, she was hysterical and knowing there was nothing she could do to get her husband out, she ran back to the lane to get help. Mercifully, Jill Aymes was driving by on her way to the Proctors with plums for the hospital. Jane all but dragged her out of her car and down to the landing stage. After one horrified look Jill realized they had no hope of pulling the man out. She had her mobile phone in the car and immediately dialled 999.'

'I'm somewhat surprised to hear our glamour girl was so level-headed,' Nigel interposed. Sarah nodded.

'From what one of the firemen told me later, immediately the police hear someone has drowned or is drowning, they summon the fire brigade and an ambulance, all of which went screaming down the lane within twenty minutes of Jill's call, nearly knocking poor Ellen off her bicycle as she was coming out of the farmyard.'

'How perfectly ghastly for Mrs Proctor!' Migs said. 'Was her husband . . .?'

'Well and truly dead!' Sarah forestalled the question. 'The firemen had got him out of the lake before the police arrived. He was still strapped in his chair. Somewhat pointlessly they tried resuscitation, but obviously to no effect. By this time, Jill had telephoned me and so there we all were by the lake in case we could help, or support Jane who was still pretty hysterical. She kept saying "It was my fault, my fault. I didn't check if the brake was on securely. It was my fault. I should have checked but he gets so cross if I fuss . . .". Next thing, the wretched woman is pulling herself away from us the better to see one of the men covering the Wing Co's face with a blanket before they lifted him on to a stretcher and carried him to the ambulance.'

Sarah looked so discomfited, Nigel put a hand on her arm.

'Look here, darling, you don't have to tell us any more right now. I expect we'll hear all about it tomorrow from the police, though heaven knows what you or I can tell them, eh, Ian? You barely knew the man and I so disliked him, I never had anything to do with him if I could help it.'

Sarah took a deep breath and gave Nigel a reassuring smile.

'It was a bit macabre at the time,' she admitted, 'but it was after the ambulance had taken the body away that things got worse. A senior policeman had arrived by then, a Detective Inspector Govern. He wanted all of us who were there, which included the Rev and Betty who'd come to see what was up – excluding the firemen, of course – to join him back at the Proctors' house for questioning. Jill and I made tea for everyone as Jane was too upset even to think about it, and that was when the inspector said the Wing Co's death could not necessarily be considered an accident having occurred in suspicious circumstances.'

'I don't believe it!' Nigel burst out. 'You mean to say he thought someone had actually pushed the old boy in? But that's crazy! Who on earth would have wanted to murder the poor chap, bore though he was.'

'You for one, darling!' Sarah said with an attempt to lighten the conversation. 'Last time we played bridge with the Proctors you came home saying if ever he told that story again about how he'd managed to land his plane on one engine, riddled with bullets, in the middle of a ploughed field but only after shooting down three Jerries, etc, etc, you'd strangle him!'

Nigel grinned.

'OK, so I might have wanted to bump him off but not by drowning the poor devil. The police don't really think it was murder, do they?'

Sarah put down her empty glass and stood up.

'Actually, I think they do. It didn't help matters for Jane to keep confessing it was all her fault. Even if she didn't check the brakes, that doesn't mean she wanted him off the planet.'

'Maybe not, but she did have a pretty strong motive, didn't she? I'm sure I remember you telling me she'd said if it wasn't for her husband, she could have gone to America to live with that son she adored?'

'I'd forgotten that!' Sarah said, linking her arm through Migs'. 'Whatever, she's such a mouse, I can't imagine her doing such a thing. Come on, boys, supper. It's nothing special, I warn you. Cold salmon and asparagus followed by summer pudding.'

'Sounds good to me,' Ian said as he followed Sarah and his wife indoors. 'Migs and I have been married nearly two years and she still can't cook a decent scrambled egg.'

Miggs turned and confronted him, an exaggerated frown distorting her pretty face.

'Say that just once again, you ungrateful man, and I'll murder you before you're a day older.'

'Steady on, old girl!' Nigel said. 'Murder isn't the most palatable of subjects right now. You should have married me, you know. I like my eggs boiled!'

The mood lightened once more as Sarah led them through to the charming French-styled kitchen where she liked to feed her friends.

Detective Inspector Govern with his assistant, Sergeant Beck, beside him, turned his car into Millers Lane. The previous day, following the death of the wheelchair-bound Wing Commander, the Reverend Hollywell had given him a list of all the residents of the lane eligible to vote – a copy of the one he had drawn up to assist him in his work as chairman of the Road Committee. There appeared to be seven couples, two spinster sisters, one recently bereaved widower and the author, Andrew Lavery. Beck, an ardent fan, had looked up Lavery on the Internet and found him to be a fairly prolific writer of whodunnits – thirty-one published books to his credit Beck had informed Govern. There was no Mrs Lavery according to the Reverend Hollywell, but from time to time there were some 'questionable young women around'. Not all at once, he had hastened to add, but they changed quite frequently so that he never really knew who was there. Having proffered this much information, he seemed reluctant to give any pen pictures of the locals and Govern now intended to investigate them all.

According to the initial report from the pathologist, Proctor's death had been by drowning and there were no other signs of injury. He himself had made an examination of the wheelchair and the landing stage, and had more or less made up his mind that the accident had to have been just that – no foul play. The brakes of the wheelchair when it was recovered from its watery grave had proved to be in the 'off' position, but were otherwise in perfect order. So either they had not been properly secured when the poor chap had arrived there or, improbable though it seemed, someone had gone down to the lake and released them. This was the alternative he and Beck now intended to consider before making a report for the coroner and the inevitable inquest.

Following the accident, he and Beck called at The Mill House to see the unfortunate wife of the dead man. Although she was no longer hysterical, she kept insisting the accident had been her fault. She seemed genuinely shocked. The lady who was comforting the woman – a Mrs Sarah Sedgewick-Jones – was more coherent.

'The Wing Co was a thoroughly crochety character,' she'd told them, having inveigled them into the kitchen where she was making coffee. 'He bullied his wife whenever he wanted to vent his bad temper and there was no one else around.'

Beck had agreed with him that the very attractive Mrs Sedgewick-Jones was best described as flippant, and her evidence, if such it could be called, should be taken with a pinch of salt. 'If I was her, I'd have bumped him off years ago!' she'd said. Govern had had to reprimand Beck for grinning when they left the house. Nevertheless, it wasn't entirely a waste of time for they'd established that Mr Sedgewick-Jones had a perfect alibi having been in London all day as had the younger fellow down the road – Ian Peters. It was he who suggested they should call first on the author who, along with the farmer Dodd and Evelyn Bateman, had lived in the lane longest.

'Miss Bateman being the old lady with the er . . . handicapped friend?' Govern had asked.

Evelyn, Mrs Sedgewick-Jones told him, had lived in Rose Cottage since she was in her twenties – some sixty-odd years ago. The mentally handicapped one was her younger sister and had only come to live with her two years ago. The sister, Daphne Bateman, had spent most of her life in a mental home but when the government began closing down such sanctuaries, and as Daphne was harmless, Evelyn took her in. 'Must drive Evelyn mad at times,' Sarah had remarked to Beck. 'Daphne never talks properly, you know, only spouts all those ghastly nursery rhymes.'

'You don't think the loopy one could have pushed the Wing Commander into the lake, do you, sir?' Beck asked Inspector Govern as they passed Rose Cottage and saw Daphne waving from one of the front windows.

'No, I don't! And I don't think anything at this stage of the proceedings, Beck. All we know for certain is that Mrs Proctor did have a motive. Now let's see what Mr Lavery has to say.'

'If he writes whodunnits, maybe he done it . . .' Beck began but received such a filthy look from his superior, he didn't pursue the joke.

Andrew Lavery came into the room carrying a tray with three mugs of coffee. He was wearing pale blue chinos, a white T-shirt and a darker blue cotton cravat tied at his neck. His jet black hair was flopping over his forehead, his skin deeply tanned. In all, his appearance gave him a look that was part rakish, part bohemian – but despite his age, Govern could see why Mrs Peters had described him as 'attractive'.

The coffee mugs distributed, Andrew sat back in his chair, one long leg crossed casually over the other.

'You said you were here about the Wing Commander's unfortunate death,' he said. 'Doubt I can be of much assistance to you, Inspector, I was in my study hard at work when I gather the accident happened.'

'I've read several of your books, sir,' Beck commented enthusiastically. 'Got one at home in fact – *The Seventh Bride*. It's—'

'Beck, I'm sure Mr Lavery is not interested in your comments!' Govern broke in, his tone of voice barely concealing his irritation with his young assistant. He turned back to the author who clearly considered this exchange amusing. 'You say you were in your study, sir. Is there someone who can verify that?'

Andrew Lavery's eyebrows rose in surprise.

'Do I gather from your question, Inspector, that you don't consider Proctor's death an accident?'

'No, sir! At the moment, an accident seems the most likely occurrence. However, I should point out that the circumstances are somewhat unlikely. We have made a very thorough inspection of the brakes on the Wing Commander's wheelchair and they were in the "off" position, but I have to consider it unlikely that he would have positioned himself on that narrow landing stage to cast his line without making sure the chair wouldn't move. Mrs Proctor assures me they were on when she left her husband.'

'Interesting point. Mind you, he'd fished from that landing stage umpteen times before. Keith Aymes telephoned me last night and said his wife was first on the scene, and that Mrs Proctor had been hysterical, saying it was all her fault, she must have left the brake off.'

'That's true, sir!' Govern said. 'However, she was in shock, and anyway I would expect a man like the Wing Commander to check such an elementary necessity himself, would you not agree?'

'Interesting point . . .' Lavery began again, when the door opened and a young female sauntered into the room.

Beck, who had temporarily lost interest in the proceedings, sat up and stared wide-eyed at the newcomer. She was wearing the briefest of bikinis over which was a diaphanous top which merely enhanced the deep tan of her exceptionally shapely legs and arms.

She crossed the room to stand behind Andrew Lavery's chair and, disregarding the visitors, planted a kiss on top of his head.

Andrew was grinning at the ill-concealed expression of surprise on Beck's face as he continued to gawp.

'May I introduce Vanessa Vantage? Dectective Inspector Govern and his assistant, Sergeant Beck, sweetie. Come to see me about Proctor's death. Miss Vantage is a . . . a friend who is staying with me for a while.'

Vanessa ran a hand through her streaked blond hair and smiled at the two men.

'Andrew is putting me up whilst I'm resting!' she said cheerfully. 'In case you don't know, that's what we actors and actresses call it when we're out of work. Andrew has promised to get me the female lead if the sale of the film rights of *Murder in Manhattan* goes through. If that comes off, I won't have to rest so often!'

'Vanessa, sweetie, I think the inspector has other matters on his mind. Before you disappear to the garden to sunbathe, could you enlighten him as to our movements yesterday?'

Vanessa's pretty face creased in a giggle, and she glanced sideways at Beck as she said, 'What, *everything* we did, Andy?'

Barely concealing a smile, Andrew said gently, 'Just an outline, sweetie. For instance, did we at any time yesterday leave the premises?'

'If you're referring to the house and garden, no, we didn't. We were late getting up and—'

'I think that is sufficient information for the moment, Miss Vantage!' Govern interrupted as he stood up. Beck dragged his eyes away from Miss Vantage's advantages, as he later referred to them in the pub, and jumped to his feet. 'Before I leave, Mr Lavery, I believe you have lived here quite a while and know everyone in the lane?'

Andrew too stood up.

'Can't say I know the new young couple at The Cottages very well, but the rest of the lane, yes. But I haven't always been in full-time residence here – an uncle died and left the cottage to me when I was at university. In those days I used Pear Tree Cottage as a weekend retreat. I've actually lived here about ten years, I suppose – when I'm not travelling, of course. But I'm certainly not the oldest resident. I gather Miss Bateman has lived in that cottage of hers nearly all her life. The dippy one joined her a few years ago – she's harmless though. She rushes out of the house when I'm passing the cottage to give me a flower or a stick of catkins or some such. The gift is usually accompanied by one of those nursery rhymes we all learned as kids.'

'Fancies you rotten, I'd say!' remarked Vanessa.

'Yes, well . . . time we were off, Beck!' Govern said firmly, thinking that it was not beyond his young assistant to ask for both the girl's and Lavery's autographs. 'I don't think I will need to bother you again, sir. Thank you for the coffee.'

As Lavery showed them to the door, he said thoughtfully, 'Have you had a word yet with Frank Dodd, the farmer? Talk in the pub is that he hates Proctor's guts – hated, I should say.'

Govern paused in the doorway.

'Now why should he do that, sir?' he asked.

'Well, the Wing Commander put a lot of people's backs up in the village because to listen to him, you'd think he'd won the war single-handed; and some of the locals lost parents, cousins, whatever, in that war and disliked his constant boasting. Apart from that, he treated the locals as inferiors: "Out of my way, Rogers", "Pass me that beer mat, Goodman!" No pleases or thank yous. You won't find anyone in the village who'll be in mourning!'

Govern nodded thoughtfully.

'Anyone in the lane other than the farmer like that?' he enquired.

Andrew shook his head.

'You can't blame Frank Dodd, who's a really nice chap. Proctor treated him like dirt. "Dodd, do this" and "Dodd do that", not to mention the fact that the Wing Co had it in for Dodd's lad, Jack. He was always complaining about the boy. Mind you, Jack's a noisy little bastard – roars up and down the lane on that grotty old motorbike of his. And Proctor caught him poaching fish on the lake once or twice – it's owned by the Aymes as you probably know – so Aymes warned Frank the boy would face a much bigger fine if he trespassed again. But I can't see poor Frank or the madcap Jack bumping the old boy off, although I suppose they could have done.'

'But you wouldn't make them suspects in one of your books, sir?' Beck said enthusiastically.

'Too true!' Andrew said laughing, but Govern was not amused. As soon as they were out of the house and back on the lane, he informed Beck in no uncertain terms that he was there to observe, make notes and keep his mouth shut.

'And your eyes shut too, Beck, if you can't control where they are looking when a there's a bit of fancy-work around.'

'OK, take your point, sir,' Beck said cheerfully. 'All the same, "fancy-work" is the right description, I'd say. Wouldn't half fancy a bit of that myself. Can't promise to control my eyes, sir, given that view!'

'Well if I'm going to let you drive my BMW, Beck, you'd better control them now,' Govern said. 'You near as damn it hit that gate post just now.'

'Sorry, sir!' Beck said cheerfully. 'I say, sir, there's that crazy old woman waving at you. Remember yesterday when you were talking to the vicar and I came down to see if Mr Peters was home? Well, the old girl was there watching the baby have its supper. When I told Mr Peters we were looking into Mr Proctor's death that afternoon, Mr Peters said, "You aren't suspecting someone killed him, are you?" That's when the batty one changed from "Little Jack Horner" and started on "Who killed cock Robin?". It was quite uncanny, and doubtless would have continued had Miss Evelyn not arrived at that moment and shushed her, or tried to. You don't think she knows . . .'

Detective Inspector Govern drew a deep sigh.

'We're not paid to make wild guesses, Beck, so stop dreaming and get moving.'

'Where to, sir? It's not far off lunch time,' he added pointedly.

Govern sighed again.

'Food! That and drink are all you think about!'

'Not all, sir!' Beck said as he steered the car past the lake where the lane narrowed. 'No pleasing you, is there, sir?' he said without rancour. 'Just now you were telling me not to think – you know – not to think about what I could do to Mr Andrew Lavery's fancy bit!'

Govern turned impatiently to his assistant.

'Shut up, Beck, and stop at the farm. I want to have a word with Frank Dodd.' Genuinely fond as he was of his young assistant, his voice softened imperceptibly as he added, 'After we've seen him, we'll go and have a bite at the pub. Food sounded OK – home-made steak and kidney pudding or bangers and mash, and gooseberry tart – although I'd have preferred Bakewell.'

'Any sort of tart is OK by me!' Beck said. Govern was not laughing as Beck got out of the car to open the farm gate.

Eight

E llen put away the mop and bucket she had been using to wash Miss Bateman's kitchen floor and glanced at the clock. It was just on eleven and time for mid-morning tea; Miss Bateman didn't think coffee was a healthy drink which suited Ellen who preferred tea anyway. She laid three pretty bone china cups and saucers on the table together with the same flower patterned sugar bowl and milk jug, and carried the tea pot to the dresser adjoining the cooker where the kettle was now whistling cheerfully. She found it a pleasure to do her once-weekly clean-through for Miss Bateman, whose cottage was more or less spotless anyway and which had so many old-fashioned, pretty things, like the tea set and the shining copper kettle the old lady used saying she had no time for new-fashioned electric things which were always going wrong.

Ellen herself would not have been without her modern gadgets: the steam iron, the pop-up toaster, the washing machine. It was her cleaning work in the lane which had paid for these extras which her husband, Ray, considered extravagant luxuries made for 'the gentry'. Years older than herself, Ray was old-fashioned in his ideas – not unlike Miss Bateman, Ellen thought, as she poured out the tea and called to her employer and Miss Daphne to say it was ready. It was only this past year that Miss Bateman had condescended to drink her elevenses in the kitchen with Ellen.

Evelyn came in from the garden, Daphne following behind in her shuffling gait. Having washed their hands under the tap, they sat down at the table, Daphne humming 'Polly, Put the Kettle On . . .' until Evelyn shushed her.

Daphne looked so woe begone that Ellen said kindly, 'Her

73

doan't bother me, Miss Bateman. Remarkable how many of them nursery rhymes she knows, isn't it?'

Like a lot of people, Ellen spoke of someone she knew to be mentally handicapped as if they weren't there.

Evelyn took a sip of her tea and said sharply, 'That's as may be, Ellen, but it's best she doesn't talk at all if she can't say something sensible. Now drink your tea, Daphne, lest it gets cold. Then we'll go and pick the sweet peas to take to the church this afternoon – you'll enjoy doing that!'

Daphne's face brightened at once and she smiled at Ellen, her rather vacant but wide-mouthed child's smile.

'Vicar must be right pleased with your flowers, Miss Bateman,' Ellen said. 'Your garden is pretty as a picture, that's a fact – all them lupins and hollyhocks and sweet peas and all-such. Ray won't grow them – says they's all a waste of space seeing we've not much garden compared with yours. Ray says his dad used to tell him that in the old days you had a lawn and flower beds all the way to the turning but you let that bit go back to nature when it got too much for you. Oh, well, it won't bother you none, will it, if Mr Aymes has his way and they chop off the corner?'

Evelyn's voice sharpened as she said brusquely, 'On the contrary, Ellen, we need some uncultivated land for the benefit of our birds and insects. People nowadays appear to have no concept of what this present day society is doing to our planet. Farmers and gardeners are spraying their crops with poisonous chemicals and a wealth of our wildlife is threatened with extinction. I shall certainly be voting against Mr Aymes' ill-advised and quite unnecessary plan at the next Road Meeting.'

Ellen nodded in agreement.

'My Ray says as how there won't be no green fields and gardens and woods and such if we go on building roads and houses and all. It'll be a concrete jungle, he says.'

'And quite right, too,' said Evelyn.

'The Dodds are all for it though,' said Ellen as she gathered up the empty tea cups and put them on the draining board for washing. 'Happen he needs the money, Ray says.'

Evelyn sniffed.

'Nobody is going to pay much for a half acre of scrub,' she said. 'It's not as if it is building land.'

'That's as may be, Miss Bateman,' Ellen persisted. 'Mary Dodd told me that after you had offered to buy it, it being your garden and all, Mr Aymes told him Frank could name his price.'

Evelyn's expression darkened.

'Unfortunately, Frank is within his rights to sell if he wishes. When my aunt moved into Rose Cottage just after the First World War, Frank Dodd's father allowed her to extend the garden right up to the corner, but that extension was never formally sold. I don't think it ever once occurred to Frank Dodd or myself to alter the status quo.'

'The what, Miss?' Ellen asked.

'The existing state of affairs, for want of a better translation,' Evelyn said. 'Come along now, Daphne, we'll go and pick the sweet peas. Perhaps you would like some, Ellen, seeing you have no flower garden?'

'Ray doesn't hold with growing flowers on our little bit of land,' Ellen agreed with a sigh. 'Wants all the space he can get for his dratted vegetables. That's men for you all over, innit, Miss Bateman?'

Realizing suddenly that the elderly spinster she was addressing probably knew very little about men, good or bad, she hurriedly turned back to the sink and busied herself with the dishes.

Evelyn paused in the doorway.

'The plums will be ripe enough for jam-making next week, Ellen. You can put in an extra afternoon to give me a hand – Monday, perhaps. I'll get young Jack to pick them for me over the weekend.'

'I'll come Tuesday as normal and stay on, if that suits, Miss Bateman,' Ellen suggested.

As Evelyn and her sister left the kitchen and went out into the sunlit garden, Ellen could hear the somewhat shrill, childlike voice of Daphne singing, ' "*Diddley, diddley, dumpty, The cat ran up the plum-tree, Half a crown To fetch her down, Diddley, diddley . . .*".' But she got no further before Evelyn's sharp tones admonished her to be quiet. Not for the first time, Ellen felt sorry for the poor simpleton who would never be any more than her sister's shadow.

Having finished the dishes, Ellen dried them and started on the washing. It would dry well on this warm, sunny day, she thought, at the same time wishing that her employer did not insist she pegged them on the wash line at the very far end of the garden. It was quite a way to walk carrying a load of wet sheets and towels. But it would spoil the aspect of the flower beds and their contents to have the wash line any nearer, Miss Bateman had insisted, and there was little enough to be seen up by the boundary of the garden and The Warren, Frank Dodd's meadow. Like as not Mary Dodd would have finished her washing by now and half dried it, too.

Mary had indeed completed her Tuesday wash and was settled at the kitchen table studying the farm accounts. No amount of looking at them made them any more agreeable. The truth was, they were simply not making ends meet and the bank manager had written a nasty letter last Friday saying that if they couldn't pay back at least a part of the overdraft by the end of the month, the bank would have to foreclose.

No one knew better than Mary how such an eventuality would break her husband's heart. It was near broken when Jack announced he wasn't going to stay on the farm and work it with his father. He wanted to join the Navy and no amount of talk by Frank could dissuade him. In the end, it was she who had talked Jack into remaining at home, at least until they were out of the financial doldrums. Two years at very most, Jack had insisted. Even if they weren't on an even keel by then, he was off.

Presently, Mary thought, she would take a can of beer out to her husband who was repairing the hen house. A fox had got in through a hole in the roof and savaged three good laying hens at the weekend so the task was a priority one. The hens weren't exactly a gold mine but they laid good, big, brown eggs and most of the residents in the lane bought from her. Even though the eggs weren't organic, they were visibly free range. No, they couldn't afford to lose any more birds.

Mary drew another long sigh. Frank seemed to think that Mr Aymes would end up paying enough for that rough old bit of Miss Bateman's garden to soothe the bank for a while – at least until he could get rid of some of the milk cows and plough up the meadows for sewing rape. But it would be autumn next year before they could harvest the rape, and anyway, she hated the stuff; hated the colour as well as the smell. Moreover, the bees all took to it and the honey they produced tasted quite horrible. As she'd pointed out to Frank, she would have to get rid of her hives.

For one of the very few times in their married life, she and Frank had fallen out over money – or rather the lack of it. Frank was a totally unrealistic optimist, whereas she looked the facts in the face and thought they should sell up whilst there was still something that wasn't mortgaged to sell. They could go and live with her widowed sister in Selsey, she'd said, and Frank had gone red in the face and said, 'And do what? Watch your sister crocheting those doilies of hers all day?' 'We'd manage on our pensions if we lived there,' she'd argued. 'Jack'll be gone any road, and you could go fishing, Frank!' He'd been really angry then, shouting that it was his n'er-do-well, lazy son who liked to sit on a river bank and stare at the water, not him. He was a farmer, born and bred, and would die one.

The way things were going, he'd end up a bankrupt, not a farmer, she told him, and after that, they hadn't spoken to one another for two whole days. A truce had been called when Jack, of all people, stood up for his father pointing out that no one knew for sure at this point how much money would be offered for Miss Bateman's bit of scrub, so his mother wasn't entitled to give up the fight for financial recovery quite yet. Mary had agreed to say no more about their precarious situation until Millers Lane Road Committee took a vote for or against the widening of the lane. It should have been decided months ago but had had to be postponed, first for poor Mrs Coleman's death and then Wing Commander Proctor's. Now half the residents had summer holidays planned and it had been postponed again.

Neither of them had been at all happy about the two unpleasant accidents so near home – not because they had any particular liking for the victims but because the Detective Inspector who had come to investigate the deaths, discovered the story of the fire in their barn last year. For a time, he appeared to suspect Jack, who had no verifiable alibi for the day the Wing Commander had drowned. Although Jack had never actually been accused of starting the barn fire, it was known they were short of money and that the insurance money would come in very handy, as, indeed, it had.

Nevertheless, the details had remained on police files and the Inspector had unearthed them. He'd managed somehow to extract the truth from the boy about his movements on the day the unfortunate Wing Commander had died, which was more than she or Frank had been able to do. Jack had sworn that although he'd been in the wrong, fishing that morning on the Aymes' lake when he should have been at work at the golf course, as soon as the Wing Commander had turned up, he'd scarpered not wanting to be caught trespassing. The Inspector had believed him.

Frank was not so certain Jack had revealed all the facts. However, knowing Mary would fly into a panic if she thought her precious son was involved in any way, however innocently, he decided to let sleeping dogs lie. It wasn't the first time either, but silence on his part had often proved the best option for peace when Jack's misdeeds were concerned.

Whilst his wife was poring over the farm accounts with a sigh, Frank walked up to The Warren, the field that adjoined Miss Bateman's garden on the north side. The old girl had asked him to take a look at the fencing as rabbits had been getting into her garden and eaten all the tender leaves of her young cabbage plants. There was no sign of her now, nor of the batty sister, but Ellen was there hanging out the sheets on the washing line. They were blowing back in her face as she pegged them.

'Silly woman!' Frank muttered. 'Not sense enough to stand on the other side of the line.'

He didn't much care for Ellen although he got on well enough with her husband, Ray, a quiet chap like himself who liked nothing more than to be left to get on with things. Ellen, on the other hand, was an inveterate gossip. 'Doing' for all the residents who could afford domestic help, she had plenty to gossip about and invariably passed on the tit-bits – grossly exaggerated – to Mary. 'A nasty cold' became 'a serious bout of influenza' and

Mary would go rushing off to whoever was ill with offers of calves' foot jelly and beef broth and the like. Privately Frank thought such donations were not appreciated and like as not got thrown away as soon as Mary departed. It wasn't her place to do such things, he'd remonstrated. She should let Miss Bateman or Mrs Hollywell, the vicar's wife, act the good samaritan. Since then, Mary had ceased such activities and the subject wasn't raised between them again.

Women, Frank thought as he bent to peg down a section of wire netting a fox or badger must have dislodged, were an enigma to him these days. There was that flighty bit of Jack's, Sandra; looked like a prostitute in that skirt barely covering her buttocks and a shirt which didn't cover her midriff. She not only had a ring in her ear but one on her belly button, too. Yet withall, she was polite enough to him when Jack brought her home and she never used bad language like Jack – even told him off when he did so. Mary thought the world of her.

Then there was Mr Lavery's harem of fancy ladies – different ones every month as far as Frank could see. The man would come walking down the lane with his dogs, arm in arm with whoever was the dish of the day. In summer, they'd be half naked – shorts so tight you could see where their legs ended and their bottoms began! As for their top halves, most of their bosoms were in full view and Frank found it hard not to stare when they called in for eggs or milk.

'It's the fashion, Frank!' Mary told him when he criticized them. But she wore sensible skirts herself, as did Ellen and, of course, the Bateman sisters. They went a bit too far the other way – dresses, usually black, down almost to their ankles. He wouldn't have been surprised to see them in those little black button boots Victorian ladies wore. 'But they almost are Victorians,' Mary had pointed out. 'Miss Evelyn's gone eighty and poor Miss Daphne is not far off seventy.'

'That's no cause for them to look like two old crows,' Frank persisted. 'Look at the Queen Mother – she still wore pretty dresses and hats and she was over a hundred!'

'She could afford it!' Mary said, ending the discussion.

Reluctantly, Frank turned back towards the farmhouse. His

dinner would be ready any moment now and Mary would be upset if he let whatever she had cooked get cold. She was a good cook and did wonders on the limited housekeeping money. He did not want to upset her but at the same time, he feared there might be more bad news as well as his tea waiting for him. Not that he had any real reason for thinking so but there had been too many accidents for his liking – unexplained accidents. 'Accidents' was what the coroner had called them but sometimes when he was drifting off to sleep, Frank thought that if he'd been the coroner, he'd have chosen a verdict of 'Cause Unknown'.

He glanced at his watch and saw with dismay that it was nearly one o'clock. He'd be late in to his dinner and Mary justifiably would be cross. Wherever had the morning gone? It was strange how quickly time seemed to go now he was older – no sooner was he up and about and it was time for bed again with only half the jobs he meant to tackle done. Mary said it was because they were slower doing things now than they used to be.

He quickened his pace and was hot and breathless as he hastened into the yard. Almost at once, Mary came hurrying out of the house and all but ran to meet him.

'Thank goodness you're back, Frank!' she said, her cheeks flushed and her hands flapping her apron in agitation. 'It's the Peters' little boy – he's gone missing.'

Frank stopped in his tracks and put a reassuring hand on his wife's arm.

'No need to get in a panic, Mother!' he said. 'Mrs Peters was over in our dairy not that long ago with the little 'un. Got a half dozen eggs, she did. So what's to do?'

Mary shook Frank's arm in frustration.

'You don't know the facts, Frank. It were Miss Daphne took him – and she hasn't come back.'

'Took him? Took young Dougal? Where?'

Mary's mouth tightened.

'If we knew that, he wouldn't be lost, would he?' she snapped.

'Better come indoors and sit down and tell me what's going on!' Frank said. 'Can't do anyone any good us standing here.'

A few minutes later, their uneaten dinner growing cold, Mary enlightened her husband. Ellen had been over at Rose Cottage doing her usual two-hour stint of housework. At eleven thirty, Miss Evelyn had gone off to Hunnington to do her weekly shop and Ellen had left Miss Daphne in the garden playing with the rag doll Mrs Hollywell had given her one Christmas. She'd locked up the house as Miss Evelyn dictated so Miss Daphne couldn't get in and cause an accident with matches or the gas fire, or electrocute herself with the iron or some such. The garden was well fenced in so Daphne could not wander off, and the gate was bolted on the outside. She always seemed quite unworried when she was left on her own in the garden. The lane residents passing by always waved to her and she would wave back. Of course, if it was raining or likely to do so, she went shopping with Evelyn.

'So what happened this morning?' Frank interrupted Mary's flow of words.

'Miss Daphne lent over and unbolted the gate. I always said she wasn't half as stupid as some make out. Anyroad, over she goes to Mrs Peters and after playing with Dougal for five minutes or so, she indicated that she'd like to take him up the lane for a walk in his pushchair. "You can go as far as Mr Lavery's house, Pear Tree Cottage," Mrs Peters said. "Do you understand what I'm saying, Daphne?" she'd asked, and Miss Daphne had nodded and smiled and off she'd gone with the pushchair and Dougal safely strapped in.'

As Mary paused to draw breath, Frank urged her to continue.

'So, what happened? Was there an accident?'

Mary shook her head.

'That's just it, Frank. Mrs Peters came rushing over here not twenty minutes ago to say Miss Daphne hadn't come back. She'd telephoned Mrs Sedgewick-Jones who'd been out on her horse riding up past Mr Lavery's house and she hadn't seen them. She'd got in her car and driven Mrs Peters all over and there was no sign anywhere of the two of them. Mrs Peters asked if Jack was home and maybe he'd go looking over our fields. They've been gone nearly two hours and even allowing Miss Daphne mebbe can't tell the time nor guess it, she'd surely be back by now. Dougal usually has his lunch at twelve and would likely be hungry and crying. I've telephoned everyone in the lane, Frank, but no one has seen them.'

'Isn't Miss Evelyn back yet?' Frank asked, beginning to understand why the womenfolk were clearly in such a state. Miss Daphne wasn't a normal person no matter how much sense Mary thought she might have. Just suppose she'd suddenly taken against the little boy – disliked him screaming, which maybe he was if he was hungry enough – and . . . well, tipped him into the lake in his pushchair, same as someone must have pushed the old Wing Commander . . .

'Make us a cup of tea, Mother!' he said as calmly as he could voice the words. 'Then I'll take a look up at Badgers Field and round Millers Lake. You'd best go sit with Mrs Peters if she wants.'

'Mrs Sedgewick-Jones is with her,' Mary said, 'and they've telephoned Mr Peters at work and he's coming straight home. I'd best go over to Rose Cottage, be there to break the news to Miss Evelyn when she gets back. I wonder what's kept her so long? Ellen said they were having a cold lunch so there's nothing to spoil but when Miss Evelyn does go off and leave Miss Daphne on her own, it's never for as long as this. Do you think I should telephone the golf club and ask them to send Jack home?'

'No, of course not!' Frank replied more sharply than he had intended. 'The two of them are probably somewhere perfectly safe and sound. Probably picking blackberries or sommat like and Miss Daphne not having no idea how worried everyone is, especially—'

'Mrs Peters!' Mary finished for him. 'She looked half out of her mind, poor thing. She's having another, you know, and having early morning sickness with it – that's why she let Miss Daphne take Dougal off for a walk – so she could have a bit of a rest. Oh, Frank, do you really think they're all right? There've been so many awful things happening down this lane of late. Suppose . . .?'

'No, we are not going to suppose anything!' Frank broke in quickly. 'Now pour out that tea you've brewed so I can get it down me and be on my way.'

He knew he should hurry lest his worst fears were realized, but at the same time, he knew that if there had been another horrible accident, by the time he got to the lake it would be too late.

Nine

B ut for Sarah, Migs knew, she might well have given way to the fear that had now engulfed her. It was three thirty in the afternoon and Dougal had been missing for four hours. Mercifully, Ian would be home at any minute to deal with the hopelessly ineffectual young policeman who had arrived in answer to Sarah's telephone call.

He had done little to assuage Migs' fears that Daphne Bateman had not only kidnapped Dougal but might well have harmed him.

'Four hours is not all that long for your little boy to be missing . . .' the young constable had said as he'd sat down at the kitchen table and taken out his notepad and biro.

'For God's sake, he's not even a year old!' Sarah had burst out. 'And the woman he's with is a mental defective.'

Red-faced, P C Jones announced that it might be best if he took a few notes. He was unfamiliar with the district having only been sent to the area a few weeks ago, and until he'd been told to look into a missing child report in Millers Lane, Delhurst, he'd never heard of the place.

Curbing her overwhelming feeling of impatience, Migs answered his questions. Yes, Dougal was her child. Yes, he was nearly one year old. Yes, she had agreed that Miss Daphne Bateman should take him for a walk. He was in his buggy. No, he couldn't possibly have wandered off without her seeing him – he could barely walk . . .

Hearing the panic in Migs' voice, Sarah took over, explaining who Daphne was and where the sisters lived over the road; that Daphne had the mental age of a very young child but was otherwise harmless; Evelyn, her sister, took care of her. No,

Evelyn had not been at home at the time, but she was back now and was out searching for Daphne and yes, of course she was desperately worried, not only for Dougal but for her sister.

Both Sarah and Migs were beside themselves as the constable decided he must take further details: descriptions, ages, addresses, even telephone numbers of all those who might be involved.

'This is wasting time!' Migs burst out as a further question was about to be posed. 'We know they aren't in the lane – we've already searched it and all the footpaths. A woman, a buggy and a child can't disappear into thin air. One of us would have seen them if they had been in the neighbourhood. Can't you put out a Missing Persons call? They can't have got far. Daphne – Miss Bateman – didn't carry a purse and she didn't have money to put in one.'

'That's as far as you know, Madam,' the constable said, scratching his head with his pencil. 'I've heard some of these loonies can be very crafty. She . . .'

To Migs' intense relief, she heard Ian's car stop outside the cottage. Relief released the tears which now coursed down her cheeks as she flung open the door to let him in.

'Come on, darling, you may be panicking for nothing,' he said as he put his arms round her and held her tight. 'Now calm down and tell me what's happening. Who's that in the kitchen?'

'Sarah with an idiot police constable aged about fifteen, I should think,' Migs said in a choked whisper. 'Ian, I'm frightened. I keep thinking about the lake, the Wing Commander . . . maybe Daphne thought . . .'

'That's enough, darling!' Ian said sharply, hearing the hysteria in Migs' voice and himself afraid to hear her express his own terrible fear. 'I'll have a word with your young policeman and then I'm going to telephone Detective Inspector Govern. I know he wouldn't normally be involved with something like this – after all, the pair of them have only been gone for less than five hours – but he and I hit it off last time he was down here and when I ran into him at the inquest, he said I was to get in touch with him if ever I suspected something strange was happening in the lane – gave me his personal mobile number.'

It was a full hour before Govern arrived. This time his sergeant was not with him because his visit was unofficial, he explained. At that moment, a white-faced Evelyn returned home from her searching and reported to Migs that she had seen no sign of the missing pair.

'There is a limit to how far my sister can walk!' she said to Ian. 'An hour at most – she has weak ankles, you see. I did wonder if she had decided to walk to Delhurst. There's a small children's playground on the green – I expect you've taken your little boy there . . . swings, a slide, a climbing frame. But the green was deserted – people gone home to their tea, I dare say. I did ask at the King's Head, and Jack Dodd's young lady Sandra was there washing dishes and promised to keep an eye out for them.'

Her voice, usually so forthright, was shaking and Migs who had come through from the kitchen, felt sorry for her. Daphne was her sister and Evelyn had every reason to be as worried for her as she herself was for Dougal.

'You look exhausted, Miss Bateman. Can I get you a drink? A cup of tea?'

But thanking Migs for her offer, she hurried back across the road to her own cottage, saying that if she could answer any questions the inspector might have, she would be at home to receive him.

Inspector Govern followed Ian and Migs back into their small sitting room and accepted the glass of beer Ian produced for each of them. The young constable was despatched back to his station to deliver his report.

Govern looked at Migs' taut face and said gently, 'Try not to let yourself think the worst, Mrs Peters. I can think of many far more cheerful possibilities.'

'But it's all my fault!' Migs broke in tearfully. 'I should never had let her take Dougal, only I wasn't feeling so good and she seemed so anxious to let Dougal go with her. She's always so good with him, plays with him and sings to him and he really loves her and . . .'

'Mrs Peters, whatever has happened, you must not blame yourself. What you did was perfectly rational. Miss Bateman – Daphne – is not known to be violent or harmful in any way.

Women like her – unmarried, childless – do sometimes take children because they are lonely and believe they can care for them better than their own mothers. They want to love them, not harm them. It's very rarely they do so. After all, why should they?'

'Yes, why should Daphne harm Dougie? The inspector is quite right!' Ian said, putting his arm round Migs as much to comfort himself as her. 'But what more can we do to find them, Inspector? They definitely aren't in the lane or on one of the footpaths, and the Dodds, Mrs Holywell, Mr Lavery, the Aymes – everyone has scoured their gardens and grounds.'

'Maybe they haven't looked in their garages, sheds, stables,' Govern said. 'I've been on to the Hunnington police station and they are going to organize an official search if the woman and your little boy are not home by six o'clock. Not altogether unreasonably, they think they might well have turned up by then, and there will still be over two hours of daylight.'

Both Ian and Migs were silenced by the horrifying thought that if Dougal was not found by nightfall, he would be out somewhere in the dark; cold, hungry, crying for his mother and his beloved piece of blanket without which he would never go to sleep.

'He hasn't got his "bankie"!' Migs whispered. 'I should have given it to him before they left. I . . .'

'Migs, darling, you had no idea they would be so long!' Ian interrupted. 'You look worn out, sweetheart. Why don't you go and lie down for half an hour? I know you won't sleep but you'll be in better shape when they do get back if you rest now.'

When Migs had somewhat reluctantly left the room, Ian gave the inspector another beer and sat down opposite him.

'I said "when they get back" just now, but you're thinking it's "if", aren't you, Inspector?'

The older man looked over the top of his glass at Ian. After years in his job, he reckoned himself an exceptionally good judge of character. He decided now that Ian was up to hearing the truth rather than platitudes.

'Last time I was down here – what would it be, a fortnight ago? – I took the trouble to investigate Miss Daphne Bateman's background – or rather, on my instructions, Beck did. He obtained access to her medical documents and throughout the decades that the unfortunate woman was kept in a secure institution, there was never any sign whatsoever of violence in her behaviour. Childlike was the most frequent description of her. She liked playing with dolls, knitting, basket work, colouring books – that kind of thing.'

He took a notebook out of his top pocket and opened it.

'From what her sister told me last time I was here, Daphne Bateman was little different in her habits and behaviour since she'd taken her in. I rather think the old girl finds her sister somewhat of a trial. Well, you can imagine what it must be like for her, a much respected, highly efficient legal secretary with an excellent brain living with a halfwit. Perhaps not very wisely, the older Miss Bateman has on numerous occasions tried to improve the younger woman's behaviour   put a stop to the endless repetition of nursery rhymes; teach her to talk more sensibly, to play with jigsaws instead of dolls – that kind of thing.'

'But not successfully!' Ian said. 'Mind you, I haven't seen her with any dolls. Maybe Evelyn took them all away!'

The inspector put down his beer mug and leant forward.

'Exactly! And your little boy could be a substitute. When I was last down here talking to your wife after the unfortunate death of your neighbour, the woman was out in the garden playing with the child in the sandpit. Quite honestly, Mr Peters, I don't think she'd do the kid any harm although she may have kidnapped him – you know, she's concealing him somewhere in case her sister takes him away the way she took the dolls.'

'God, I hope you're right, Inspector. All the way down from London, I kept thinking about those two accidents you told me you thought might be murders . . . motiveless murders as far as you could see. I thought, suppose the murderer had been Daphne and now she'd decided for whatever crazy reason to despatch our Dougal.'

Inspector Govern shook his head.

'No, Mr Peters, you're way off the mark. I never said I thought they might be murders – only that they *could* have been. As to Miss Daphne Bateman, she had irreproachable alibis. On each of the days in question, she was at the day care centre – Beck verified she attended. She was certainly not responsible even if it were conceivable that she would give Mrs Coleman some poisoned soup; or had the intelligence to release the brakes of the Wing Commander's chair and tip it into the lake. I doubt she would have realized wheelchairs have brakes and that they'd most certainly be on. No, if she was guilty of anything, it might just conceivably have been that barn fire the Dodds had a while ago. It was never satisfactorily explained. A mad woman might have lit a match, assuming she had one, just to see the flames and then panicked and shut the door and run away.'

He glanced down at his watch and stood up.

'I think I'll have a word with the other residents,' he said. 'You'd best stay here in case there's a phone call or Miss Bateman turns up with young Dougal. I know it's a stupid thing to say, but try not to worry.'

Ian, too, stood up. Perhaps he should stop imagining the worst possible scenarios: Daphne pushing the buggy along a busy road and a car running into them; Dougie terribly injured in some hospital, no one knowing who he was; Daphne dead or humming one of her sickening nursery rhymes. Maybe Dougie was dead! Or drowned? Perhaps Daphne had tipped him into the village pond and, too frightened to come home and tell them what she'd done, she'd run away. Maybe she'd taken him into a hay barn, helped him climb to the top where the fumes could be lethal and they were both suffocated. Maybe a paedophile . . .?

A few minutes after Inspector Govern had driven off in his Rover, Evelyn Bateman appeared in the open doorway of the cottage. She was no longer pale but brightly flushed, her customary neat bun in disarray straggling to her shoulders. She was trembling visibly.

'What is it?' Ian shot at her. 'What's happened? Is Daphne back? Have you heard anything?'

Evelyn drew a deep breath, her hands twisting together at her waist as she stammered, 'No, I've not heard anything, Mr Peters, but I've found out something I think you ought to know. The money, the loose change I always keep to pay Mary Dodd for the eggs – it's gone.'

She paused for a second to draw another deep breath.

'I keep it in an old tea caddy on the mantelshelf. Daphne's seen me putting coins in and taking money out many a time. I think she must have taken it, Mr Peters – that's why we haven't been able to find her in Millers Lane or the village.'

Ian felt his heart lurch.

'But why would she want money? Was there something she wanted to buy?'

The colour left Evelyn's face which was once more a pale parchment white.

'For the bus, Mr Peters. She loved going on busses. We didn't use them because I have the car but when she was at St George's, the staff would take them to the seaside once a year by bus. That's the only song Daphne knows other than her nursery rhymes: "The wheels of the bus go round and round . . ." The inmates sang it on their outings.'

Ian lent forward and grabbed hold of his neighbour's arm as the first clue to Dougal's whereabouts might be unfolding.

'Is there a bus from the village? Where does it go? When does it go? We must ring the bus company . . . No, they'll be shut now. I must ring Govern – he'll chase this up.' Aware that he was still gripping Miss Bateman's arm, he released it with a hurried apology. Leaving her to make her own way back to Rose Cottage, he dialled Govern's mobile number. The Inspector was at Andrew Lavery's house. Within minutes, learning what was afoot, Lavery produced a local bus timetable.

'Had to use the wretched thing last month when my Land Rover was in the body shop – had a bit of a bump in that M25 pile-up last month. Here, should be up to date.'

He handed it to the inspector who quickly turned to the right page. Running his finger down he stopped at a specific time.

'Leaves the King's Head in Delhurst at five minutes past twelve. Stops at Hunnington at twelve twenty. Thanks, Mr Lavery. I'll keep this if I may.'

He did not stop to return Ian's telephone call but drove straight back there.

'I'll get on to this right away,' he said. 'I dare say the driver of the midday bus has gone off duty but we'll find him. He's sure to

89

remember if he had to help an old woman with a buggy on board outside the King's Head. If Mrs Peters is awake, you can tell her we have a lead but don't raise her hopes too much. Even if Miss Daphne was on that bus and did get off at Hunnington, we've still got to find her.'

And that, thought Ian as he went up to talk to Migs, was a very big 'if' without the problem of locating Daphne. There was another very big question mark, too – supposing they found Daphne and Dougal wasn't with her?

Having second thoughts, Ian decided not to go into the bedroom. Were he to do so, Migs might well see how truly terrified he was that they would never see their little boy again.

Ten

J ack Dodd dropped his bike down outside the front gate of No. 1 The Cottages and dashed up the path just as Ian opened the door to look for the hundredth time to see if by some miracle, Daphne had decided to come home.

'It's her – I seed 'em top of the lane!' Jack gasped out breathlessly. 'Young 'un's in the buggy and she – Miss Daphne – is pushing it.'

For a moment the enormity of the feeling of relief so overwhelmed Ian that he couldn't speak.

Misunderstanding the expression on his face, Jack said, 'It's the truth, Mr Peters. I was on my way up to the King's Head to meet Sandra and when I seed 'em, I turned round right quick to come and tell you. Look, you can see 'em now just coming past the big oak tree in Barley Meadow.'

Following Jack's pointing finger, Ian saw that the lad was not mistaken. Daphne's bulky figure was coming towards them, her voluminous black cotton skirt fluttering in the evening breeze. She was limping, he noticed, and, thank God, the buggy she was pushing was not empty.

Ian had his hands on Jack's bike intending to use it to reach the couple more quickly when Govern drew up in his Rover.

'They're back – they're back!' Ian shouted. 'Up the road . . . coming home . . . Jack's seen them and it really is them. I'm going . . .'

Govern was by now out of the car and he hurried round to the passenger side to put a restraining hand on Ian's arm.

'No, don't go rushing up to them. Gently does it, Mr Peters, if we want to find out what's been going on. If you rush up all hot and bothered, Miss Daphne may think you're angry with her.

She took her sister's egg money so she probably knows she's done something wrong even if she's unaware how long she's kept Dougal from his mother. Let her come to us – see how she reacts.'

Curbing his impulse to race up to the buggy, grab his little son and be reassured that no harm had come to him, Ian did as the inspector suggested. The pair of them stood by the car pretending to be checking one of the windscreen wipers.

After what seemed to Ian to be at least half an hour but which was, in fact, less than five minutes, Daphne Bateman, looking extremely hot and untidy but smiling broadly, stopped by the car. In the buggy lay the inert body of the little boy, only the top of his curly head visible beneath the baggy pink hand-knitted cardigan that covered him. For one indescribably dreadful minute, Ian feared he was staring at the motionless body of his dead child. Then, with an even wider smile, Daphne started to sing:

> Diddle, diddle, dumpling, my son John,
> Went to bed with his trousers on,
> One shoe off, and one shoe on!
> Diddle, diddle, dumpling, my son John.

At the sound of her voice, Dougal opened his eyes and struggled into a sitting position. Seeing his father, he smiled as he handed him one of his little canvas shoes. As if she had been gone for no longer than her usual afternoon walk, Daphne bent and lifted him out of his seat. Handing him cheerfully to Ian, she delivered a noisy, wet kiss on one of Dougal's cheeks.

' "*Bye Baby Bunting*",' she sang as, waving to the two men, she made her way across the road to Rose Cottage. Before she could unfasten the gate, Evelyn came hurrying out of the front door to confront her.

'Dear, oh dear!' said Inspector Govern. 'I'm afraid the poor old thing is going to be hauled over the coals and no mistake, but judging by what we've just seen, I'm sure she intended your little boy no harm whatever.'

Dougal seemed to have dropped off to sleep again in Ian's

arms, his breathing steady and unhurried, his cheeks a healthy if somewhat grubby pink. As far as Ian could ascertain, absolutely no harm had come to him no matter what Daphne had been doing with him for the past six hours.

'Six hours!' he said aloud to the inspector as they walked together up the path to the front door. 'What in heaven's name could they have been doing?'

Govern looked thoughtful.

'We'll find out in due course. I've a dozen men out looking for them in Hunnington. What with her untidy hair, extraordinary dress, our Daphne Bateman is unlikely to have gone unnoticed, especially with your boy in his buggy. She looks old enough to be his great grandmother, let alone his granny.'

He broke off as his mobile phone started to ring.

'You go on in and break the good news to your wife,' he told Ian. 'If I may, I'll use your kitchen table to make some notes.' He pressed the 'play' button on his phone and followed Ian indoors.

When Ian and Migs came downstairs half an hour later, the kitchen table was littered with pages torn from Inspector Govern's notebook.

'Migs has given Dougie a bath and put him to bed. He didn't seem to want anything to eat but enjoyed a mug of milk,' Ian said. He held a chair for Migs to sit in and sat down himself. 'Any news for us?' he asked.

The inspector smiled.

'A great deal! Seems your little boy has had quite an exciting day, Mrs Peters.'

'Migs, please!' she said. 'Please tell us what's been going on!'

Govern put down his pen and gathered the spread notes into a heap.

'One by one!' he said as he lifted the first. 'This was a call from the driver of the local bus. He helped our Miss Daphne and the buggy with the child into his bus at midday outside the King's Head. Couldn't make out where they were going to but as the old lady didn't seem to have much money on her – no purse or handbag but only a fistful of change in her pocket – he assumed they were going to Hunnington. Sure enough, they got off when the bus stopped at Hunnington Park. He didn't report it because the child seemed perfectly happy and she was singing to it and didn't appear agitated or act like someone who didn't know what she was doing.'

'Seems she knew exactly what she was doing!' Migs said. 'I've often wondered about her, Inspector. It's so strange the way she talks only in nursery rhymes – yet I've noticed that the words are so often completely apt.'

Ian nodded.

'You're quite right, darling. Just now it was "Diddle, diddle dumpling" and that line: "*One shoe off and one shoe on . . .*"! Dougie had one shoe off which he gave me. I left it downstairs when I rushed up to tell you the wonderful news he was back.'

'Well, Miss Daphne's rhymes drew quite a lot of attention to herself,' Inspector Govern said taking up another couple of notes. 'This was a call from a woman in Hunnington Park; she was at the boating pool with her little boy and saw Miss Daphne with the buggy throwing bread in for the ducks. The woman went over to chat to her but all she could get out of her was: "I had a duck and the duck pleased me, I fed my duck by yonder tree". She remembered the couplet because it was quite catchy and it made the little boy in the buggy laugh.'

Her eyes full of unshed tears, Migs took Ian's hand in hers.

'Then there was a sighting by a cashier in Asda. Seems when Miss Daphne, with Dougal in the buggy, had reached the checkout, Dougal had eaten most of the banana and opened the packets of crisps and chocolate biscuits so it was quite difficult for her to check the bar code. Not only that but the old woman, as the girl referred to Miss Daphne, had no handbag or purse and simply drew out a handful of coins from her skirt pocket. The girl hadn't made a fuss about Dougal's attack on the food because there was only three pence change from the money Miss Daphne handed her, so she reckoned she must be very poor. The return bus ticket to the village was amongst the coins, so she gave it back, telling Miss Daphne to take care of it.'

'No wonder Dougal wasn't hungry,' Ian said.

'Or thirsty!' Govern added. 'An elderly pensioner sitting on a bench in Hunnington Park had a bottle of lemonade he intended to drink with his sandwich. He said the woman just helped herself and the little boy as if it belonged to her; and the little boy gave him such an angelic smile, he decided not to question the old girl, who he rightly thought a bit odd!'

'Daphne must be totally exhausted,' Migs said thoughtfully. 'I must go over and tell Evelyn not to be too angry with her. After all, she meant no harm and did no harm.'

'All the same,' the inspector interjected, 'however much the poor woman loves your little boy, she can't be allowed to whisk him off to heaven knows where without so much as a by-your-leave.'

'This will be the last time she'll be allowed near Dougal,' Ian said forcefully but Migs shook her head.

'That would be cruel, Ian. I know she loves him. She can come over here to our house to play with him. We just won't let her take him off for a walk again.'

The inspector stood up.

'I'll pop over and have a word with Miss Bateman – tell her to keep a closer eye on her sister in future; then I promised I'd go back to Mr Lavery's house for a quick drink. Interesting chap, don't you agree, Mr Peters? He deals with imaginary murders and I deal with real ones, so in a funny sort of way, we have a lot in common. Then I must get back to my office. It was fortunate you got hold of me on a quiet day.'

'Migs and I are tremendously grateful,' Ian said, rising to show the inspector to the door. 'Next time you come down to Delhurst, it must be a social visit – come and have lunch with us. Are you married? Bring your wife if you have one.'

'Did have!' the inspector said dryly, 'but she didn't care for the day and night demands of my job and I didn't care to change my occupation, so we agreed to call it a day. No kids, fortunately, although I must say your youngster could have made me change my mind. Glad he's back safe and sound!'

Dougal was still sleeping soundly when Ian and Migs went upstairs to check on him. Despite the quick bath Migs had given him, there was still a streak of chocolate round the side of his neck. His small fingers were clutching his piece of blanket which was pressed against his mouth.

'Seems he went all day without his "bankie"!' Ian commented

as he in turn bent to kiss the sleeping child. 'He must have had a happy day without a single worry or he'd have yelled for it at the top of his voice. It's sad in a way, isn't it? Daphne loving kids the way she obviously does and never having one of her own.'

Migs closed the Bob the Builder curtains across the window and followed Ian out of the room.

'If she'd had a child, it would be nearing fifty at a guess, or thereabouts!'

'Then she might have had grandchildren, great grandchildren . . .'

Migs' laughter interrupted his geneological surmising, but her eyes were thoughtful again as she put a ready-made lasagne in the microwave for their supper. She glanced at her husband who was studying the TV evening programme guide. Could he have recovered so quickly from the dreadful fear that must have engulfed him, she wondered?

'Ian, did it once cross your mind that . . . that Daphne might have had an accident with Dougal? Let the buggy run out into the road under a car, tipped it into the duck pond like the Wing Commander . . .?'

'Stop it, darling!' Ian's voice was as stern as his expression. 'Of course it did, but we were wrong to think the worst. As for suspecting the wretched Daphne, well, I know strange things have happened in this lane, but Govern is in no doubt that she was not involved. How could she be anything else but harmless with those ridiculous nursery rhymes of hers? Do you know what she said to the cashier at Asda's? "Pat-a-cake, pat-a-cake, baker's man"!'

Despite the residue of fear that still lurked at the back of her mind, Migs smiled. After all, it was one of Dougal's favourite games, trying to match his little palms with hers. Her thoughts were interrupted by the telephone ringing. It was Sarah saying how truly delighted she was to hear the news that Dougal was safely home.

'You know this lane, Migs, the grapevine always red hot with the latest! I heard it from Andrew Lavery's latest bit of enter-tainment. She'd gone out for a stroll whilst that nice inspector was chatting to Andrew. Needless to say, I rang Jane Proctor and

Colin who both said to tell you how pleased they were for you. I'll come down tomorrow for a cuppa and hear all the gory details. And by the way, Migs, the Rev is sending Jack round tomorrow with a notification about the next Road Meeting. Betty said he's concerned because it's been postponed twice and Mr Aymes is anxious to get the work started before the winter sets in.'

'I sincerely hope not,' Migs said. 'We haven't even voted for the plan yet, have we?'

Sarah laughed.

'Exactly what Nigel said. He's got the bit between his teeth now and is going to lobby all the "against" so we can out-vote the Aymes. You and Ian will come, won't you? Gotta go now, sweetie, Nigel's shouting for food as usual. See you *demain*!'

As the line went dead, Migs stood by the telephone smiling. Sarah was just the tonic she needed. The awfulness of the day receded to the back of her mind as she went through to the kitchen. She was almost back to her normal cheerful self when she told Ian about the forthcoming Road Meeting and Sarah and Nigel's plans to hijack the scheme.

Eleven

M igs and Ian sat at one end of the room with Sarah and
Nigel, and Keith and Jill Aymes, with one empty chair
beside them. Robert and Betty Hollywell sat halfway along on
the window seat, and at the far end of the room in a group sat
Frank and Mary Dodd, Colin Coleman, Jane Proctor and
Evelyn Bateman. Daphne was in the Peters' house being
'minded' by Dougal's babysitter.

'I think we're all present and correct now, Robert,' Betty said
looking round the room for the third time.

'Hang about! Andrew Lavery's not here yet!' Colin said. 'I
know he's coming – saw him this morning and he said so.'

'Wouldn't miss it for the world!' were Andrew's actual words
when Colin had mentioned the evening gathering. Colin had
looked more than a little surprised.

'But these meetings are so indescribably boring!' he'd declared.

'Not to a writer like myself!' Andrew had replied. 'A group of
such incredibly diverse characters at odds with one another but
bound together by one inanimate object – the lane! Why, there
may even be a real murderer amongst us!'

As Andrew and his girlfriend set off belatedly down the lane to
the meeting, he recalled his remark and momentarily grinned as
he remembered Colin's shocked expression. Reproaching himself
now, he realized that it had not been a very tactful remark to
have made seeing that quite a few people wondered if indeed
Colin had bumped off his wife in order to benefit from her will. It
was well known she held the purse strings – and that the purse
was quite heavy! She was one of those women who always had to

be one up on her friends and neighbours, he reflected. According to Jill Aymes, the moment she'd told Caroline the name of her London hairdresser, Caroline had to go there, too. It was the same with her clothes and decor. It was quite easy to see why, if old Evelyn's parsnip soup was universally approved, Caroline would have determined to make hers as tasty, or better!

As for Colin, Andrew was by no means entirely convinced of his innocence. Certainly the man had been away birdwatching, or some such, on the day of his wife's death; but that wasn't to say he hadn't dug up some of the poisonous roots before he left the house, telling her they were parsnips! He was a strange individual; creeping around peering out of those bottle-glass spectacles from behind hedges, trees, bushes; hiding himself in ditches or staring up at the treetops through his heavy binoculars. When spoken to, he rarely smiled and never, ever saw a joke. Feeling sorry for the chap after his wife's funeral, Andrew had invited Colin back to Pear Tree Cottage to meet his new 'popsie' as he called his current girlfriend; but he'd made some ridiculous excuse about a great crested grebe he was hoping to see on the lake.

Andrew sighed as he and his girlfriend hurried along the road to Ivy Lodge. It was nearly dark and the lake was a black ominous blur. A vixen called suddenly from the woods behind the lake, sounding like a child being tortured. The girl beside him shivered, clinging more firmly to his arm.

'Isn't that where that airforce chap drowned himself?' she asked nervously.

Andrew nodded. No point in frightening her further by saying that he was a hundred per cent certain Proctor hadn't committed suicide but had been pushed in. Anyone could have hidden themselves in the trees behind the landing stage and stepped forward and let off the brakes of his wheelchair. Colin could have been lurking there watching a rail or a coot or something. But what motive could he possibly have had? Or must he have had a motive? Research Andrew had done for his murder stories had shown him that men sometimes killed just for the kick it gave them. It was a thought – one he might share with Nigel who often dropped in for a drink and a chat.

He was, needless to say, late for the start of the Road Meeting. Ellen let him into the house, staring goggle-eyed at the Liz Hurley lookalike, the tall, auburn-haired girl with the unmissable cleavage and skintight jeans, as she showed them into the Hollywells' sitting room. There was a sudden hush as all eyes turned to the young woman in the tight-fitting blue sequinned T-shirt with its plunging neckline, bare midriff and gold chain hanging loose round the low waisted jeans. Andrew now cheerfully introduced his latest acquisition as Perdita Purdy.

'If my school Latin is anything to go by, Perdition means utter destruction,' Nigel said with a wicked grin at Sarah. 'With a body like that, she'd destroy me in no time.'

Sarah gave a mock scowl.

'What you really mean is, lucky Andrew. Well, I say, lucky Purfleet, or whatever her name is!'

They were both silenced by the sepulchral voice of Robert Hollywell.

'. . . all gathered together under one roof, it would be appropriate for us to have a minute or two's silence in order to say a little prayer for our dear, departed friend and neighbour, Wing Commander Cecil Proctor.'

'D.F.C., O.B.E., V.C. and all the rest of it, why not!' Nigel muttered, loud enough unfortunately for Keith Aymes to hear.

'No need to make fun of him, Sedgewick-Jones!' Keith Aymes never used Christian names if he could help it. Surnames savoured of public schools and although he'd never been to one, he very much wished he had. 'He was a very brave man!'

As if echoing Keith's voice, Robert Hollywell was now saying exactly the same thing.

'Not many of us here are old enough to have had the privilege of serving our country in the last war, but we, sons of those brave men, will never forget the gratitude we owe them – in particular those heroes like Wing Commander Proctor who was one of the magnificent few Battle of Britain pilots to survive. It is all the more regrettable that so brave a man should lose his life in what the coroner described as "a tragic accident". Tragic, indeed . . .'

'Oh, God!' Nigel said in a whisper to Sarah. 'At this rate we're going to miss the football on Sky!'

Now occupying the empty chair next to Ian which he was happily sharing with Miss Perdita Purdy, Andrew said in a loud, clear voice, 'Can we possibly proceed with tonight's agenda, Robert? We're going out to dinner when it's over and at this rate, we'll lose our reservations.'

Robert Hollywell's mouth tightened in annoyance but beside him Betty muttered timidly, 'It is getting a little late, dear. Do you think . . .'

'As you seem to be in a hurry, Andrew, I'll forgo the few little opening remarks I had been going to make and allow Keith to explain better than I can why his plans for the lane are important and urgent. Keith? Would you like to take the floor?'

There had been a barely audible sigh of relief when the parson had announced he would not be giving his usual 'sermon'. All heads turned now to the large portly figure of Keith Aymes. His brown hair was carefully brushed, his dark blue London business suit perfectly tailored, his pink hanky and tie with its ruby tie pin, coordinating colourwise with his striped shirt.

'Clear to see our Keith is used to public speaking!' Andrew remarked softly to Migs. 'The careful pause as he glances round the room to make sure everyone is paying proper attention, then . . . off he goes . . .'

'A great deal more attention seems to have been centred on the proposed resurfing of the lane.' His clear, articulate voice was audible to everyone. 'That is not the important issue here. It's the chopping off the corner of the lane, which I know you will all agree is quite lethal, and putting in the culvert and drains underneath to take the surface flood water. We have all suffered from this tiresome and unnecessary regular winter occurrence.'

Evelyn Bateman's high thin voice broke in as she said, 'Quite a few residents live further down the lane than you, Mr Aymes. They are not affected by the flooding.'

She spoke with a degree of authority not unlike that of a barrister in court. She had after all been a legal secretary most of her working life. Because of her scholastic record and exceptionally good brain, she had been accepted into a prestigious legal partnership, quickly gaining promotion to become the invaluable PA to one of the country's most able barristers. As a result of this past background, she was not intimidated by any of the neighbours.

'Yet you yourself must suffer more inconvenience than most with water lying outside your own gate, Miss Bateman!' countered Keith Aymes.

'I have perfectly good wellington boots, Mr Aymes,' Evelyn replied. 'As for any inconvenience to myself, it is my garden you wish to appropriate for your culvert!'

Aymes' mouth tightened.

'I am well aware of it, Miss Bateman. However, as I think you are very well aware, that piece of what you call your garden belongs to Frank Dodd who has already agreed to sell it to me. Nor can you honestly describe that piece of land as a garden. It's a positive wilderness.'

Evelyn's face flushed as now she stood up, her diminutive black clad figure making her look like an irate small bird.

'I do not wish to be rude, Mr Aymes, but you will not deny that you are new to country life. You have only to read your daily paper to hear how our English heritage is slowly being corroded. Our fields and woods, moors and fens are being covered in concrete. Slowly but so surely, future generations will not understand Blake's famous line of verse: "*Green and pleasant land . . .*". Many of our birds, animals, insects, butterflies are becoming extinct – and more will do so, those which at this very moment are enjoying the thistles, dandelions, rose hips and blackberries which thrive in my so-called piece of "wasteland". You have, I know, offered to cover the cost of widening the lane but this will reduce the grass verges if not eliminate them altogether. Your offer is a generous one but to the birds who nest in the hedges and feed off the vegetation in the verges, you are destroying their livelihood. We are living in a very beautiful part of the country, Mr Aymes. I propose we continue to enjoy it without unnecessary alteration or "improvements".'

'Well said, Evelyn!' Colin Coleman, the ornithologist, broke the silence that followed Evelyn's impassioned speech. 'Agree with every word.'

'Me, too!' said Nigel ungrammatically. 'I suppose you're all for it, Frank?'

Flushed but undaunted, Frank Dodd said, 'No objections to what Mr Aymes wants to do. Plenty of grass and trees and such on my land for Miss Bateman's wildlife.'

'Well, I'm against upgrading the lane,' Andrew Lavery said, shifting himself on his chair to make more room for his girl-friend. 'Any improvement is bound to speed up the traffic and one of the reasons I bought Pear Tree Cottage was so I could walk my dogs round about in safety.'

Now Robert Hollywell stood up, raising his arm as if to give his congregation the blessing. Instead, he said, 'It is over three months since our last meeting and we have all had plenty of time to consider Mr Aymes' proposal with two of our Road Meetings postponed. Now we have to consider that it will soon be winter and if work is to be done on a culvert, then it should be started very soon. As you all know, Mr Aymes has generously offered to fund two thirds of the cost. The remaining third would require the rest of us to subscribe about a thousand pounds each – not too great a sum considering the advantages. I will now take your votes.'

He glanced round the room and decided to begin with Frank. Beside him, Betty nervously fingered her pencil and note pad as she waited to take down the votes.

'Frank? For. Mary? For . . .'

Slowly he went from head to head. Jane Proctor? For. Evelyn? Against. The Aymes, two more for the proposal. The Sedgewick-Jones, two more against. Migs and Ian? Two more against. Colin? Against. Betty and himself? For.

'How does that add up, Betty?' Robert asked as she bent low over her note pad and furiously totted up the figures for the second time.

'Seven votes for and six against!' she announced.

Evelyn lent forward in her chair.

'You quite clearly indicated there was one vote for every resident, Mr Hollywell. You have not allotted a vote to my sister and, unquestionably, Daphne would be as opposed to the proposal as I am. As you know, she enjoys walking up and down the lane by herself.'

The room fell silent, no one having the nerve to suggest that a mentally handicapped person like Daphne Bateman was hardly capable of a considered opinion. Betty Hollywell was the first to speak.

'That would make the voting equal.'

'Hold it!' Keith Aymes stood up, looking less composed knowing as he did that there had to be a majority for the motion to be carried. 'You've not had a vote from Andrew Lavery. Am I right, Lavery?'

'Absolutely, old fellow. I'm sorry but I'm against. So is Perdita!'

There was a sudden buzz of voices and Sarah's barely concealed laugh. The Reverend Hollywell was not amused.

'The voting is for residents, Mr Lavery!'

'Quite! And Perdita is currently resident at Pear Tree Cottage, aren't you, sweetie?'

The girl nodded, not altogether sure whether she was doing the right thing or not. There was a distinct air of disapproval in the room.

'Mr Lavery, the young lady is not a *permanent* resident, is she? Therefore it would be undemocratic to give her a vote.'

'Well, why not?' Nigel put in mischievously. 'Nowadays, partners are treated like wives or husbands, aren't they?'

Sarah, Migs, Colin and Andrew were all grinning but the Reverend Hollywell was red in the face.

'This is no place for tomfoolery, Nigel. We like to consider ourselves a proper democracy. In any event, the question of Miss . . . er, Miss Purdy's right to vote is irrelevant. She is a temporary, not a permanent resident. The voting now stands at eight to seven against Mr Aymes' proposal, am I not right, Betty?'

'Yes, of course you are, Robert!' Betty said quickly.

Looking anywhere but at Keith Aymes, the Reverend said apologetically, 'Then I'm afraid to say you are outvoted, Keith. Personally I am sorry but—'

'Excuse me, everyone!' Frank Dodd's voice interrupted Hollywell's. 'If every resident is to be allowed a vote, like Miss Daphne, what about my boy, Jack? He's of age now and I'll tell you this, he'd be behind his mother and me.' Fearing that at this eleventh hour, his chance to sell his piece of land to Keith Aymes was slipping away, his tone became even more emphatic as he said, 'You can count young Jack's vote as for the proposal, Mrs Hollywell.'

'Eight all! It's as good as a tie break at Wimbledon!' Nigel muttered, delighting in putting the cat among the pigeons. 'What about the Brigends?' he said. 'They haven't voted.'

'I think they opted to abstain,' Betty said.

Keith jumped quickly on to the bandwagon.

'Since we have no deciding vote, I think we should make quite certain they do not have an opinion. Isn't Mrs Brigend, Ellen, here in the house? I think you should call her in, Robert, and see what she has to say. Whichever way she and her husband vote, it should be recorded.'

'I don't think Ellen should have pressure put upon her, Mr Aymes!' Evelyn said and beside her Jane Proctor nodded her agreement.

'If she doesn't mind either way, she has a right to abstain.'

'Ask her!' said Keith. 'Surely she's more than capable of speaking for herself? She's not a stupid woman. Can you go and call her in, Betty?'

Obediently, Betty scuttled out of the room. It was a moment or two before Ellen returned in her place. She had removed her apron and stood looking round the room curiously. Nearly everyone here employed her. Mondays she did for Mrs Proctor; Tuesdays for Miss Bateman; Thursdays for Mrs Proctor again; Fridays for the Hollywells. Wednesdays she went to the market so she had a day off. Saturdays she sometimes worked for the Aymes if they were entertaining, which they did on a lavish scale and which she rather enjoyed.

When the Reverend Hollywell put the question to her as to why she and her husband had abstained, she was not in the least flustered.

'I'm all for getting rid of rainwater like Mr Aymes says it will,' she said bluntly. 'Get me legs soaked through every winter coming up this end to work. But Ray, well, he doesn't like getting mixed up in things like votes and that. I said we'd got a vote same as everyone else and he said it was a free country and I could do as I pleased.'

'Does that mean you will vote, Ellen?' Robert Hollywell said. 'We won't hold it against you if you prefer not to do so.'

'I'll vote if you want me to, Reverend,' Ellen said cheerfully. 'It's Ray as don't want to . . . says he don't mind either way.'

'Of course you can vote without him, Ellen!' Aymes broke in. 'So if you are for getting the lane dried out, that makes the deciding vote to carry the proposal, if I'm not mistaken. Is that now agreed, Robert?'

'Lucky devil!' Nigel whispered to Sarah as Aymes stood up and moved across the room to talk to Robert. 'We'd have pipped him at the post if he hadn't cooked up our Ellen.'

'What now?' Migs asked.

As if in reply to her question, Robert held up his hand for silence. When the room quietened, he said, 'I very much regret that Keith's very generous proposal for our benefit has split the lane in this way but I'm sure you will all agree that it is a great relief to have a final decision at last. Keith is going to get a detailed estimate for the proposed work and will notify each of you what your exact portion of the expenditure will be. If anyone is . . . er . . . not in a position to meet this sum over and above the yearly subscription, they have only to notify Keith and he will . . . er . . . cover the shortfall.'

'Would you call that offer patronizing or generous?' Andrew asked as arm in arm with the luscious Perdita, he followed Nigel and Sarah out of the room. 'Reckon old Keith knew all along he'd carry the day. He who pays the piper calls the tune, isn't that right? Take Ellen for one – Sarah says Jill pays her double the going hourly rate when she goes up on a Saturday for their lunches. Bet Keith's going to pay Frank Dodd way over the odds for Evelyn's bit of garden. Not that it's any skin off my nose.'

'It's not the end of the world, is it?' Nigel replied. 'Now, how about you and Perdita coming to us to have a decent drink? The Rev's sherry is like cough mixture! You, too, Ian? Migs?'

'Thanks, Nigel, but Migs is off alcohol at the moment, and I expect she wants to get back to The Monster, don't you, darling? We're both a bit paranoid after his disappearance last month – keep thinking we can't find him when we're looking in the wrong room! Come and have a drink with us tomorrow; you, too, Andrew and Perdita.'

'Great!' Perdita said with a radiant smile. She lifted her arm to wave them off, the noise of her multitude of bangles all but drowning the sound of the Peters' car engine as, to everyone's surprise, she added in French, '*A tout a l'heure!*'

Nigel and Sarah were out riding most of the following morning but dropped in for a pre-lunch drink. Migs was giving Dougal his lunch in the kitchen so Sarah took her glass of white wine in there where the little boy was making a not very great success of feeding himself.

'He needs a bath after each meal!' Migs said as Sarah sat down at the table to watch Dougal spoon mashed potato, spinach and minced chicken into his hair. She laughed.

'He really is something, Migs! I have to say, I'm almost tempted. It's the not being able to ride whilst I was pregnant that puts me off the idea of having a kid. I suppose I'll come round to it eventually, before time runs out on me. Nigel doesn't seem overanxious to start a family yet. By the way, what's happened to Andrew and his girlfriend?'

Migs smiled.

'He telephoned to say they'd decided to spend the day in London but would pop in tomorrow if that was OK. I have to say, his Perdita's quite something, isn't she?'

The girls continued to gossip whilst outside, Ian and Nigel sat in the warm early October sunshine discussing the lane.

'I had a feeling Keith Aymes would get his way in the end,' Nigel remarked. 'His sort usually do get what they want, although I can't quite see how with the voting the way it was. I'm surprised he didn't kick up when poor old Daphne was allowed a say – well, a proxy vote might be a better way of putting it.'

Ian laughed.

'Well, the remaining seven of us who were against the proposal could have followed up with a refusal to allow young Jack a say. After all, it was supposed to be two per household.'

Nigel nodded.

'Which included Caroline when this plan of Keith's was first proposed. I'm sure she was all for it – make the place a bit more like Potter's Bar!'

They both smiled but then Nigel's expression became thoughtful.

'I suppose you'll think I'm as dotty as Daphne if I tell you I've started wondering if . . . well, if things aren't quite above board!'

'What's that meant to mean?' Ian asked, aware that Nigel's voice had dropped a tone or two as if to ensure that neither Sarah or Migs could hear him through the open kitchen window.

Confirming Ian's thoughts, Nigel said quietly, 'Don't breathe a word to the girls of what I'm going to confess. For one thing it sounds crazy even to me; but for another, I don't want to scare either of them, Migs in particular.'

'Scare them?' Ian repeated stupidly. 'What's on your mind, Nigel? Spit it out whatever it is!'

Nigel paused briefly and then leaning forward to clasp his hands together between his knees, he said, 'The two so-called accidents we've had in the lane – perhaps the fire in the barn, too – it's crossed my mind that they may be connected in some way with this ruddy road plan of Keith's.'

'What on earth do you mean, connected?' Ian questioned.

Nigel sat up and looked directly into Ian's eyes.

'I know it sounds crazy, but if you think about it, if the old Wing Co and Caroline Coleman had been alive, that would have been two more votes in favour of Aymes' plan.'

Despite the gravity of Nigel's voice, Ian laughed.

'I never heard anything so far-fetched in my life!' he said.

Nigel did not join in his amusement.

'Is it so far-fetched? What about the Dodds' barn fire? Maybe Frank was meant to be bumped off and whoever it was trapped young Jack instead. Frank is for the proposal. After all, he is selling the land Keith wants for cutting the corner and the culvert.'

'Look, Nigel, I think you're doing your best to emulate our friend Andrew Lavery. He's really good at imagining murders. Did he put this idea in your head?'

Nigel grimaced.

'No, he didn't, and I said you'd think I was bonkers. But the thought has niggled ever since the last meeting.'

Ian was silent whilst he opened two more cans of beer and passed one to Nigel. Then he said quietly, 'Look, let's suppose for a moment that you've hit a nail on the head and someone felt sufficiently passionately about the alterations to Millers Lane actually to commit two murders to prevent them. I ask you, Nigel, who? We can write off all those residents in favour of the plan, Hollywells, Dodds, Aymes, Jane Proctor, Ellen Brigend; then there's yourself, Sarah, Migs and me who I'm sure you will agree are above suspicion. So who's left?'

Nigel sighed.

'I know, I know! It only leaves Andrew Lavery, Colin Coleman, and the two Batemans. We can discount the two old girls opposite. I know Evelyn is pretty passionate about the wildlife etc and she'll lose that rundown bit of garden, but you don't go bumping your neighbours off at eighty-something to preserve a few toads and thistles!'

'But the dippy sister?' Ian queried. 'You don't know what goes on in her head.'

'But she was fond of Caroline who, if you remember, had befriended her. As for pushing the Wing Co into the lake, if she really did do such a crazy thing, she'd have found some stupid nursery rhyme to boast about it! Seriously, Ian, Andrew is a possibility. Inventing all those murder stories may have affected his brain! I don't know . . . maybe he's been experimenting or something.'

He gave an apologetic shrug of his shoulders as he realized how implausible this was.

'Not very likely, I know,' he remarked. 'But Colin Coleman, now . . . well, he's pretty fanatical about the environment and birds and suchlike – twenty times worse than our Evelyn – but not sufficiently so to commit murder, for heaven's sake!'

'But he *is* fanatical, and your Sarah told Migs she thinks he might well have bumped off his wife because she'd decided she hated country life and wanted to sell Siskins and go back to Potters Bar! What's more, she held the purse strings so Colin couldn't have bought her out and stayed here. As for who killed the Wing Co – *if* he was killed and it wasn't an accident after all – what about his wife? I gather he was a dreadful bully and made her life hell. She had every reason to get rid of him.'

Nigel emptied his beer mug and stood up.

'I have to admit Colin sounds the only reasonable suspect, but why kill the Wing Co as well as his wife? I can see you think I'm nuts. All the same, I shall expect you to eat your hat if there's another "For" destined for the high jump!'

'Seeing that you're scraping the barrel, Nigel,' Ian said, 'what about that chauffeur of Aymes', Parker? Nobody seems to know much about him. Maybe he's one of those early release prisoners the papers are on about, and he's getting his own back on society? Come to that, how about my next-door neighbour, Ray?'

'Come off it! What possible motive could Parker have? As for Ray – he's a man of the soil if ever there was one. Besides, even if he wanted to go round killing people, Ellen wouldn't let him!'

Both man laughed, but despite their restored good humour, neither one related their conversation to their wives.

Twelve

I t was five thirty on a late October afternoon. Jack had finished helping his father with the milking, washed out the dairy and cleaned the milking apparatus. If he got a move on, he told himself, he could get in a couple of hours fishing before dark. It was now two months since the ghastly morning when he'd seen the shadowy figure of the murderer tip the old Wing Commander into the lake, and he'd not been fishing since that scare. All the same, he'd thought it best to give Millers Lake a miss for a bit longer. Then, out of the blue last night in bed, he'd remembered the Baldwins' pond in Briar Field.

He knew there were trout in this large pond because Brenda Baldwin, whose husband owned Rogan Farm, had said he was going to stock it with fish. Mr Baldwin had been told they'd do all right, the pond having a good flow of water. They'd be rainbow trout, of course, not like the brown trout in Millers Lake, but Jack had little doubt he'd catch more fish and he could do with the money.

There was a slight drizzle falling as Jack left the farm taking care that neither of his parents saw him leaving. They'd want to know where he was going and when he'd be back. The autumn air had a slight chill presaging the winter weather to come. However, the water would still be warm after the Indian summer they had enjoyed at the beginning of October and conditions for fishing would be ideal, he decided. He'd just have to be careful to find a place to conceal himself when he got there. There was a narrow overgrown footpath leading across Briar Field but before he reached it, he'd have to risk being seen when he walked up the road as far as the corner where the footpath began. He certainly couldn't afford to be caught poaching again.

Jack had barely left the farmyard when he was startled by an unexpected noise. He slipped across the road hoping to conceal himself behind the bushes bordering the gate into Barley Meadow. Then the noise came again and he nearly laughed out loud – it was only the hooting of an owl.

He was about to resume his walk along Millers Lane to Bracken Footpath when he saw a shadow moving towards him across the meadow. In the dusk it was impossible to identify the person but whoever it was had no reason to be there on his father's land. Granted he or she was not disturbing the cows who were lying down at the far corner, but there was no public right of way across the field and Jack decided to wait until the figure came closer.

'Is that you, Jack?' he whispered. 'Don't make a noise. There's a tawny owl in that oak tree – a grey one; quite unusual.'

It was that creep, Coleman, Jack realized, up to his usual tricks birdwatching – only owls and such weren't the only sort of birds he watched. Sandra had told him the dirty old man had tried to touch her up in the pub one night when she'd been on duty collecting empty glasses. If he tried it on again, she'd told him, she was going to report him.

Not wishing to get into conversation with him, Jack merely nodded and when Coleman put his binoculars up to his eyes and gazed up at the tree, he took the opportunity to slip away up the lane.

Lights in the downstairs windows of Nos 1 and 2 The Cottages had already been turned on, sending a faint orange glow on to the small squares of their front gardens. He could see the flicker of a TV screen through the Brigends' kitchen window – probably watching *Richard & Judy* he guessed with a grin. In the Peters' cottage, Mrs Peters, who Jack quite fancied, was giving the kid his tea. Chirpy little fellow – Jack liked him, and Mr Peters too, who employed him from time to time doing odd jobs and often gave him a beer as well as always paying him on the nail.

On the opposite side of the road, the sitting-room curtains of Rose Cottage were drawn but Jack could hear the unmistakeable sound of the *Neighbours* signature tune. He was surprised, Miss Evelyn having once told him how she 'abominated' modern soaps. Maybe Miss Daphne liked *Neighbours*? He shifted his gear on to his other shoulder and, keeping well to the verges of the lane, he was about to turn into the footpath when he heard a high-pitched voice calling his name. His first instinct was to dive down the footpath as quickly as possible, but he paused long enough to recognize Miss Evelyn's voice.

'Jack, come quickly. I need your help. Quickly, Jack!'

There was no doubting the urgency of the old lady's tone so Jack quickly dropped his rod and gear into a clump of withered cow parsley and hurried to the corner of Millers Lane where he could make out the shadowy figure of Miss Bateman waving at him. She grasped his arm, her thin, bony fingers surprisingly strong as she held on to him.

'It's the Reverend Hollywell, Jack, poor man. I think he must have had a stroke. Run quickly to Siskins and ask Mr Coleman to ring for a doctor and an ambulance. Maybe someone can resuscitate Mr Hollywell.'

Shocked almost to incoherence, Jack stood still echoing her words. 'A stroke? You mean he might be . . .'

'Don't stand there gawping, boy. And yes, I do think Mr Hollywell's dead. Now go and find Mr Coleman, and if he isn't at home, go to the Sedgewick-Jones'. Someone will be in. I'll stay at the house in case Mrs Hollywell returns. I don't want her to find . . .'

She broke off, realizing that she was detaining Jack who now sped off down the road, his fishing entirely forgotten. Evelyn went back to Ivy Lodge and entering the sitting room, stood staring with extreme distaste at the sight of the Reverend Robert Hollywell sprawled on the floor by the unlit fire. By the agonized expression on his face and the way his fingers clutched at the collar of his shirt, it was clear he'd not experienced a peaceful death.

A long time ago, she'd been in court when a member of the jury had had a heart attack. The memory came back to her now but was quickly forgotten as she became aware of a sickly smell pervading the room. She went across to open one of the double casement windows. As she did so, a damp breeze rustled the shabby cretonne curtains, one of which knocked over a photograph frame. The sound of breaking glass momentarily disturbed the breathless silence in the room.

Evelyn shivered as instinctively she bent to pick up the broken shards. Knowing the distorted figure of Robert Hollywell was behind her, it was with reluctance that she turned round as she heard voices in the hall.

'Is that you, Mr Coleman?' she called out, anxious now to see a familiar face. It was Jack who answered.

'It's me and Mr Aymes' chauffeur, Miss. Mr Parker were just passing. I'll fetch Mr Coleman now!'

After one horrified look at the vicar's body, Jack disappeared back through the front door. Evelyn regarded the pale unfriendly face of Stewart Parker who had not thought fit to remove his fleece cap, the least he could do in the presence of the dead, she thought.

'He's a gonner all right!' the man said as he looked up from the vicar's body at Evelyn. 'Best not touch anything, Miss.' He looked round him uneasily. 'Don't seem no sign of a break in. Where's his missus then?'

'If you are referring to Mrs Hollywell, she is in London,' Evelyn replied coldly. She glanced at her wristwatch and automatically corrected herself. 'Mrs Hollywell will be on her way back from London as a point of fact.'

The coach taking a party of W.I. members to a matinée of *Chitty Chitty Bang Bang* followed by tea at the Ritz, was due back that evening. Betty Hollywell had invited Evelyn and Daphne to join them. Of course, there was no conceivable way Daphne could be included in such an outing, Evelyn had replied, and excused herself on the grounds that she could not leave her sister alone. As it happened, one of the assistants at the day care centre had offered to look after Daphne if ever Evelyn felt in need of a day off, but *Chitty Chitty Bang Bang* was certainly not to her taste and in any event, she had no intention of imposing on the assistant's goodwill.

'Living it up with the other old sheilas, was she?' Parker's voice with its strong Australian accent broke into Evelyn's thoughts. 'Can't say I blame her married to that old—'

'Will you please be quiet!' Evelyn's voice was very much that of a law court official reprimanding an unruly member of the public. Somewhat surprisingly, the man did shut up but only for a minute or two. With another curious look at the dead man, he turned back to Evelyn, a leering grin on his face.

'What've you been doing here, if I may enquire? Bumped the old geezer off, have you?'

Evelyn's mouth tightened to a thin line. Since the Australian's arrival with the Aymes, she had avoided Stewart Parker whenever possible. To his employers, he was obsequious, over the top with his 'sirs' and 'madams', bowing and scraping as he opened car doors for them. Jill thought the world of him and often remarked how lucky they had been when he'd answered their advertisement for a live-in handyman/driver. They had had the flat over the garage entirely redecorated and modernized for him and provided a smart grey uniform for when he was on duty. But at the moment he was not on duty and wore jeans and a black turtleneck jersey which, Evelyn thought, gave him a decidedly sinister appearance. This she might have overlooked had she not quickly observed that whenever he was not within the Aymes' ear shot, his manner was openly cheeky, bordering on insolent.

Disliking the vulgarity of his last remark, she was stung to reply, 'Perhaps I might ask what *you* were doing outside Ivy Lodge, Mr Parker?'

But before he could reply, Nigel came hurrying into the room followed closely by Jack.

'Good God!' Having taken a quick look at the body, Nigel turned to Evelyn, his customary good-natured expression replaced by one of serious concern. 'I was on my way home from the station when I saw the lights blazing in Ivy Lodge and the front door wide open. Next thing Jack tells me you and he found . . . found poor Robert like this. You look very pale, Miss Bateman – been a shock I dare say. Jack, hot foot it down to The Paddocks and tell my wife to get up here as quick as she can – and bring a bottle of brandy with her.'

Evelyn was now trembling quite visibly. Nigel put an arm round her.

'Steady on, old thing. I think you should get out of this room.

115

Sit yourself down in the kitchen. Anyone called a doctor? The police?'

Evelyn shook her head.

'I sent Jack down to your house to ask someone to make the calls . . . so silly . . . I could have telephoned from here . . . really, I can't think why . . .'

'Don't worry about it, my dear,' Nigel said gently as he lead her out of the room. 'Shock can make the best of us behave oddly. Now you sit here until Sarah comes.'

'I think I ought to go home,' Evelyn said faintly. 'Daphne will be worrying. I said I'd only be a minute or two . . . I wanted to see if Betty, Mrs Hollywell, was back. I had some of my home-made elderberry wine to give her and this is a good time for me to be out of my cottage because Daphne always watches *Neighbours* and *The Simpsons* on television, so—'

'Yes, I do understand!' Nigel broke in, aware that the need to call the doctor was long overdue and, he decided, the police. He did not have enough medical knowledge to know if his neighbour had committed suicide or if this was another 'accident', which he and Ian had thought might even be murders. One thing he did know, this was not a heart attack. He'd seen his own father's sudden death of heart failure and knew by the vicar's appearance that his had been a violent death.

As he went to the telephone on the hall table by the front door, he was aware of Stewart Parker's figure standing by the sitting-room door staring at him. Only now did it occur to him to wonder what he was doing here.

As if divining his thoughts, the man waited until Nigel had made the necessary telephone calls and then said, 'Young Jack stopped me on me way up to the pub, sir! I came in to see if there was anything I could do. Bit too late, I'm afraid, sir.'

Nigel nodded. The Australian was not his favourite person but he seemed an efficient chap. Sarah said there'd been one occasion when Jill Aymes had lent him and their car to drive her to the station and he'd 'eyed her up and down', to use Sarah's description, and given her 'the look'. When Sarah had explained what that meant, he'd thought it unsurprising seeing what an attractive girl his wife was, particularly when she had her London party gear on.

'Well, you'd better hang around, Parker!' Nigel said now. 'The police are sure to want to question everyone who might have clues as to what happened.'

The chauffeur nodded.

'It's just that I could maybe help out by meeting Mrs Holly-well. Madam told me she'd gone by coach to London and Mr Hollywell was to take and fetch her from Delhurst. Seeing the weather, sir, I thought perhaps I should take Mr Hollywell's Morris and meet her, seeing he can't do it himself!'

Nigel hesitated. It was a very logical – indeed, thoughtful – idea, yet he had the strangest feeling of antipathy towards the man's suggestion. It was almost as if it was too kind, too considerate; yet even as the thought struck him, he knew he was being ridiculous. Nevertheless, he told the chauffeur that he should remain in the house until the police came. He'd read enough Agatha Christie whodunnits to know that no one was permitted to leave the scene of a crime until told by the police they might do so.

Scene of the crime! Nigel repeated to himself as he went to the front door to open it for Sarah and Jack. What crime, for heaven's sake? Surely to goodness no one could possibly have wanted to murder poor old Hollywell.

The sight of Sarah carrying not only a bottle of brandy but a bottle of whisky, too, restored Nigel's equanimity.

'Good girl!' he said. 'Jack told you the news, I imagine?'

Sarah nodded as she followed Nigel into the kitchen.

'It's true, then? Robert's dead?'

'Afraid so, darling. Now, find some glasses and pour us all a drink. Poor Miss Bateman has had a horrible shock. And don't say you don't drink spirits, Miss Bateman. I'm well aware it's not your custom, but in this case, a small brandy is what the doctor ordered – or would, if he was here.'

With Nigel's prescribed shot of brandy in her, Evelyn, who had been silent until now, became more voluble.

'It seems so untimely, so unseemly, that so young a man as Mr Hollywell should have died in his comparative youth,' she said looking from Sarah to Nigel. She quickly corrected herself. 'Well, if not exactly in his youth he would still have had a good two more decades of life to carry on his good works.' She paused momentarily to finish the last dregs of brandy before adding thoughtfully, 'He was not a particularly well educated man, one has to say, but he did try to be helpful to his parishoners in the years before Delhurst Church was closed. That was before your time, of course.'

Evelyn had little in common with Betty Hollywell, Sarah thought as Evelyn's precise, punctilious voice rambled on. Betty, like Jane Proctor, was a timid little woman who would never stand up to her husband's dictates. Not that Robert Hollywell was a bully like Cecil Proctor had been. His worst fault was that he had so loved to hear the sound of his own voice as he asseverated his lengthy sermons – or, indeed, his summing up of their road meetings!

But she mustn't think critically of the unfortunate man, Sarah told herself. He had meant well, as Evelyn had said. He always left his front door unlocked, as if Ivy Lodge was a church and, he insisted, must be open to any of his former parishioners who might wish to seek his spiritual guidance. As Nigel had said on several occasions, it was a crazy thing to do in this day and age. Anyone might have gone in and cut his throat . . .

With a little gasp at the direction her thoughts had taken, Sarah quickly turned her mind to the elderly woman opposite her.

'Would you like me to pop down and see if Daphne is all right?' she asked. 'I could bring her back here, if you like.'

'I don't think that's advisable with the police and medics who will be all around,' Nigel broke in. 'Tell Migs and Ian what's up and ask them to have Daphne over with them until Miss Bateman gets back.' Seeing that Evelyn was about to protest, he added with a smile: 'Migs told us your sister could be very helpful. I gather she sings nursery rhymes to Dougal to get him off to sleep.'

'How kind . . . how very kind of you, Sarah. That would be most helpful.' Evelyn said. 'Oh dear, I do wonder where Betty is. She should be back by now.'

'I'll nip up to the King's Head after I've seen Migs and Ian,' Sarah said. 'It's turned out such a foul evening, I dare say the coach is late back. I can hear a car outside now.'

It was, in fact, Doctor Grainger's car, followed closely by a police car. Half an hour later, whilst the local constabulary was still questioning the occupants of Ivy Lodge and an ambulance had removed the dead man's body, to everyone's intense surprise, Inspector Govern and his assistant, Sergeant Beck arrived. None of the residents of Millers Lane were aware that the inspector had followed Ian and Nigel's train of thought with far more suspicion than theirs. He'd had a substantial bet with Beck that there would be a third death, and so certain was he that both the previous so-called accidents were murders, he had left word that any future violent action in Millers Lane was to be reported to him instantly.

Shutting the files he was working on when the duty officer had informed him of a further death in Millers Lane, he'd driven as fast as he dared to Delhurst. There he had all but collided with the coach which had just deposited an exhausted Betty Hollywell outside the King's Head. The drizzle had now turned to a steady downpour of rain and seeing the poor woman who he recognized from his previous visit, he had offered her a lift home, omitting to tell her the reason for his presence until she was safely inside Ivy Lodge.

Sarah greeted all three arrivals and with a swift glance at the inspector who shook his head, she took it upon herself to break the terrible news to Betty that her husband had been taken to hospital and was unhappily beyond medical aid. Despite the measure of brandy Sarah insisted she drink immediately, the newly bereaved woman lapsed into hysterics. It was not so much caused by the news of her huband's demise as by the nature of his death which Doctor Grainger immediately identified as asphyxia. His estimate of the time of death was between midday and two p.m. Since the death was not a natural one, he said, there would of course be a post mortem but the doctor doubted if the pathologist would find any alternative cause of death to that of suffocation. He, too, now departed to attend to an emergency in Hunnington but had left some sleeping pills with Sarah for Betty Hollywell's use should she need them. He could be contacted at his surgery the following morning, he told Detective Inspector Govern.

Whilst Sarah was helping the sobbing Betty upstairs and into her bed, Inspector Govern turned to look at the four people now seated round the formica-topped kitchen table. Nigel Sedgewick-Jones; Miss Evelyn Bateman; young Jack Dodd from the farm and the Aymes' chauffeur, Stewart Parker, who was fiddling with his cigarette lighter. It was now time, he told himself, to see just what true or false alibis these four potential suspects came up with.

Thirteen

'I spent the morning dictating to my secretary, lunched with two of my co-directors and then attended a meeting with the Chief Executive of Allied Investment Management, which ran on until about four o'clock. After that, back to my office until I left shortly before five to meet up with Ian Peters to catch the five twenty train home.'

Nigel's voice was level-toned and although, as a matter of routine, the inspector nodded to Beck to check on these sundry activities, he did not doubt their veracity. They had moved to the chilly and somewhat spartan dining room so that each person could be interviewed separately. Nigel's statement tallied with the one he had given the local policeman and Govern told him he need not retain him any longer and he could go home with Sarah.

As it happened, Nigel had asked his secretary to telephone Sarah at lunchtime to enquire whether the vet had come as requested to check on his favourite hunter who had developed a slight cough. This his secretary had done at twelve thirty at which time the vet had not yet arrived. Exactly three quarters of an hour later, Sarah had rung back to say the vet had been, prescribed an antibiotic, and assured her there was nothing serious to worry about. It seemed highly unlikely, to say the least, that Sarah Sedgewick-Jones would have found time to nip up the road to smother a man as heavy as herself, and with no conceivable motive.

'Thanks for your help, Mr Sedgewick-Jones. I'm sure Miss Bateman was grateful for your intervention when she and the lad discovered the . . . er, body. Now would you be so good as to ask young Jack Dodd to come in?'

Jack was a bundle of nerves. Not least, he told himself, because

121

his father would soon hear about Mr Hollywell's death and him and the police being there and all, and heaven help him if it got out he'd been down that end of Millers Lane in order to go poaching from Mr Baldwin's pond! Whilst waiting in the kitchen to be interviewed, he had decided to say he'd gone to look for a piece of metal which had dropped off his motorbike when he'd delivered the Sunday papers to Mr Lavery. Fear that he might not be believed as he told this lie to the inspector caused his voice to shake and he could see by the expression on the detective's face that he'd not convinced him.

'This is the third time, Jack, that you've been connected to some very strange happenings here in Millers Lane . . . Happenings that until now have been called "accidents".' Govern's face was impassive as he made this statement, but sharpened as he continued, 'The Reverend Hollywell's death, however, is no accident. According to Doctor Grainger's findings and my own, there was no way Mr Hollywell could have smothered himself. It is a murder we are dealing with now, and I would strongly advise you to tell me the truth. Let's begin again, shall we? This morning – mid morning – what were you doing, Jack?'

This much was easy, Jack thought as in firmer terms he described his morning at the golf club, the steak and kidney pudding his mother had cooked for lunch, his activities on the farm after lunch finishing with the evening milking and cleaning out the dairy.

Inspector Govern, recognizing truth when he heard it, nodded.

'So far so good, but what brought you up the lane this evening?'

Jack's hesitation was so palpable that the inspector was in no doubt that the boy had been up to mischief. He decided to take a chance.

'Perhaps you might find it easier to give me a truthful answer if I promise you it will be confidential? Unless, of course, you happen to have been the person who murdered the unfortunate vicar?'

Jack gave a sickly grin which quickly disappeared as, haltingly, he confessed to his illegal fishing sorties. Noting the barely concealed smile on Sergeant Beck's face, he was encouraged to elaborate and proceeded to confess to the full story of his presence at Millers Lake when the Wing Commander had drowned.

Inspector Govern's expression became suddenly alert, reminding Beck of a pointer he had once owned when it scented game.

'You saw someone? This is extremely important, Jack. Who did you see? A man? A woman? Come on, boy, out with it.'

Jack swallowed. He had not expected his confession to elicit further questioning.

'That's just it, sir. I couldn't see, I couldn't see proper it was that far away – opposite side of the lake, you know? And I was trying to hide myself behind twigs and that. I'd been trespassing there before, you see, and the Wing Commander'd told me dad and—'

'Yes, I do understand, Jack, but you're an intelligent lad and you must realize that what you witnessed that morning means the Wing Commander's death was no accident despite the coroner's verdict, if what you are saying is true.'

'Cross me heart and cut me throat!' Jack replied, adding with an anxious glance at Beck, 'I was in the Boy Scouts till I left school.'

The inspector was looking thoughtful. When he'd promised the boy confidentiality, he'd never dreamed Jack would confess to witnessing a murder. Such a thing was of vital importance and it wouldn't be long before the press would get hold of the story . . .

'Look, Jack, I made that promise of confidentiality with every possible intention of keeping it but I'm afraid I've jumped the gun. I should have waited first to find out what you had to say. I thought it would be something like a trespass – maybe a bit of scrumping, meeting a girl . . . But you have just told me you saw someone push the Wing Commander's chair into the lake. You're an invaluable witness to a murder and I'm going to have to ask you to make a statement to that effect.'

Seeing the horrified expression on Jack's face, he added quickly, 'If it's your dad finding out about your fishing sorties, I'll do what I can to make it all right with him. You're a very important witness, you know. The coroner's accidental death verdict could become murder by person or persons unknown.'

Jack was effectively silenced, remembering how reporters had swarmed up and down Millers Lane, getting people to give them a story about the Wing Commander's drowning. Ellen had been paid a hundred pounds just for saying how she cleaned The Mill House on Mondays and Thursdays and how the Wing Commander had hated being in a wheelchair and how brave he was! Like as not they'd pay a whole lot more for *his* story, especially as this time round the 'accident' would be 'a murder' – and all because of what he, Jack Dodd, had seen that morning. There'd be no need for anyone to know he hadn't been given permission to fish the lake. As for his dad, who'd know better, maybe he'd turn a blind eye if he, Jack, could help him out with all those bills he kept worrying about. If he was really rich, he might even be able to afford the Ducati 998, or the Honda Fireblade . . .

For a brief moment, Jack dreamed of glory, but then his face fell once more as another thought struck him.

'Me mum wouldn't like us being in the newspapers, no way!' he said doubtfully.

Inspector Govern stood up and patted Jack on the shoulder.

'Let's worry about that when and if the time comes,' he said. 'I'm sure she will want to see justice done at all costs. Now, you're quite sure you have no idea who that person was at the lake that day? If it was a man or a woman?'

Jack shook his head frowning.

'I couldn't see proper, like I said. First I thought it were Mrs Proctor but I couldn't see no skirt; there's tall yellow flowers – irises I think they're called – along that bit of bank by the landing stage, which would have hid their legs like. And I was far away. Could've been Mr Coleman, I s'pose – he's always creeping around behind bushes and things. He were up in Barley Meadow this evening when I come out of our farm – watching owls, he said, but he didn't have no right to be there.'

Inspector Govern glanced across at Beck who was busy making notes, before he turned back to Jack.

'If you do remember anything – anything at all about that

morning at the lake, you will tell me, won't you, Jack? As I said before, you're the only witness we have.'

He might have been a more important witness if he had been able to identify the murderer, Jack thought, reverting once more to the idea of being courted by the newspapers for his story. He grinned suddenly, imagining the effect he would have on his friends and the girls if he went zooming up to the King's Head on a brand new Ducati! He'd no need to let on he'd been fishing without Mr Aymes' permission. In any case, it wasn't him who'd objected to him pinching a few fish, but that bad-tempered old git, Proctor. Mr Aymes wasn't interested in fishing and probably wouldn't even care if he knew Jack was poaching a few now and again. He liked Mr Aymes, who tipped him quite generously when he delivered the Sunday papers; even bought him a beer when they'd run into each other in the pub.

He realized suddenly that his mind had been wandering and turned his attention back to what the inspector was now saying to him.

'I want you to come to Ferrybridge police station tomorrow, and Sergeant Beck here will help you write out a formal statement. Nothing for you to worry about, young man . . . just repeat everything you've told us. I want you to know I'm extremely grateful for your help. Now I expect you are anxious to push off. I shan't need you again tonight.'

'But what am I to say to me mum and dad?' Jack asked, realizing suddenly that his parents would have more than a few questions to ask once someone told them about Mr Hollywell's death – Ellen, probably; she was always first with the gossip.

From his chair by the window, Beck said, 'How about a sort of half truth; that you'd thought of going fishing and then thought better of it seeing it was illegal; that when you'd got to the footpath, the old lady, Miss Bateman, had called you. Then you can keep strictly to the letter, can't you? And Jack, be sure to warn your parents to lock up carefully. There's no doubt there is a murderer round these parts . . . madman by the look of it.'

'No doubt whatever!' Inspector Govern confirmed as he told Jack to ask Miss Bateman if she would be so good as to come and see him now.

As Evelyn entered the room, it struck the inspector how utterly exhausted the old lady looked, and he felt a pang of conscience for not interviewing her first so that she could have gone home earlier.

'Do sit down, Miss Bateman. I apologize for keeping you so long. I have here the statement you gave to Police Constable Green. Would you be so good as to read it and confirm the facts as you related them? It will save you having to go through your story again.'

Evelyn nodded, appreciative of the inspector's thoughtfulness. The facts, she told him as she sat down in the chair opposite him, were indeed as she had related them to the local policeman, was it one or two hours ago? She had spent most of the morning dividing dahlia tubers and potting up next year's geranium cuttings in her greenhouse. She had nipped down to the farm some time before lunch to get some eggs which Mary Dodd sold to her. She had stayed for a short chat. She couldn't recall the exact time she was at the farm. Then she'd gone home and given Daphne and herself lunch after which she had syphoned some of the elderberry wine she had made into clean bottles she had prepared for the purpose. Some of these bottles she kept for a future contribution to the village summer fête; some she intended to give to neighbours to whom she owed hospitality or favours, and one or two she kept for herself for special occasions such as the recent Jubilee, Christmas and New Year.

As for the evening, Evelyn explained, she remembered that she'd promised to give the vicar a bottle of her wine for his Harvest Festival. Knowing Daphne would be perfectly happy watching the children's programmes and *Neighbours* on television, she decided to pay a quick visit to Ivy Lodge whilst she had a spare minute to do so. She had arrived to find the front door unlocked as was usual.

'Reverend Hollywell liked to keep it open at all times,' she explained to the inspector. 'Just as one would a church before the days of vandals. As I told the constable, I called out to Mr Hollywell and when he did not answer me, I called a second time. It was getting late so I knew he wouldn't be in his garden, and his car was in the garage so I was certain he must be at home. By now

I was a little anxious about his welfare. He suffered from high blood pressure, you know, and from time to time he had spells of giddiness. So I opened the sitting-room door and realized at once from the terrible sight that met my eyes that poor Mr Hollywell was dead.'

By now, Evelyn herself was feeling faint and, noting this, Govern said, 'Please take a rest if you wish, Miss Bateman. Beck, fetch the lady a glass of water.'

Evelyn shook her head, one of the hairpins falling out as she did so, releasing several strands of grey hair from her bun.

'No, I'm all right, Inspector, I assure you. You see I worked for many many years for Mr Headington-Lock, the Q.C., with whom I'm sure you are familiar. I am therefore fully aware how important my findings will be for you as I must have been the first person to find the vicar.'

When Govern nodded, she stiffened her back and in a clear voice continued, 'Seeing such a dreadful sight, I was very shocked. I ran out of the house intending to go to Mr Coleman whose house is nearest, but then I saw Jack Dodd, the farmer's boy. So I called him over and asked him to fetch help whilst I waited here in the hall. I'm afraid I did become a little confused at this point and can't be sure when Mr Parker, my neighbours' chauffeur, arrived, or Mr Sedgewick-Jones, who then took charge. Some short while after his wife, Sarah, arrived and about the same time, our nice local doctor, Doctor Grainger and two policemen. I don't know which of us was the more shocked,' Evelyn continued, 'when Doctor Grainger informed us that Mr Hollywell had died of asphyxia.'

As she paused, Govern said gently, 'The doctor informed me that death had occurred several hours before your visit, Miss Bateman – somewhere between midday and two o'clock, he suggested.'

Evelyn nodded.

'Mr Hollywell was a good man if not a very intelligent one, if I may say so,' she announced as Inspector Govern stopped speaking. She gave a little sniff of disparagement as she added, 'I seem to recall he only got a third at Cambridge.' She did not see the look of amusement on Beck's face as she made this pronouncement since he was standing behind her chair.

'I don't suppose you have any idea who might have wished the vicar ill?' the inspector asked as he stood up. 'As far as you know, Miss Bateman, did he have any enemies?'

'None that I know of!' Evelyn answered. 'He and his wife spent a very quiet uneventful life here in Delhurst. Mrs Hollywell's day in London I would say is a fairly rare event. As far as I know, neither she nor her husband have many friends, although Betty does have a sister who visits occasionally. In fact, entertaining the residents of Millers Lane at Road Meetings are probably the only social occasions they enjoy. The meetings are always preceded by a little drinks party, you see.'

'Ah, Road Meetings!' the inspector echoed. 'If things go on as they are, there soon won't be any residents left to attend these events.'

Evelyn looked at him, her expression, he decided, very much lacking even a glint of humour – in fact, it was deliberately disapproving.

'In case you are unaware of it, Inspector, there are ten houses in this lane and ever since I can remember, decisions as to what happens to our road are made democratically at periodic Road Meetings. The newer residents on the whole are for modernizing the lane but older members such as myself, prefer to keep it in its former state – a simple bridleway. Now the vicar has departed this world, the numbers will equalize so there will have to be another meeting convened at the end of the month; however, a new chairman will need to be elected before we take a further vote as Mr Hollywell will have to be replaced.'

'Very interesting – very democratic!' the inspector commented thoughtfully, 'but I am detaining you, Miss Bateman, and I'm sure you must be very tired. Thank you again for your cooperation and now, if you have nothing further to tell me, you must be anxious to go home.'

'There's just one thing, Inspector,' Evelyn said as she stood up to leave. 'I brought round a bottle of my new elderberry wine for the Hollywells but I can't remember where I left it – it was such a shock seeing Mr Hollywell, you understand. Could you make sure someone gives it to poor Betty? I shall call to see her, of course, but . . . well, it ought to be put somewhere cool.'

Inspector Govern looked at Beck who nodded.

'No problem, Miss Bateman. An unopened bottle of wine was in the sitting room on the table near the vicar's armchair. Mrs Hollywell will receive it in due course.'

Once it had been analyzed, he thought wearily; not that he expected it to contain anything that could account for Mr Hollywell's violent death since it was not only full but was firmly corked.

Evelyn turned towards the door and with an unconscious movement born of many years habit, she straightened her back.

'I shall be at your disposal if there is anything further I can help you with,' she said. 'Goodnight, Inspector!'

'Goodnight – and thank you, Miss Bateman,' Govern replied feeling a little like a very junior clerk in the presence of a highly efficient legal secretary who had just dismissed him. 'As you go,' he added, 'would you be so good as to send in Stewart Parker.'

Evelyn's face took on an expression of acute distaste.

'Oh, *him!*' she exclaimed. 'There's a two-faced Machiavelli if ever there was one. The Aymes who employ him think the world of him but I've lived long enough to tell good from bad. You should watch out for him, Inspector.'

'I'll do that – and thank you for your advice, Miss Bateman. Sergeant Beck will run you home.'

'But I only live a little way down the road!' Evelyn protested. 'It won't take me a minute to walk.'

'Nevertheless, we don't know who might be lurking in the dark, Miss Bateman – and besides, it's raining heavily now.'

'Then I'll accept the offer of a lift,' Evelyn replied, and for the first time that evening, a thin indeterminate smile hovered about her lips.

Damned if I can make that woman out, Govern thought as Beck followed Evelyn out of the room. She might look like a bird with her tiny black-clad figure in old-fashioned floor-length skirts, but she was certainly no bird brain. Her summing up of Stewart Parker was nearer the bone than she could know. There was something shifty about the chauffeur which had triggered his instincts on his last enquiry into Wing Commander Proctor's drowning accident. Jill Aymes had insisted the man had excellent references and that although she could not recall taking them up – it was, after all, six years ago – she was sure she or her husband would have done so. In all that time, they had never had cause to reproach him or mistrust him. In fact, they gave him the keys of the house whenever they were away so he could act as caretaker, being more trustworthy, in their opinion, than the Filipinos they employed as cook and houseboy.

Despite this eulogy, something had prompted Govern to look further into the man's background, but an email enquiry to his counterpart in the Australian state from which Parker had emigrated had shown no criminal record against him or anyone else of that name.

As Parker now came into the dining room, Govern once again felt that prickle at the back of his neck which past experience told him never to ignore.

'Sit down, Mr Parker!' he said. 'You understand this is an informal enquiry but you will be required to make a formal statement tomorrow at the station.'

Stewart Parker's head turned sharply to look directly at the inspector.

'What for? I haven't got anything to make a statement about.'

His voice was truculent rather than belligerent. Govern chose to ignore the question.

'Jack Dodd said he was on his way to ask Mr Coleman to come to the house when he met you coming down the lane from the direction of the Manor House. He told us you were on foot and not in your uniform, so what exactly were you doing outside Ivy Lodge, Mr Parker?'

'I wasn't doing nothing. I was on my way to the pub for a few beers. Mr Aymes didn't have no need for me this evening seeing as how they wasn't going out anywhere, so he gave me the evening off.'

There was something about the man's tone of voice which caused Govern to probe even further.

'How well did you know the Reverend Robert Hollywell, Mr Parker?'

For some reason, the chauffeur's face paled and Govern realized he could actually smell the man's fear.

'No more'n anyone in the lane – less, probably. I don't go to church.'

'Did you like him?'

Parker shrugged his shoulders.

'Sanctimonious old geezer, tried to push God down me throat.' His face contorted suddenly into a bitter grimace. 'But I didn't smother the old fool to shut him up, if that's what you were thinking.'

Govern ignored the barely concealed grin on Parker's face which faded as Sergeant Beck came back into the room and went to stand behind his chair.

'Someone did!' Govern said pointedly. 'Usually when a person has been murdered, the murderer has a motive. I suppose you didn't have a motive, Mr Parker?'

This time he deliberately spoke light-heartedly – almost as if he was joking. But on noting the sudden tension in the man's face, the tightening of the jaw, the furtive side-to-side glancing of the eyes, he knew he had chanced upon something. His voice sharpened.

'As I said earlier, Mr Parker, this interview is informal. If there is anything you would like to tell me it would be greatly to your advantage to do so now, voluntarily. Perhaps I should add that at this time I am not interested in anything unconnected with this murder. Where exactly were you mid morning?'

Parker's mouth tightened as quite noticeably he struggled to make up his mind how to reply to his inquisitor. He knew from past experience how these detectives operated. They were like dingoes hunting prey.

'Chopping logs mostly and then twelve thirty's me lunch hour – go back to me quarters for that. Afternoon I took logs up to the manor.' He paused, turning to look briefly at Beck and then back at his inquisitor. 'As for what happened here, I don't have the slightest idea.'

The inspector stood up, his face impassive.

'Thank you, Mr Parker. You can go now, but I will expect you over at Ferrybridge police station tomorrow morning to make a statement.'

'What for? I'm not a suspect, am I? That's ridiculous. I—'

'No, of course not, Mr Parker!' Govern broke in. 'It's simply to help us in our enquiries. It helps us to eliminate the innocent, you understand?'

For a brief moment, there had been an unmistakeable look of fear on Stewart Parker's face but at the inspector's interruption, his face cleared.

'That's all right, then!' he said as he stood up to go. 'Sorry I can't be more help.'

After he had left the room, the inspector turned to Beck.

'I suspect he has been a great deal of help. If the man's not guilty of murder, he's certainly guilty of something. Lock this room and the sitting room, Beck, and see there's a constable on duty to stop anyone getting into the house. I want the fingerprint chaps down here first thing tomorrow morning and they are to pay particular attention to the arms of that chair where Parker was sitting – a really good set of prints if possible; and as soon as we have them, you're to get them checked in Australia.'

Beck looked puzzled.

'You said he'd given his former address as Sydney but police records had nothing on him.'

'There are plenty of other states besides New South Wales, Beck. Well, I suppose we'd better have a word with the ornithologist – Coleman, isn't it? Where was it young Jack said he'd seen him earlier?'

'Barley Meadow – that field full of cows opposite the farm,' Beck replied. He glanced at his notes. 'Colin Coleman, husband of the woman who died last June – food poisoning. You thought he might have done it!'

'Came into a hell of a lot of money she'd left him!' Govern agreed. 'Told us he was going to sell up and go down to the coast somewhere or other. Obviously changed his mind. So he had a motive for killing his wife, but I can't imagine why he'd want to kill the parson, can you, Beck? Nip across the road and tell him I want to see him but don't put the wind up him.'

Either the man had a spectacularly strong nerve or he was innocent, Govern decided as he questioned the unprepossessing Coleman a few minutes later.

He'd been birdwatching most of the afternoon and evening, he informed the inspector . . . Trying to spot the sparrowhawk he'd seen the previous day tearing a rabbit to bits; and later, tracking down a rare grey tawny owl up by Millers Farm.

'And in the morning?' Govern asked.

Colin Coleman's face flushed suddenly an angry red.

'I know you think I killed Caroline!' he burst out, his former equilibrium suddenly deserting him. 'I've heard what's happened here. I suppose you think I killed Robert, too. Well, I'm not into murdering people for kicks and, if that's what you're suspecting, you can think again. I was in Hunnington this morning, getting the bridge of my glasses fixed. The optician will confirm he saw me. I called in at the garage for petrol – got the receipt at home, and at midday I was having a beer in the King's Head. Does that satisfy you?'

'For the time being, yes, Mr Coleman!' Govern said calmly. 'And for your information, we are questioning all the residents in the lane – you have not been singled out as you seem to think.'

Colin's face cleared and he gave a sheepish grin.

'Then I can go? There's a programme on birds in the Amazon jungle on TV this evening I particularly want to see.'

Beck saw him out and turned back to his superior.

'Can't say I take to the fellow,' he said, 'but he seems to be in the clear. I'll check his alibis of course.'

Govern nodded.

'I reckon Parker is our most likely suspect so far although I can't imagine what possible motive he could have had. But you know me, I can smell fear and that man has something to hide or I'll eat my hat, as they say!'

'Well, let's have something a bit more appetizing. I'm starving!' Beck said grinning. 'King's Head?'

Inspector Govern gave a deep yawn and stretched his arms above his head to relieve his stiffening back.

'If the pub has got rooms, we'll stay the night. I want to question the rest of the residents first thing in the morning.' He drew out Constable Green's list from his pocket. 'There's Mr and Mrs Aymes, of course; Farmer Dodd and his wife – we met them briefly last time we were down; the Brigends – he did occasional gardening work for the Hollywells. My note says to eliminate

Sedgewick-Jones and young Peters – they were both in town all day. Mrs Peters is a very pregnant mum and therefore hardly likely to commit murder! Nor can I see the sloaney Mrs S-J as a psychopath either.'

'What about the church organist whose husband drowned?' Beck added with a glint in his eye. 'Mrs Proctor, wasn't it? Maybe she's a serial killer and bumped off all three of them – plans her next victim whilst she's churning out hymns!'

'Don't be silly, Beck!' Govern chided him, carefully hiding a smile.

'Well, how about the local Lothario, our good-looking author,' Beck said, his voice serious now. 'Unless he's got a damn good alibi, that's who I'd put my money on. After all, who more likely than a writer of whodunnits, to want first-hand knowledge of what it feels like to choke someone to death.'

'Look, Beck, there's no doubt now after what that silly young chap confessed, Wing Commander Proctor's death was no accident. He was murdered – and unless I am very much mistaken, we've another murder on our hands right here. I don't thank you are right about Lavery,' he added wearily as he joined Beck at the door of the dining room. 'I think Parker is our man. What's a middle-aged, unmarried chap like that doing in a backwater like Millers Lane? It's not as if he was an old family retainer. I'd be interested to know what he did in Australia before he came to live in England and was employed by the Aymes.'

'Maybe Interpol will be able to enlighten us tomorrow,' Beck said, very obviously eyeing his watch. His gesture did not go unnoticed.

'OK, Beck, we'll push off. Lock this door whilst I go and make sure Mrs Sedgewick-Jones will stay here in the house with the unfortunate widow. Mrs Hollywell's lucky to have good neighbours. And tell Green he's to stay here, and not let anyone else in except the doctor, if he's needed.'

'If good neighbours is what they all are!' Beck commented, smiling once more as he followed Govern out of the room. Seeing his boss's expression, he added, 'Well, one of them made her a widow, presumably!'

'We don't know that. It could have been a complete stranger. Now get going, Beck, or we never will get that meal.'

A complete stranger? Beck thought as he locked up and went outside to start up the inspector's car. A bitter wind hit the side of his face as he emerged from the house into the darkness. The driving rain that had been falling earlier had ceased but the wind was just as unpleasant. It made a strange, screeching noise as it blew through the bare branches of the sycamore tree that leaned perilously over the Ivy Lodge drive.

Shouldn't be growing that close to the house, Beck thought as he stumbled over the gravel towards the car. Something dark appeared suddenly out of the hedge and brushed past his legs. A fox or a cat, he thought as he paused to let his quickened heartbeat slow again. Whatever it was had given him a nasty, if momentary, fright. 'A complete stranger,' his boss had suggested. Could such a person still be lurking in the darkness? More likely the Manor House ghost, he told himself with an effort at jocularity.

Aware that hunger was making him totally irrational, Beck unlocked the car door and switched on the headlights as he waited for Inspector Govern to come out of the ivy-clad house.

Fourteen

'They have arrested the Aymes' chauffeur, Stewart Parker!' Ian's face clearly showed his deep concern as he put down his briefcase and went to stand in front of the log fire. Holding out his hands to the blaze, he continued, 'Sarah met us at the station and told us the grizzly news. Nigel said if they bail him, he wants Sarah to go to her mum's.'

Migs handed him his customary homecoming whisky regarding him anxiously.

'Stewart Parker? You mean they think *he* was the one who . . . but why? I can't say I ever liked the man but . . .' Once again her voice faltered. She shivered, pulling her thick Arran wool cardigan more tightly around her. The cottage had no central heating, which they intended to install as soon as they could afford it, but for the present cold autumn months they were dependent on the localized heat coming from the logs in the inglenook fireplace.

Ian turned and, standing behind her, put his arms round her bump and drew her gently against him.

'Millers Lane hasn't turned out to be quite the idyll we imagined, has it, darling? Let's hope Parker *is* responsible and that it was he who did the Wing Commander and Caroline Coleman in as well – that is, if they were murdered. With him out of the way, we can all relax.'

He drew Migs down beside him on the sofa.

'Look, darling, I think Nigel is right. If they do bail Parker, I'd be happier if you went to stay with your mother for a week or two. She'd love to have you and . . .'

'I won't go, Ian!' Migs interrupted fiercely. 'I'm not leaving you here on your own. You're tired enough commuting as it is without you having to come home and cook for yourself and spend the weekends washing and ironing and doing the housework.'

Ian sighed.

'I knew you'd say that. Sarah was just as stubborn when Nigel asked her to leave. But you've got Dougal to think of, Migs, and the coming baby and—'

Once again, Migs interrupted.

'I don't want to even think about it,' she said. 'Anyway, what makes Nigel think Stewart Parker might be bailed? Why arrest him if they aren't sure he did it?'

Ian paused long enough to pour himself a second drink. He was sufficiently worried to feel he needed it. If Hollywell could be murdered in broad daylight, who was to look after Migs and Dougal when he was in London at his office?

Without any real hope of her agreeing to leave, he once again put his fears to her. Migs shrugged them off.

'Ian, you sound as if I'm completely isolated here. I've Ellen and Ray next door within shouting distance and the redoubtable Miss Bateman opposite. Anyway, who on earth would want to murder me?'

Ian sighed.

'Who would imagine anyone would want to murder the unfortunate vicar?'

'Well, *why* do they think Stewart Parker did it?'

Ian hesitated, uncertain whether or not to pass on the information Keith had told Nigel at lunch that day and which Nigel had told him in the train coming home. Of course, Migs would hear it from Sarah soon enough, he told himself, so there was little point in trying to keep the unpleasant news from her.

'Seems Inspector Govern decided to make enquiries in Australia about Parker's background. Cutting a long story short, Stewart Parker isn't the man's real name – he was born John Hudson but changed his name by deed poll when he came out of prison. He'd served fifteen years in Australia for murdering his best friend. Seems there'd been a drunken fight over money and he stabbed his chum with the hunting knife he always carried. Anyway, he was still only in his mid thirties when he was released at the end of his sentence and decided to come to England to try to make a new life for himself. The only qualification he had was as a driver. He took a job as a delivery man for a florist and a few years later, when he saw the Aymes' advertisement for a chauffeur, he jumped at it – quiet position in the country with accommodation and a salary big enough for him to save for the independent future he had in mind. He's worked for them for a long time – moved to Millers Lane with them from Esher two years ago . . . led a blameless life as far as anyone can ascertain.'

'Then why would he want to kill poor Mr Hollywell?' Migs broke in.

Ian shrugged.

'Nigel thinks the rev may have found out somehow about Parker's background and threatened to expose him. He'd settled in England illegally, you see. But that's only a supposition and they need proof to convict someone. They may *have* to bail him.'

Migs stood up and went through to the kitchen to put a casserole in the oven which she had prepared for their supper. When she returned, she said, 'Will Keith and Jill continue to employ him if they do bail him?'

'Your guess is as good as mine, but I doubt it.'

For a few minutes Migs was silent. Then she drew a long sigh.

'I'm finding all this extremely hard to believe,' she said. She gave a half smile. 'You don't think Nigel made all this up?'

Ian returned her smile.

'Unfortunately not! Inspector Govern was in touch with Keith because he reckoned he was entitled to the information about Parker's past. Whether Keith should have told Nigel or not. I don't know. But as they were lunching together, it was the obvious topic. Nigel has promised to keep me up to date. You know what he's like and he'll surely tell Sarah who will tell you, my darling, so you can have a good girlie gossip about it tomorrow.'

'Yes, well, let's not talk about it any more for now,' Migs suggested as a feeling of apprehension took hold once again.

Sensing her change of mood, Ian said cheerfully, 'Guess what,

Migs. We're all going to get a circular from Keith proposing himself as the new chairman of the Road Committee. We'll have to replace Hollywell, I suppose, so it's not a bad idea. Anyway, Keith's calling a meeting at his house, which he says he will chair and we'll all have to vote him in or out. Very democratic but I can't see anyone having the nerve to put their hand up and vote against him, can you?'

Migs' smile returned.

'Sarah might – she can't stand him! I suppose Evelyn Bateman might as I don't think she has a lot of time for him and his "Improving Millers Lane" proposals. Still, now he's decided to go organic, she's warming slightly towards him. Ellen says poor old Ray is fed up with the extra work turning the Aymes' old croquet lawn into a chemical free vegetable plot – not that he's ever favoured chemicals. According to Ellen, "there's naught better'n well rotted farmyard manure".'

Ian laughed, glad to have the mood lightened.

'So when is this meeting going to take place?'

'Sarah said she thought the week after next, though whether this awful business will mean it's postponed, I wouldn't know. There'll be the coroner's report and presumably the funeral. I suppose we'll have to go to that to support poor Betty.'

'You can get out of both in your condition and with young Dougal to look after. As for Betty, you told me she'd been a huge support to Jane Proctor after the Wing Commander's death. Jane can return the compliment – give her something to occupy her mind.'

Migs looked at him reproachfully.

'That's hardly being very sympathetic, Ian,' she said. 'Now I'd better get that casserole out of the oven or there'll be nothing for you to eat.'

'I'll just pop upstairs and say goodnight to Dougal, change my clothes and be back down before you've dished up,' Ian said as he stood up.

As Migs looked at him, her blonde hair slightly dishevelled, her cheeks still flushed from the heat of the stove where she had been cooking, he thought how immensely attractive she was despite her size, even when she wasn't 'dolled up' as she called it,

139

and how much he loved her. For the time being, the question of whether or not she should go away to her mother's could be shelved. It could be brought up again when and if Stewart Parker returned to Millers Lane. True enough, English law pronounced a man innocent until he was proved guilty, but equally, a man who had committed one murder was well capable of committing another. With Parker in the vicinity, he was not going to let Migs and Dougal take any chances.

A few weeks later, the coroner reported on the Reverend Robert Hollywell's death. He had died from suffocation by person or persons unknown, suicide being ruled out since no plastic bag had been found close at hand which might have enabled him to suffocate himself. Despite Stewart Parker's ominous past history of violence and the murder he had committed in Australia as John Hudson when he'd been a young man, the CPS had decided not to prosecute him, there being no proof whatever that he had killed the vicar or that threat of exposure of his past had provided a motive. Shortly afterwards the man was deported back to Australia.

'I gather Keith is getting a new chauffeur.' Nigel said in a soft voice to Ian and Migs when, a month later, the Road Meeting finally convened.

Sarah nodded. 'I wasn't going to vote Keith in as chairman but I am now,' she told Migs. 'Jill was telling me that Keith said Stewart Parker was one of the best, most conscientious chaps he'd ever employed and that he'd served his time for what he'd done before he came to England and done nothing wrong since, so he deserved to be given a fresh start.'

Migs nodded.

'Too many people knew he'd been arrested on suspicion of murdering Mr Hollywell. However unjustified, mud sticks, doesn't it? I think Ian still worries he's going to turn up and bump off Dougal and me. As for Keith, I've nothing against him and I should think he's a good organizer. It's not as if voting for him to be chairman means we are voting in his road repair proposal, is it?'

Nigel handed Migs a glass of chilled white wine from the tray

140

Keith's Filipino houseboy was serving. He, Sarah and Ian took glasses of Buck's Fizz.

'Bit better than poor Robert's cooking sherry!' Sarah said wryly, but stopped talking as Keith Aymes called the room to order. Everyone in the lane was present with the exception of Ellen who was babysitting Dougal, and Betty Hollywell who was minding Daphne at Ivy Lodge. For once, Andrew did not have one of his glamour girls with him but was flirting with Jill Aymes, much to young Jack Dodd's fascination.

Frank and Mary pretended not to notice and sat in a small group with Evelyn, Jane Proctor and Colin Coleman who, until the meeting was under way, regaled Evelyn with an account of the herons and other birds he had seen on Bewl Bridge reservoir that afternoon.

Having been duly elected, Keith asked Jill to read Betty Hollywell's minutes of the last meeting and losing no time, once again put forward his former proposal.

'You will recall my proposal was carried by one vote at the last meeting,' Keith said, his tall frame towering above everyone in the large, sumptuous drawing room. 'However, as Nigel Sedge-wick-Jones has pointed out to me, Robert Hollywell's unfortu-nate death does mean the lane is now equally divided for and against. I have agreed with him to put the proposal forward once more for a new count. Ellen and Betty have given me their proxy vote.'

'If he puts on any more weight, he's going to lose his looks!' Sarah whispered.

'That's why he has started jogging, silly girl!' Nigel whispered back. 'Haven't you seen him in his little white shorts pounding up the lane at 6 a.m. every morning?'

'Training for the London marathon?' Sarah giggled but a sharp look from Keith who had observed them talking, called them to order.

To Migs' relief, the first count of hands revealed that the numbers were indeed equal. Surprisingly, Keith did not look unduly disappointed.

'Eight for the idea and eight against!' he said. 'I expect most of you know that it's common practice for the chairman – in this case myself – always to have a casting vote. Robert, poor man, did not wish to employ this right but I'm sure none of you will consider it undemocratic if I now do so.'

There was a stunned silence. Taken by surprise, nobody could think of a reasonable objection. Unperturbed, Keith continued, 'We do need to get properly prepared so that work can start next spring as soon as the weather improves. As you all know, planning permission has already been given so we can now proceed. In anticipation, I have had copies made of the building plans so that you can all see exactly what is going to be done.'

He paused momentarily to drink from the glass beside him and Evelyn took advantage of the moment to say, 'Should George Baldwin not be consulted? After all, he owns Briar Field and if the culvert you propose to put in is to run under the junction of Bracken Footpath and Millers Lane, Rogan farmland is bound to be affected.'

Undaunted, Keith turned to look at the elderly woman.

'Nothing to worry about, my dear. I've had words with George – friendly words, I might add . . .' he paused to laugh at his little sally. 'He's perfectly willing to let us go ahead provided I make good any damage the earth-moving machinery might do. Incidently, I want you all to know that if anyone suffers any similar damage or inconvenience, I will cover all costs. After all, this is my proposal, isn't it, so it's only right I should bear the brunt.'

'"... *wine maketh merry: but money answereth all things.*" Ecclesiastes, chapter 10, verse 19,' Nigel said in an undertone.

'Great Scott!' Sarah whispered, using her grandfather's favourite expression. 'I never knew you were a Bible puncher, dear one.'

'Man of mysteries, that's me!' Nigel whispered back. 'My grandpapa was a devotee of the Old Testament and made us learn a wise quote each time we went to stay with him.'

'Ssh!' Sarah whispered as Andrew Lavery began to speak in a clear voice.

'So do we know what all this is going to cost us? I, for one, don't particularly wish to contribute to what I consider a quite unnecessary expense.'

For a moment, Keith's expression darkened, but his voice was neutral enough as he replied, 'That would be somewhat against the lane's democratic agreement, Andrew. However, I've had a look at Robert's accounts and there's a couple of thousand unspent cash in the bank – cash from our annual subs. I plan to make use of this – no point leaving the money lying there – and it's entirely up to each of you what you'd like to contribute – or, as in Andrew's case, not to do so.'

'I say, Aymes, that puts those of us against your ideas in rather an unpleasant light, doesn't it? I mean, if you're going to pay for most of it . . .' Colin Coleman's voice trailed into silence. Someone coughed and Keith cleared his throat.

'I don't want any of you to think I'm . . . well, trying to shame you into putting your hands in your pockets when you have no wish to. Nor am I trying to impress anyone when I say money's not a problem – I can easily afford to shoulder the burden . . .'

'Well said, Branson!' Nigel quipped in an overloud stage whisper.

Seated on the far side of Migs, Andrew heard him and grinned.

'Honestly, darling, you men are like schoolboys when you get together!' Sarah remarked as, huddled against the cold wind, Ian and Migs followed them back to The Paddocks for supper. 'Just because poor old Keith boasts a bit, you have to take the mickey. I think he's being very generous. It'll cost thousands, won't it, Ian?'

'Certainly will! Ah, well, it'll take all our minds off the Millers Lane murders and give us something else to think about.'

'Then you still think Cecil Proctor's death wasn't an accident?' Sarah asked as Nigel bent to unlock the front door.

'Wouldn't surprise me if someone told me Caroline Coleman had been a victim, too.'

'Shut up, Ian!' Nigel said as he shepherded them indoors to the welcome warmth of the drawing room. 'You'll be having us all believing next that the wretched Stewart Parker was a serial killer and should not have been allowed to leave the country. Now, drinks, everyone. what's it to be?'

The expression on the girls' faces remained uneasy as they attempted to forget Nigel's remarks and concentrate on the pleasant evening ahead.

Fifteen

I t was a brisk February day. Nigel and Ian had just finished
their regular Saturday morning game of squash at the sports
centre in Hunnington and were enjoying glasses of beer. Nigel,
always so voluble, was unusually silent, so much so that Ian
asked, 'Anything wrong, mate?'

It was a moment or two before Nigel's head lifted and he met
Ian's anxious gaze.

'Not exactly wrong . . .' he said tentatively. 'That's to say it
could be. I just don't know. It seems so stupid and yet—'

'You're not making sense!' Ian interrupted. 'Whatever it is, it's
clearly bothering you, so out with it – *now!*'

The older man took a drink from his glass and replacing it
carefully on the table between them he said slowly, 'Despite what
most people seem to believe, I agree with Keith and Jill. I don't
think Stewart Parker killed Robert. What's more, Govern obviously doesn't believe it or he'd never have countenanced him
leaving the country. There's been plenty of time for the rev's
papers to have been investigated and they've only found one
reason why Stewart might have had it in for the poor chap – that
Robert knew he'd been in prison. Apparently Parker had "confessed" it when he'd had a burst appendix shortly after his arrival
at the Manor House and thought he was going to die! However,
as Parker pointed out and Inspector Govern agreed, he'd had
two years to silence the rev if he'd wanted, and Robert was
hardly the type to suddenly start blackmailing him.'

'Makes sense,' Ian said thoughtfully.

'Betty said Parker had only come to their house once; and on the one occasion he had given her a lift to the station, he'd been very polite, friendly and considerate.'

'So what's all that leading up to?' Ian asked, his face showing his puzzlement.

'Well, it's obvious, isn't it, that if Parker didn't do it, someone else did? "Person or persons unknown" said the coroner. A passing stranger? I don't think so and I'm pretty sure Govern didn't think so, either. Anyway, Millers Lane is a dead end and people aren't just "passing by".'

Ian frowned.

'I take in what you're saying, Nigel, but in point of fact, Millers Lane is a bridleway and people do walk or ride up and down it. For example, posses of hikers use the lane to get to the footpaths over Millers Farm and Rogans Farm fields. However, you've obviously thought beyond that possibility. You're not on your old hobby horse, are you? That one of us residents did it?'

Nigel gave a shamefaced smile.

'Well, I am, actually. I know it sounds mad and Sarah says I'm off my trolley. Of course, she knows me and she's quite right – once I get the bit between my teeth, I can't seem to let go.'

Ian laughed.

'Just plain stubborn, you mean. All the same, if you really are worrying yourself to death about it, let's examine the possibilities a bit deeper. So, there were twenty of us living in Millers Lane – twenty-one counting Stewart Parker. Three died, or were murdered, which leaves eighteen possible murderers. Now, will you agree we can eliminate Sarah, Migs and our two selves?'

Nigel gave another sheepish smile.

'OK, OK! And you can eliminate the hapless Daphne, I think. Even if she wanted those three people dead, she hasn't the nous to have carried out the murders without being caught.'

'And Evelyn watches her like a hawk!' Ian agreed. 'So that leaves thirteen possibles – impossibles, some of them. Take Betty Hollywell – she was on an outing with the W.I. when her husband was bumped off. Andrew Lavery was lunching with his literary agent in London; Colin Coleman was at that wildfowl place near Lewes. So that brings our suspects down to ten – nine if you cross off Ellen. She was doing a full day's domestic work with Jill Aymes – turning out the attic, or something.'

'Cross them off and it leaves eight!' Nigel agreed frowning. 'Three in the Dodd family, Keith Aymes, Ray Brigend, Stewart Parker, Jane Proctor and Evelyn Bateman.'

'Well, Stewart Parker was proved innocent, so we can eliminate him, which leaves seven and as for Evelyn and Jane – well, not exactly the part-time occupation of a law-abiding old lady, and the church organist is hardly likely to despatch a parson. Anyway, they certainly wouldn't have had the strength to smother poor old Robert.'

'So we're left with the Dodds, Keith Aymes and Ray Brigend,' Nigel said, adding with a sheepish grin, 'I doubt Mary Dodd would have been physically strong enough to overpower Robert either. I know he wasn't a large man but he'd have fought like hell if someone had put a cushion over his face – wouldn't you?'

Ian put down his now empty glass and scratched his chin, his eyes thoughtful.

'Yes, I would. But let's suppose he'd been knocked out first – chloroform, ether or whatever?'

'That was considered at the time, if you remember,' Nigel said. 'There'd have been traces in his lungs which the pathologist would have discovered. So we're left with the Dodds, Keith Aymes and Ray Brigend, and can you in your right mind even consider Frank or Jack as murderers even if they had a motive, no, motives in the plural. Don't you see, Ian, if there have been three murders connected in some way, and I don't doubt they are, then there has to be a motive which applies to each of the victims – three different motives. If not—'

Ian fidgeted uneasily with his empty glass, turning it round and round in circles on the table top as he broke in saying, 'I can see why someone might want to bump off poor old Keith, but there's no earthly reason why he should want to bump off Caroline, the Wing Commander or Robert. So that leaves only Ray Brigend on our suspects list. Are you still harping on to that crazy idea the murders are linked in some way to Keith's road improvement scheme?'

Nigel leant forward, his expression intent.

'So, what if I am? The previous two murders brought the number of "fors" to equals – until Ellen voted. So someone else had to go if the "againsts" were to equalize – hence Robert's demise.'

'That simply made it impasse again,' Ian argued.

'Yes, until Keith took advantage of the chairman's right to a casting vote. Now, if I am right, there will be another murder soon – and in the not too distant future since roadworks are scheduled to start next month.'

Ian cleared his throat, his eyes uneasy.

'Well, the next victim won't be one of us, will it? If your idea isn't a complete pipe dream, we're on the same side as the murderer!'

Nigel made no reply while he took his own and Ian's empty glasses and went to the bar for a refill. When he returned, his face had still not resumed its customary cheerfulness.

'To tell you the truth, I'd like to sell up and move somewhere else. Even now, three months after Parker's arrest, you can't put your head out of the door without a reporter nosing round for another story. You'd have thought the "Mysterious Murders in Millers Lane" would be yesterday's news by now. It merely seems to have added to the interest that it's all speculation – no one has proved there was even one murder, let alone three.'

Ian nodded. Like all the other residents, they too had been pestered by reporters.

'You aren't really going to sell up, are you?' he asked, knowing he would seriously miss his company; not to mention Migs who would be heartbroken if Sarah left the area.

Nigel shrugged his shoulders, grinning now.

'Sarah nearly went spare when I suggested it. Says we'd be rats leaving the sinking ship . . . and moreover, the horses would hate it! Honestly, women! Still, I don't suppose we'd get much of a price for The Paddocks after all this hoo-ha.'

'Well, we certainly couldn't afford to move. Besides, the new baby is due at any minute and Migs has our dear Ellen lined up to give her extra help. I suppose I do worry about Migs' safety – and Dougal's. But as she says, with Ellen and Ray next door and Evelyn opposite, there would be plenty of help at hand if anyone unpleasant approached the house. When all those reporters were prowling round, good old Evelyn used to come scurrying across the road to send them packing. It was quite funny at times. She used that tight-lipped voice of hers and they'd slink away like guilty school kids!'

Nigel laughed.

'Oh, well, we'll just have to hope I'm completely off track and if murder was committed it was by an outsider. By the way, did you know that Jane Proctor has sold The Mill House? She's off to America to live with her married son. Sarah said she was a changed person – a cat with two tails – and clearly that's what she had wanted to do for years and couldn't because of the poor old Wing Co.'

'Good for her!' Ian said. 'Maybe she did bump him off after all.'

They both laughed and on their way home in Nigel's Range Rover, they forgot about the possible danger lurking in the future as they speculated how good or bad a price Jane Proctor had been offered for her home; and what the new people would be like when they finally moved in.

They finished the short drive home in silence, neither one wishing to reveal their similar thoughts, that had Jane sold The Mill House nine months sooner, the newcomers might have voted against Keith's proposal at that first relevant Road Meeting, carrying the motion 'against' and thereby quite possibly saving three lives.

Despite the cold frosty air of the February morning, Daphne was standing at her garden gate as Nigel stopped at Ian's house. Wrapped up in a thick black coat reaching to her ankles, a bright red scarf round her neck and a woolly cap pulled over her head, Daphne beamed at the two men. As Ian climbed out of the car, she waved and chanted:

> 'Bring Daddy home
> With a fiddle and a drum,
> A pocket full of spices,
> An apple and a drum.'

Then she turned, waving cheerfully to Nigel as he drove off.

Migs stood by the open door waiting to let Ian in. She tucked her arm through Ian's and drew him into the kitchen where lunch was bubbling on the old range.

'You can't help laughing sometimes although I do think it's quite remarkable how apt so many of Daphne's nursery rhymes are. Not to mention her repertoire. I think she knows every one in Dougal's nursery rhyme book. Which reminds me, darling, I meant to tell you before you shot off to your squash, when Keith jogged by this morning, the window in Rose Cottage was open. I was at the gate getting the milk in and I heard Daphne chanting at the top of her voice, "Wee Willie Winkie runs through the town". The thought of burly Keith Aymes "in his nightgown" made me laugh out loud.'

Migs collected Dougal from his cot where he had had his morning rest and they sat down to lunch. They discussed Daphne's inability to recite the whole of a nursery rhyme but had she seemed to be able to extract the lines appropriate to the occasion.

'I sometimes wonder if she is quite as mentally disabled as we all suppose,' Migs said. 'Not that Evelyn will consider such a possibility – she was quite sharp when I mentioned it. Anyway, Daphne must be nearly seventy if not older and seeing she is perfectly happy living as she does, there wouldn't be much point having her mental health investigated. I dare say when she was a young girl, fifty-odd years ago, the medical profession didn't know much about psychiatry so she was just bunged into a lunatic asylum.'

'And there she would have stayed if the place hadn't been closed down.' For a brief moment, Ian recalled the terrifying day last summer when Daphne had taken Dougal out in his buggy and not returned . . . at least, not until evening when she had come trundling down the lane with a chocolate-smeared Dougal. When he and Migs had recovered from the shock of having thought their precious little son kidnapped – perhaps dead – they had slowly realized that Daphne's intelligence was little more than that of a child of five or six. Believing – quite rightly as it happened – that she and Dougal would enjoy a day out, that's what she'd supplied for them both. Now Dougal adored her and Evelyn had finally had to accept that Daphne's greatest pleasure in life was to be in Dougal's company – and to permit the time they spent together provided Daphne never again went beyond the boundaries of Millers Lane.

Ian looked at his small son, whose head was bent over his pudding bowl carefully picking out the raisins he didn't like from the delicious bread and butter pudding Migs had made. At the rate Dougal was progressing, he'd soon be requiring more intellectually stimulating company than that of the hapless Daphne, Ian told himself as he spooned Dougal's unwanted raisins on to his own plate. Migs was already talking about getting the boy into the crèche run by the nursery school in Hunnington. He could already say a few words, totter around, if a little unsteadily, and feed himself with real enthusiasm, albeit messily, spooning most of his food into his hair and round his face.

Then Ian remembered that, in a month's time, there'd be a new baby for Daphne to take out in the pram. With all the extra expense of the addition to their family, any thought of moving was quite out of the question. Unlike Nigel, he didn't really want to move despite all the awful things that had happened to their neighbours in the year since they'd bought the cottage. Yet Nigel's totally uncharacteristic forebodings left him with a nagging doubt at the back of his mind. It was more a fear than a doubt, he told himself as he helped Migs clear the table and stack the dishwasher. Crazy though Nigel's ideas had been, they did explain three possible murders all happening in one small locality.

The very last thing Ian wanted to do was to communicate his unease to Migs in her condition, yet he longed to talk it over with her, knowing how level-headed she was. What he would like to ask her was: Suppose Nigel was right? Suppose there was another murder? Suppose it was to stop Keith's road improvement plan going ahead? Who on earth cared that deeply about moderate changes to a country lane to kill not one but maybe four innocent people to obstruct such an innocuous scheme? It simply didn't make any more sense than had the mysterious fire in Frank Dodd's barn.

Sixteen

March

'Fancy her relenting after all these years!' Jack's voice mirrored his astonishment when Mary told him Evelyn had finally agreed to Daphne having one of the kittens from the twice-yearly litters the farm cats regularly produced.

His mother nodded.

'You can understand her not wanting a cat the way she is about her blessed garden. Miss Daphne's ever so pleased. You should have seen her face when Miss Evelyn brought her down to choose!'

But Daphne's face was very far from happy two days later. The kitten had disappeared. Evelyn took her across the road to ask the Brigends and Migs if they could look in their greenhouses and sheds in case it had wandered in. They also went down to the farm where Mary, seeing Daphne on the point of tears, offered her another kitten if hers was not found.

'That's very kind of you, Mary,' Evelyn said, handing Daphne a handkerchief to wipe the tears dripping down her cheeks and off the end of her nose. 'We'll give it another day or two, I think. Maybe it will just turn up. It might have crossed the road to Ivy Lodge.'

'Maybe a fox got 'im!' Jack suggested, which prophecy brought a sharp rebuke from his mother.

Migs saw Daphne later that day, standing by the garden gate, her face so forlorn that she went across the road to talk to her.

'I'm so sorry about your little kitten,' she said. 'You mustn't worry about it, Daphne. Maybe it wandered off and a passer-by found it and has given it a nice home.'

Whether or not Daphne understood, Migs could not be sure. Tears welled up in her eyes and she chanted sadly, ' "*Pussy cat, pussy cat, where have you been . . . ?*" '

'Maybe that's just what happened – she's gone to see the Queen!' Migs said quickly and was rewarded by a sniff from Daphne followed by a beaming smile.

But Daphne's kitten was neither lost nor had it 'gone to see the Queen', Evelyn thought wryly having heard this interchange from the open bedroom window. The animal was in an old chicken coop at the furthermost end of the garden. Its faint mewing could not be heard from the house or by Frank Dodd if he were to go up to Badgers Field. It had cat food and a bowl of milk as well as a hot-water bottle to cuddle against. Anyone seeing it would know at once that its gaoler had every intention of keeping it alive.

Tomorrow, Evelyn thought as she closed the bedroom window, would be The Day. Except once or twice at Christmas and the New Year, Keith Aymes never missed a morning's jogging. She could tell the time by him – passing her cottage on the way up the lane at five minutes past seven and returning half an hour later. This timetable, his wife had once told Evelyn, enabled him to shower and change before catching his train to London at eight thirty-two. But on Saturdays, of course, he did not go up to London to his office – and tomorrow was a Saturday.

Daphne was still asleep when soon after six o'clock, whilst it was still dark, Evelyn rose, dressed and went up the garden to fetch the kitten. It seemed pathetically pleased to see her but she made no attempt to pet it. Instead, she put it in the old drawstring shoe bag she was carrying. The white of the cotton fabric had faded to a dull biscuit colour, but the untidy red and blue wool embroidery, done by Daphne, was as bright as if it had been stitched the previous day.

The eight-week-old kitten at once began to mew on seeing Evelyn, but it was quiet now as, with a quick glance around her, Evelyn hurried back across the garden to its southernmost corner – the corner Mr Aymes had purchased from Frank Dodd and which was to be bulldozed next week.

She was wearing an old grey gardening coat which reached

almost to her ankles and as she made her way through the tangled undergrowth, thick brambles caught at the hem and hindered her progress. Impatiently, she tore herself free and laying the shoebag on the ground, she proceeded to pull the melée of weeds away from the rotten wooden boards the foliage had covered. Kneeling down, she pulled at one of the wooden sleepers which crumbled in her hands.

She paused now to glance anxiously at her watch. Five minutes past seven. She had only twenty-five minutes left, perhaps less if Mr Aymes returned home earlier than usual – something he might well do as it had started to drizzle. Wasting no time, she hurriedly tackled the second of the rotten boards before pausing once again to catch her breath.

Glancing across the road to the Peters' cottage, she saw the light in the little boy's bedroom go on and knew Migs or her husband must be awake. Her sense of time running out increased, and she turned her attention back to the last of the boards. The old railway sleepers had been placed over the disused well after Brigadier Horsborough's dog had been found drowned in it thirty-odd years ago.

A cold dank vapour now rose from the murky depths. It was too dark beneath the overhanging trees for Evelyn to see the water level but again this winter the lane had flooded on the corner and she could expect the water table to be high. At this time of year, both in Millers Lake and in Rogan Pond, the water lapped the edges of the banks.

With considerable difficulty, she pulled the mounds of rotten wood into a thick patch of brambles. She now brought out a ball of string from the pocket of her blue serge skirt, and having securely tied the neck of the shoebag, she proceeded to lower it until she could no longer see it. Cutting the string, she tied the end over a fallen log and covered it with leaves and moss. Meanwhile, the unhappy kitten was mewing pitifully.

Her watch now showed her she had a scant ten minutes to wake Daphne and position her on the front path. Daphne was the weak link in the chain of events Evelyn had planned so carefully this past week. Fortunately, if she failed to play the part Evelyn had designated for her, it would not be total disaster. But her own ability to successfully hide the kitten for a further twenty-four hours without discovery would be very difficult. It was essential she kept it alive and it might easily die if she left it down the cold, damp well. There was, too, the danger that Daphne or someone else would hear it crying.

Daphne, however, was unusually co-operative. There were mornings, particularly on chilly winter ones, when Evelyn had difficult in persuading her to get out of bed. But this morning, hearing Evelyn's voice, she sat up in bed, an expression of eager excitement on her face as her sister said, 'I've been up the garden to have a look and I'm quite sure your kitten is down the old well, Daphne. Do you understand? It's alive so it must have found a ledge to climb on. I can hear it mewing, but it's too far down for me to reach. You must get up, Daphne, *now*. Put your dressing gown on – no, not the cotton kimono, the warm woolly one. Now come downstairs with me.'

She ignored the fact that Daphne had not yet put on any slippers and hurried her down to the tiny front hall where she took hold of her hands and looked closely into her eyes.

'Mr Aymes will go past the house at any minute, Daphne. You're to stand by the gate when I tell you and call him. Do you understand? You're to call Mr Aymes. We need him to rescue your kitten which has fallen down the well. Meanwhile, I shall go back to the well and look after your kitten. You must bring Mr Aymes to the old well. Have you understood me, Daphne?'

Something of Evelyn's urgency penetrated Daphne's consciousness.

' "*Ding, dong, bell, Pussy's in the well* . . ." ' Daphne's sing-song voice was loud enough for the young couple across the road to hear. Horrified lest one of them came over to see what was wrong, Evelyn quickly put her finger to Daphne's lips.

'Not now, Daphne. Keep very quiet until you see Mr Aymes. Wave to him and when he stops, shake his arm. That's when you can say, "*Pussy's in the well*". Are you listening to me?' Evelyn glanced once again at her watch and hurriedly opened the front door. 'Off you go, Daphne – to the front gate. Remember, wait for Mr Aymes and then stop him.'

Daphne's face was blank and Evelyn could not be certain that she had understood what she was to do. It was too chancey, she decided. Even if Ian or Migs weren't aware of Daphne, they might come out of their cottage on some other pretext. Or even more likely, Ellen or Ray might appear, and it was not their help she wanted. Of course, Daphne couldn't know that . . .

'I'll stay here in the house,' she said. 'Just wave when you see him coming and I'll come out and speak to him.'

Daphne's face remained blank but suddenly cleared and she looked happy.

'Pussy's in the well?' It was more or a question than a sing-song nursery rhyme and Evelyn glanced at her sharply. Then one of the dogs at the farm barked and, remembering the time, she opened the door and all but pushed Daphne down the path.

A pale wintry sun was breaking through the clouds above Millers Farm and staring up the lane from her position by the front door, Evelyn could just make out Keith Aymes' burly figure. He was pounding down the lane towards them, his white shorts, T-shirt and trainers clearly visible. Daphne had seen him, too. Her blue wool dressing gown flapping about her legs, she jumped up and down, holding on to the little wooden gate, as she waved to the jogger. Watching from the hallway, for one anxious moment, Evelyn thought the man was not going to stop. But Daphne had fully understood the urgency of Evelyn's command, or else sensed the exigency of it.

At the sight of the crazy Bateman female flapping her arms wildly as she waved to him, Keith slowed to a near standstill. He was not at his ease with this mentally handicapped woman – or her sister, come to that – but he decided this must be an emergency and perhaps the old lady was in some sort of trouble.

'Morning, Daphne!' he proffered. 'Anything wrong?'

Leaning over the gate, Daphne caught hold of his arm.

'Pussy's in the well,' she said. And again: 'Pussy's in the well.'

Daphne's extraordinary propensity for nursery rhymes was known to everyone in the lane. Keith was about to make his escape when he saw Evelyn hurrying down the path.

'Oh, Mr Aymes, how fortuitous you being here!' Her voice was high pitched as she pushed her sister to one side and took her place at the gate. 'It's Daphne's kitten,' she announced. 'It's been missing since Wednesday and everyone has been searching for it. I thought it must be dead but as I was on my way to the orchard this morning I heard this noise like the mewing of a cat coming from the well. I think it must have fallen in. I can't see anything but I wear bifocals, you see. Do please come and see if you can see it. Maybe you could reach it, Mr Aymes? Daphne would be so very happy to have it back.'

As she spoke, Evelyn had opened the gate and was drawing Keith up the path.

'It's the old disused well, you see. We used to draw water from it before we were connected to the mains. I think the Water Board may have left the wooden cover off when they were checking the water table for your culvert.'

'Ah, the culvert!' Keith echoed uneasily. Evelyn had been one of the most steadfast opponents of his road improvement scheme. Of course, he did understand that she was to lose part of her garden but, he now thought as she led him to that corner he had purchased from the Dodds, it was more a jungle than a garden.

Neither she nor Frank Dodd had invited him in to see his half-acre purchase but he'd had no reason or wish to do so. He'd seen the area on the ordnance map and that was good enough for him to make his decision to buy. Now he came to think of it, one of the Water Board fellows had said something about a well but he hadn't wanted to know about that either. One of the reasons for his business success was his art of delegating. He'd got a good man from Ferrybridge handling the culvert and the widening of Millers Lane and, having agreed a price, that was all he wanted to know about it.

'It's very good of you to stop by,' Evelyn was saying. 'I do hope we aren't making you late for your breakfast. I wouldn't have asked for your help if Daphne was not in such a state about her kitten. There now, Mr Aymes, I think I heard it again. If you kneel down here . . .'

She pointed to the edge of the well. The brickwork was moss covered and crumbling. 'It's a bit muddy, I'm afraid. Here, let me hold on to you. That well is very deep, my father used to say. You wouldn't want to fall down it!'

'Indeed not!' Keith said with a brief smile. He, too, could now hear a faint mewing. Unlike his wife, he was not a cat lover and although Jill did not know it, he'd drowned a fair few unwanted kittens in buckets, and if it had been up to him, he'd have left this one to drown. But clearly, neither of the two old girls would think of such a thing. He'd have to do what he could to rescue the wretched animal.

Hearing their voices, the kitten mewed louder. Evelyn had not fed it since the previous day and it was painfully hungry – and thirsty – for there was no food or water in the shoe bag, nor anywhere firm to cling to. The air was dank and it sensed that the darkness was not that of night.

'Can't see much down there!' Keith called, his voice muffled by the old stone bricks of the well head. 'Water's a fair way down though. You must be right and it's on a ledge. Have you got a torch by any chance?'

Evelyn's voice sounded almost complacent. She had anticipated this request and her answer.

'I did have a very good one, Mr Aymes, but I dropped it down there in the water when I first heard the cat crying. I did catch a quick glimpse of it and it wasn't all that far down. If my arm had been a little longer – perhaps if you could lean a little closer, Mr Aymes, you could reach it. It was this side of the well, just below where you are kneeling.'

Seeing him hesitate, she knew exactly what tactic to employ to force his hand. It was the way she had nearly always succeeded in making the male sex bend to her will. *Surely you are not afraid to lose your case? . . Act as a witness?* Grown men were never afraid, was her challenge, and she used it now.

'Of course, I quite understand if you think it's too dangerous, Mr Aymes. I could pop over and ask Ray or Mr Peters if . . .'

'No, no, of course not. There's no need for that. Just hang on to one arm, will you, whilst I reach down with the other.'

She could feel the weight of his body pulling against her handhold. Just for a moment, she used her own body as a counterweight. Then she saw Daphne coming towards her. She was wringing her hands and saying over and over again,

' "*Pussy's in the well. Pussy's in the well*".' And then in a different tone? ' "*Who pushed her in? Who pushed her in?*" '

Evelyn's face contorted into an ugly grimace.

'Shut up, Daphne. Just *shut up!*' she shouted.

'Hang on! Pull me back a bit, I'm slipping!'

Keith's voice had an edge of panic. Evelyn stared down at his large body poised so precariously over the edge of the well. He looked fit, strong, the very epitome of manhood. In a way, it seemed a shame he had to die. If there had been any other way . . . anyone else instead of him . . . but days and nights of considering an alternative had produced no result.

'It was, after all, your idea to take away my garden!' she said as Keith struggled desperately to keep his balance. 'We were all perfectly happy here until you had these grandiose ideas. I'm sorry. I really am, but you've got to go.'

Somehow she managed to loosen his grip on her arm. His head turned and his eyes stared at her disbelievingly. Surely . . . surely she could not be meaning to . . . ? As he struggled to raise himself from his crouched position, she stepped quietly behind him and with maniacal strength, tipped him forward. Just for one moment, he was able to grip the edge of the well with one of his hands. But the green slimy moss gave him no safe handhold. In the split second left to him before he knew he must fall, he saw Evelyn reach for a nearby fallen tree branch. He realized in that same instant that she was going to strike him. He had time for only one other thought as he fell – Evelyn had said the well was deep so even if he landed on his feet, he would surely drown.

Ice cold water enveloped him, filling his mouth, his eyes, his clothes. By some miracle he seemed to have fallen feet first and as he struggled to surface, he felt something solid beneath him. Tearing his fingernails as he searched desperately for a handhold on the sodden brick walls, he found his balance and realized that on tiptoe, he could just manage to keep his head above water. Spitting out the water he had swallowed, he thought irrelevantly that it tasted quite pleasant – neither stagnant nor dank – and at the same time, realized that it was moving past his chest from left to right . . . exactly as the surveyor had told him was the movement of water between George Baldwin's pond and Millers Lake.

Such momentary thoughts went out of his mind in a flash as the urgent necessity to save himself took precedence over any other considerations. Looking up, he could see Evelyn's figure silhouetted against the sky, pulling the string of a bag with the kitten in it to the surface. Was it possible she had pushed him in by mistake? If so, why wasn't she going for help to get him out?

A minute later, he realized that this was the very last of her intentions. His would-be murderess was struggling to drag the tree branch over the well opening. Aghast, he realized that she was going to bury him alive as the debris from the tree branch drifted down on to his upturned face. As further branches cut off most of the sparse daylight, he started to shout. He could hear his own voice echoing strangely round the dripping walls as he gulped in more air to shout more loudly. Pray God someone would hear him! But who? He could see no sign of the mental sister, Daphne, nor hear her sing-song voice. Dodd would probably be up milking his cows but he'd be too far away to hear. As for Ray Brigend, he was almost certainly in his vegetable garden preparing the soil for planting.

Keith was now no longer in doubt that Evelyn was trying to cover the well head completely. Aware that he was becoming numbed by the cold water and that whatever he was standing on felt very unstable, Keith faced the fact that unless help came soon, he might very well die. Try as he might he could not comprehend why the elderly straight-laced little woman intended to kill him. It crossed his mind that, crazy though it seemed, maybe it was she who had killed Robert, Wing Commander Proctor and Caroline Coleman. *But why?*

Fear of what now seemed like certain death took hold of Keith. High above his head, he could hear the intermittent mewing of the kitten – Evelyn's method of luring him to his death, he now realized. How cleverly she had planned it! Only yesterday at breakfast, Jill had remarked on Evelyn's totally unexpected change of heart in allowing Daphne to have a pet, especially a cat which species she abhorred even more than dogs. Now he might never have a chance to tell Jill the reason.

Using every last bit of power in his lungs, Keith began once more to shout for help.

Ian was more than a little confused. Opening the kitchen door to take in the fresh delivery of milk Migs wanted for Dougal's breakfast, he was suddenly aware of Daphne Bateman hurrying across the road and struggling to open their garden gate. The sight of her in an old blue dressing gown did not so much surprise as concern him.

'What is it, Daphne? Is something wrong? Do you want to come inside? You'll catch your death of cold out here in your night things—'

Daphne interrupted him as she caught hold of his arm.

'*"Pussy's in the well"*,' she exclaimed, not once but continuously, a look of unmistakeable anguish on her face.

'Maybe she's making sense!' Ian said as Migs came to the door to see what was delaying him. 'Perhaps her kitten has fallen in – not that I knew there was a well in Evelyn's garden.'

'Best go with her and see!' Migs said, handing him his thick oilskin jacket. 'Evelyn could be trying to get the kitten out and needs help.'

It was not Evelyn who needed help, Ian quickly realized as he followed Daphne into the unkempt part of Rose Cottage garden. He could hear a man's voice, muffled, but the word 'HELP' quite distinguishable. Evelyn seemed to be in shock, standing motionless looking down at the foliage covering the well.

'Someone's down there!' Ian said unnecessarily. 'Help me, Evelyn. We must try and get him out.'

Evelyn remained unmoving and without wasting any more time, Ian began to drag away the branches. He was now able to identify the voice as Keith's.

'Get me out of here!' the man begged as Ian struggled to clear the opening. 'Is that you, Ian? Get a rope or something. I don't think I'm all that far down.'

Ian lent over the edge and could see a dark shape and the faint gleam of water. Beside him he could hear the occasional mewing of the kitten. As he ran back towards Evelyn's house where he hoped to find a ladder, he guessed that an attempt to rescue the animal had brought about Keith's fall. The door of Evelyn's tool shed was unlocked. Stacked tidily against one wall were two halves of an aluminium ladder . . . Doubtless the one someone had suggested she got to replace her old wooden one after the Dodds' barn fire. Grateful for its light weight, Ian hurried back to the well head. Evelyn still had not moved. Daphne was now kneeling on the ground hugging her kitten and chanting, ' "*Pussy cat, pussy cat, where have you been?*" ', over and over again.

Five minutes later, Keith emerged from the well soaking wet and shivering uncontrollably. Ian quickly took off his jacket and put it round the man's shoulders.

Keith gave a shaky smile.

'Pretty chilly down there! Didn't fancy staying much longer!'

'Come on! I'll get Migs to give you a really hot cup of coffee with a shot of brandy in it? You all right, Evelyn?'

'Bloody well ought not to be – she's just tried to kill me!' Keith exclaimed.

Evelyn was standing with one hand supporting her against a tree trunk. As Ian stared at her disbelievingly, he saw on her face a look of helpless resignation.

'I had to! I didn't want to, but I had to!' she murmured. 'Don't you see, it was the only thing I could do?'

Uncomprehendingly, both men turned to look at the old woman's sister. Daphne was holding the kitten in her arms, her face radiant with happiness as she sang softly to it:

> I love little pussy
> She'll do me no harm.
> She shall sit by my side,
> And I'll give her some food;
> And pussy will love me
> Because I am good.

Seventeen

During the half hour following Keith's emergence from the well, events moved quickly. Clearly Evelyn could not be left unsupervised, so Keith would have to stay in Rose Cottage with her, Ian realized, until he could summon help. He was certainly not going to involve Migs who, only two weeks ago, had given birth to their new daughter.

His mind made up, Ian led Evelyn back into her kitchen. Remarkably composed, she sat quietly down at the table whilst Ian hurried upstairs to to pull a couple of blankets off a bed to wrap round Keith who was huddled against the Rayburn cooker shivering with cold. Daphne sprawled happily cross-legged on a rug by the window feeding her kitten.

'I'm going to telephone Doctor Grainger and the police,' Ian told Keith quietly. 'Then I'll run you home. Meanwhile, I shall have to lock you in the house, Evelyn, until the police arrive. I'll take Daphne over to Migs. She'll look after her until we know what's to happen.'

For the first time since she had mustered all her strength to push Keith Aymes into the well, Evelyn spoke. Her face was paper white but she remained stiff-backed as, in a barely audible but precise voice, she said, 'When the police arrive I shall be taken to the police station to make a statement, Mr Peters, and I think it's most unlikely I shall be allowed to come home!' She gave a brief, wry smile as she made this last remark.

'You will need a lawyer, Evelyn. Is there someone you would like me to ring?' Ian asked.

Once again, Evelyn allowed herself the briefest of smiles.

'You forget I was working in law for over forty years and am probably far more aware of proceedings than you are. I'm not obliged to have a lawyer, nor do I wish to have one as it happens, but thank you for your consideration.'

It was Keith's turn to speak. Surprising Ian, his tone was far from vengeful despite the fact that Evelyn had a very short while ago tried to kill him.

'I take it you're not going to deny you tried to kill me, Evelyn? Do I understand you are going to admit it?'

Evelyn's white face flushed and her back stiffened as she said, 'It is my intention to make a full confession, Mr Aymes. It has not been easy for me this past year, as you will doubtless realize, and it will be a relief to unburden myself.'

Her face was devoid of expression as she added, 'I do want you to know, Mr Aymes, that I have nothing personally against you.'

Keith's expression was one of incredulity.

'Nothing against me?' he repeated. 'Yet on your own admission, you tried to kill me?'

Evelyn drew a long sigh before saying quietly, 'It was not you but your proposal I hoped to destroy.'

'Good God, woman! Surely you didn't need to go to such lengths . . .' He broke off and turning to Ian said, 'She's insane – she and her sister both.'

Ignoring Keith's comment, Evelyn now addressed Ian.

'I doubt I shall be permitted to return home from the police station, so could I impose on your kind nature and ask you or your wife to explain matters to Betty Hollywell? I believe she will take care of my sister.'

She glanced briefly at Daphne who was now lying on her back, her dressing gown barely covering her skinny bare legs, the kitten curled up on her chest.

'Get up at once, Daphne!' she said sharply. 'I shall take that cat away if you can't behave decently!'

She sounded utterly normal and Ian was unable to hide his look of astonishment at Evelyn's extraordinary coolness at a time when she was on the brink of being arrested for attempted murder. He paused before saying, 'As you know, Evelyn, Migs has only recently given birth to our baby and I will not have her involved. However, I'm sure she will willingly make some arrangement with Betty that will ensure Daphne's well-being.'

Not waiting for any further comment from Evelyn, he hurried out to the hall to use her telephone before ushering her into her sitting room, and without protest from her, securely locking the door. Five minutes later, having handed Keith over to Jill's care, he drove back to his own house taking Daphne and her kitten with him.

Migs was just coming downstairs having bathed and fed the baby. Dougal was playing happily with a pile of Leggo bricks. The domesticity of the scene was about as far removed as it could be from the scenes he had so recently been witnessing. Migs looked anxiously at her husband as she motioned to Daphne to sit down by Dougal who was immediately entranced with the kitten.

'What's happened? Has Evelyn had an accident? Why is Daphne here? Why was she trying to make you go over to Rose Cottage?'

'Calm down, darling. Sit yourself down and I'll explain. Yes, there was an accident. Keith fell into a disused well in Evelyn's garden trying to rescue Daphne's kitten which had fallen in . . .'

Or had it, he now asked himself. But, of course, Evelyn had put it in in order to entice Keith to try to rescue it.

'Fortunately Daphne must have grasped what had happened which was why she was indicating she needed my help. I got there in time to pull Keith out. So you see, sweetheart, there's nothing whatever for you to worry about. I've asked Doctor Grainger to come and give Keith a quick check over, for hypothermia, that sort of thing. You may see a police car, too.'

Migs regarded him in astonishment.

'But why the police? It was an accident, wasn't it?'

'I must go back, darling,' Ian said evasively. 'By the way, Evelyn asked if you'd contact Betty, see if she'd mind Daphne for her as she may have to go down to the police station – as a witness of something. I expect I shall have to go, too,' he added vaguely. He turned briefly to look at the woman still in her old blue dressing gown, now seated at the other end of the table playing Pat-a-Cake with an enchanted Dougal.

'Look, Migs, I must get back,' he repeated. 'I can't explain things now but Keith's OK and I promise you everything's under control and there's nothing you can do other than make arrangements for Betty to take care of Daphne. I know you're busy with the kids so you might walk up to Ivy Lodge and see if Betty would take over until we know what's happening.'

Looking even more mystified but trusting Ian to know what he was doing, Migs said, 'If Betty's at home – which she should be – she'll jump at having Daphne. She's been pretty lonely since Robert died and only last week she said she envied me having the children, and looking after Daphne was like looking after a child again. She has been teaching her to cook and knit and cut out scraps for a scrapbook she gave her.'

'I'll be back the moment I can,' Ian said planting kisses on Migs' and the baby's heads. 'And you're not to worry if I'm not back for a few hours.'

He kissed Migs again, waved to a laughing Dougal, and hurried back to Rose Cottage.

He had barely entered the house before there was a ring at the doorbell and Dr Grainger arrived stating cheerfully that it was as well Ian had called him before the start of morning surgery. After hearing a very brief outline of what Ian described as 'an accident', he promised to look in on Keith as soon as he'd checked Evelyn, who he presumed to be suffering from shock. Ian was not privvy to Dr Grainger's examination of Evelyn but on his return from the sitting room, he detained Ian, saying, 'Is there anyone who can come and look after Miss Bateman? She has obviously had an extremely nasty shock, and between you and me, her heart's a bit dicky. I've given her a shot which should help but she's refusing to go to bed . . . Some nonsense about making a statement at the police station. Witnessed it all, I suppose. Ah, well, these things happen, don't they? I'll pop up now and see Aymes before I dash off to surgery. Other than a bit of hypothermia, I imagine he'll be OK. Strong man, Aymes!'

From her front window, Migs saw him go, followed almost immediately by the arrival of a police car. She recognized Constable Green but not the female P.C. who went with him into Rose Cottage. They were there little more than ten minutes before they reappeared, Evelyn carrying a small overnight case between them.

165

Momentarily distracted by Dougal who was demanding his second box of Leggo, she did not see Ian returning to collect their car, but she heard him driving away. It was then she realized that something a great deal more serious than an accident must have occurred.

Eighteen

B y the time Ian returned from the police station shortly after midday, Keith and Jill Aymes were still the only two residents of the lane who knew that Evelyn had been arrested and charged with attempted murder. Migs had only the limited information she had gleaned from Ian, and was unable to give Betty Hollywell any reason why she was needed to look after Daphne until further notice. Sarah dropped by mid-morning and left as mystified as Migs, who promised to have Ian telephone as soon as he returned and passed on more of the facts.

It was, however, their old friend, Detective Inspector Govern who elected to return to Millers Lane that afternoon and relate the shocking news that Evelyn had confessed – not only to her attempt to kill Keith, but to the successful murders of Wing Commander Proctor, the Reverend Robert Hollywell and Mrs Caroline Coleman. He asked if Ian would record his report so that he would have a factual account with which to inform the other Millers Lane residents.

'There will be no court case, you see,' he explained, 'so I think it only fair to those of you who live here to know the truth.'

Migs was not only deeply shocked but totally disbelieving.

'Are you saying Evelyn has actually confessed to *murder*? I can't believe it! Moreover, I don't see how she could possibly have carried out such – such appalling deeds,' she said. 'And if she did, why? For whatever reason? I really can't believe Evelyn, of all people, resorted to murder in order to preserve the flora and fauna – that's crazy.'

Inspector Govern took the cup of tea Ian was proffering and sat back in the faded cretonne-covered armchair sighing.

'A lot of people's reasons for murder appear crazy to everyone else, Mrs Peters. Miss Bateman maintained she was trying to prevent Mr Aymes' scheme for the road improvement from going ahead, not only for the flora and fauna but to preserve Millers Lane as a quiet bridleway, not, as she put it, as an airport runway.'

'But you don't kill people for reasons like that! If Evelyn did so, then she must be mad.' Migs looked from the inspector to Ian whose face was noncommittal. 'If she really is guilty, what will they do with her? Surely they won't send an eighty-odd-year-old woman to prison?'

The inspector glanced at Ian and seeing him nod, said gently, 'That won't happen, Mrs Peters, which is one of the reasons I'm telling you all this. Whilst we were still in the interview room at the police station, after making her confession but before she could be sent back to the cells, Miss Bateman had a heart attack.' Hearing Migs gasp, he added quickly, 'She died almost instantaneously. We called the doctor, of course, but by the time he came, it was too late to save her.'

Knowing how fond Migs had been of Evelyn, Ian moved closer to her on the sofa and took her hand in his.

'Best thing for her, don't you agree, darling? She would have loathed prison and perhaps hated it even more if she'd been sent to Broadmoor. *Was* she crazy, Inspector?'

'I think she must have been, although I have seldom interviewed anyone more lucid, more graphic when making their confession. Between you and me, hardened as I am to the criminal fraternity, I did feel the poor woman was more misguided in her ecological obsession than evil. To care so much for the environment as she seemed to do is undeniably obsessive, is it not?'

He proceeded to describe the interview with Evelyn before her death. Ian and Migs sat listening to the inspector's calm, matter-of-fact voice in disbelief. Evelyn had repeated her earlier statement that she had intended to kill Keith if she possibly could. To succeed in doing so was her last hope of putting paid to his road improvement scheme. By allowing Daphne to have the kitten, she obtained the means for getting Keith to the well head.

'At this point,' Inspector Govern said, 'Miss Bateman took the trouble to enlighten me as to the fact that, personally, she abhorred both cats and dogs which, when they got into her garden, broke her flowers and dug holes in the beds. She followed this statement by enlightening me further as to the detrimental effect Mr Aymes' plan would have on the part of her garden which she had set aside for the birds, butterflies and suchlike as well as some old fruit trees.'

'But it's a wilderness, Inspector!' Migs broke in. 'Preserving it cannot be worth the cost of a life!'

'Three lives,' Govern reminded her, adding that Evelyn had expressed deep regret that she had been obliged to kill three other people – as well as having intended to kill Mr Aymes.

Ian turned to the inspector.

'I know she said she'd killed them, but how could she possibly have done so? Take Caroline Coleman for a start. Surely the coroner's verdict was food poisoning?'

Govern nodded.

'But Mrs Coleman was not the first on Miss Bateman's list of victims. It was over a year ago when Mr Aymes discovered that Miss Bateman did not own that corner of her garden; that it had been leased to her aunt a generation earlier by Frank Dodd's father. Aymes realized then he could get rid of that tiresome corner of the lane, widen it and eliminate the flooding if he purchased the land from the farmer down the road, Frank Dodd. He promptly put in an offer greatly exceeding the real value. Mr Dodd told his wife, who told Miss Bateman of Mr Aymes' offer; she also told her that they were in dire need of money and would almost certainly sell.'

The inspector paused to glance down at his notes.

'That was when Miss Bateman decided she must act. It was arson and not murder she had in mind at that stage. She knew of a barn fire over the far side of Ferrybridge and that the insurance company had paid the farmer in full for the loss . . .'

'That was before we came to live here,' Ian said. 'So it was Evelyn who set fire to Frank's barn, unaware, I imagine, that Jack was in the loft.'

'Exactly! She liked young Jack who often did small tasks for her which she couldn't manage herself. After tossing in a couple of matches, she shut the barn doors so no one would realize a fire was building up inside and put it out before sufficient damage was done.'

'But her plan went a little wrong,' Ian said thoughtfully as he refilled the inspector's tea cup.

'The Dodds did get the insurance money,' the detective acknowledged, 'but it didn't clear all their debts and they agreed to sell the piece of land Mr Aymes wanted if his plan were to go ahead. Miss Bateman considered she had no alternative then but to resort to murder.'

'But why on earth dispatch poor Caroline?' Migs questioned. 'Why not Keith, whose plan it was?'

'I asked the same question,' Govern replied. 'Miss Bateman's reasons made sense: one, that she had no ready means of killing Mr Aymes in a manner which would make his death look like an accident; and two, that she did have a more or less foolproof way of killing Mrs Coleman who intended to vote for the proposal.'

'And foolproof it was!' Ian broke in. 'The coroner's verdict was misadventure, wasn't it?'

Inspector Govern nodded.

'Knowing Mrs Coleman had some extremely poisonous Hemlock Water Dropwort growing in her garden and that it was often mistaken by the uninformed for common parsnips to the partaker's detriment, Miss Bateman showed the poor lady how to make soup of it. It's deadly poisonous as you probably know. Miss Bateman had learned this from the barrister she worked for, Mr Headington-Lock, Q.C. He had once defended a case dealing with just such a poisoning.'

'It sounds so . . . so cold-blooded,' Migs whispered. 'To kill someone in so horrible a fashion – just to prevent them voting for something you don't want! She has to have been mad!'

'She was sane enough when, despite the lawyer's advice, she confessed to killing Wing Commander Proctor and the Reverend Hollywell for the same reason,' the inspector said wryly. 'Her voice was quite steady although I have to say, she did seem suddenly to have aged. I thought perhaps she was not feeling very well and would like a break, a cup of tea. But she refused both, thanked me for my consideration and proceeded to explain how she, a frail eighty-one year old, had managed to tip the Wing Commander's chair off the landing stage into the lake – and without detection.'

He paused while Migs went upstairs to ascertain that Dougal had not yet woken from his afternoon nap and Ian went out to see that the new baby was still safely tucked up in the pram under the apple tree. When they returned, the inspector resumed his account.

'I think you might call the Wing Commander's death an opportunist murder,' he said. 'Miss Bateman had discovered that after the count of votes at the last Road Meeting, she was again out-numbered and must despatch another person who had voted "for" the scheme. She'd not made up her mind who it must be, when, on her way one morning to pick the blackberries she knew to be plentiful along the footpath on the far side of Millers Lake, she saw Mrs Proctor going into her house. Looking down to the lake, she also saw Wing Comander Proctor fishing.'

'From the landing stage,' Ian said. The inspector nodded.

'Apparently, there was no one about. Miss Bateman said it took her only a moment to slip off the road down to the lake where she knew she would be hidden from the view of anyone passing by.

'Jack Dodd was also fishing on the lake – illegally as it happened – opposite the landing stage. He was too far away to see if it was a man or a woman approaching the Wing Commander. He didn't hear Evelyn when she told the unfortunate man that his wife had been taken ill and had asked her to push him back to the house.'

At this point in his account, Inspector Govern gave a brief smile.

'One has to appreciate Miss Bateman's next caustic comment. She told me that the Wing Commander wasn't nearly so much concerned for his wife's health as for the fact that his fishing had been interrupted! It was a simple matter for her to let off the brake and instead of pulling the chair backwards, she pushed it forward so that one wheel went over the edge of the landing stage and the chair tipped into the water. It had made a fearful noise, she said, but luck was with her and she was able to make her way back to the road and continue on past Mr Lavery's cottage where she proceeded to pick the blackberries.'

'If Jack had recognized her—' Ian began but Migs interrupted him.

'Evelyn would have been apprehended a great deal sooner, and Robert would not have been killed!' she said.

'But Jack didn't even suspect her!' Inspector Govern said. 'I did question his movements at the time but he produced a reasonable alibi. Anyway, the Wing Commander's passing equalled the voting at the next Road Meeting, so the motion would not have been carried had Mr Aymes not co-opted Ellen to his way of thinking. Once again Miss Bateman felt obliged – as she put it – to remove another of the "for" voters.'

'The Reverend Hollywell,' Ian broke in. 'But the post mortem revealed he died of suffocation. How could Evelyn possibly have smothered him? He was quite a large man.'

'Because,' the inspector said with a sigh, 'she used aconite, which she gave him, telling him it was her elderberry wine.'

'Aconite? I'm not familiar with it!' Ian said,

'You may know it as monkshood,' Govern replied. 'Miss Bateman said she had learned about it from watching one of those *Midsomer Murders* stories on television last year. Basically, it paralyzes the victim almost immediately, it numbs the mouth and the alimentary canal with an excruciating burning sensation. Since the victim can't breathe, it gives the appearance of suffocation. It's undetectable by a pathologist as the only post mortem signs are those of asphyxia.'

'That's horrible!' Migs said with a shudder. 'Evelyn just has to have been insane.'

'It takes a very clear mind to plan such a murder without it being detected,' Govern said wryly.

'Yes, but to carry it out and see someone you knew – had known for years – die in agony—' Migs argued.

'Since Evelyn is no longer with us, we'll never know the answer, will we?' Ian broke in. 'Personally, I'm inclined to agree with the inspector, Migs. There wasn't even a motive such as revenge. She may not have liked Proctor or had a lot of time for Caroline, but she respected Robert.'

'Be that as it may, Miss Bateman would have remained undetected in each case had she not failed to finish off Mr Aymes!' the inspector reminded them. 'But to continue, Miss Bateman knew Mrs Hollywell would be away all day on a W.I. outing. She also knew that it would not seem particularly strange to any chance visitor to find the front door locked despite the fact that her husband usually kept it open as if it were a church – pretentious, Miss Bateman said. However, he did lock up if he was not accessible.'

At this point in his account, the inspector was obliged to wait whilst Migs went upstairs to fetch Dougal who had woken from his nap. When she had brought him downstairs and settled him happily with a box of toys in his playpen, Govern picked up where he had left off.

'Miss Bateman went up to Ivy Lodge that morning after Mrs Hollywell had left in the coach for London. She went to the house unseen and the vicar let her in. She pretended to have forgotten that his wife was out but insisted that, nevertheless, he taste the elderberry wine she had brought for Mrs Hollywell. It was around eleven o'clock. She knew from the television murder play how long it would take for the unfortunate man to die, and as the death might not be immediate and someone might call or telephone him, she took the receiver off its rest and left the house, taking the empty glass and bottle with her. She also locked the front door, and making absolutely certain no one was about to see her, she returned home.'

He paused once more when Migs said she must put the casserole she had prepared after breakfast in the oven. Having given Dougal the mug of orange juice he was demanding, she rejoined Ian and the inspector.

'It was almost dark when Miss Bateman returned to Ivy Lodge, carrying a new, unopened bottle of her elderberry wine with her. This time she didn't mind whether she was seen or not. She knew the pathologist would discover in due course that the vicar had died much earlier and since she was not seen to go into the house, there was no reason why she or anyone else would be suspected of murder. But first she had to get into the house before the vicar's body was found in order to put the telephone back on its rest and leave the door unlocked again.'

'What if someone had telephoned Mr Hollywell during her absence and found it out of order?' Migs asked.

The inspector shook his head.

'The old lady must have thought of that, too. A caller would have heard an engaged signal, not an out of order one until it had been reported to the engineers. Even then, it would be unlikely that a B.T. engineer would have turned up to repair the supposed damage before Miss Bateman returned. As it was, she replaced the receiver when she went into the house with young Jack. He was on his way to Rogan Farm and, luckily for her, was at the road junction just when she needed an accomplice – someone to find the door *unlocked* and the phone on its rest.

'By the time she called to Jack for help, all was as normal.'

At this point in her confession, the inspector said, he had noted a faint film of perspiration on Evelyn's face and decided that the interview had gone on quite long enough. Evelyn, however, would have none of it.

'Miss Bateman refused to have a rest when I suggested it,' he said now. 'She wished to complete her confession. She drew a deep breath, clasped her hands tightly together and said in a matter-of-fact voice that the voting was once again equalized by the elimination of the Reverend Hollywell's vote; but unfortunately, fate was not on her side. Mr Aymes all but sealed his own fate when he announced that as chairman, he had a casting vote and intended to use it. Miss Bateman was obliged, therefore, to commit what she hoped and prayed would be her last murder.'

The inspector paused at this moment, almost as if he were regretting what he must now say. When he began talking again, his voice was sombre.

'It was after that meeting that Miss Bateman conceived the idea of pushing Mr Aymes down the old well. She knew she couldn't force him into it without good reason for him to be near enough for her to push him in. So she let Miss Daphne have her kitten. Two days before Miss Daphne thought it was lost, but Miss Batemen had got it safely imprisoned in a chicken coop at the top of the garden. After starving it overnight, she tied it up in an old shoe bag and lowered it down the well in the very early morning. She knew that Mr Aymes jogged down the lane every day whatever the weather and that at this time of year, he passed her house at five minutes past seven returning thirty minutes later. She described him as a most methodical man, totally dependable which had, doubtless, helped him to the success he now enjoyed. Far from wishing him dead because she didn't like him, she clearly had a certain degree of admiration for him.'

Inspector Govern's mobile phone interrupted his account. It was Sergeant Beck telling him that he was urgently needed back at the station. Promising to call in again in a few days' time, he said his farewells and left Ian and Migs to talk things over.

'I still don't understand why events happened as they did,' Migs said as they sat down to lunch, Dougal in his highchair and, as always, banging his spoon on the tray when his mother didn't serve him quickly enough. It always made Ian smile and, to tease Migs, he swore he'd teach Dougal how to chant '*Why . . . are . . . we . . . wait . . . ing?*' But now, neither of them smiled. 'Why didn't Evelyn kill Keith first? It was his scheme, and if she had succeeded, there'd have been no need to kill anyone else.'

'Inspector Govern asked her that very question,' Ian replied. 'Her answer was simple – if Keith had been killed, there would have been a hunt for a motive and everyone in the lane knew of her strongly-voiced objections to his plan. A weak motive, I accept, but not obviously so in Evelyn's eyes. I must go up there after lunch and see how Keith is.'

But Migs' mind was not on Keith but on Evelyn who, despite all that had been said to her detriment, deserved some pity. She had left her pretty cottage and beautiful garden and was never coming back; to see the carpet of snowdrops and crocuses; if her fuschia cuttings had survived the frost; if her spring bulbs were visible. Her eyes filled suddenly with tears. Seeing them, Ian put his arms round her.

'Darling, if I'm thinking what I think you are thinking, you mustn't feel sorry for Evelyn. She was an old lady with a weak heart and a great many people would say she was exceptionally evil. One thing is perfectly clear, she was not stupid. She must have known the risks she was taking . . . nothing less than

Broadmoor or prison if, as did happen, she was caught in her last act of murder.'

Migs wiped her eyes and sniffed audibly.

'All the same, she did look after Daphne and that must have driven her mad at times. Thank God Betty wants to adopt Daphne. She told Evelyn she would if anything ever happened to her. And you, Ian, you used to enjoy those evenings when Evelyn was persuaded to come in for a cup of tea or a glass of sherry, both of you expounding your views on the latest political crisis or scandal.'

'Well, you've got to remember her father was headmaster of a public school, and was fanatically strict with his two daughters. At least, that's what I gathered when Evelyn was telling me about her upbringing. He'd actually wanted sons to continue the family name and Evelyn felt it her duty to try to make up for the fact that she had been born female instead of male. Anyway, darling, I'd better start getting a precis of the details Inspector Govern gave us from my tape recorder on to the computer. Then I can run off enough copies to give one to everyone in the lane. I suggest you give Sarah a ring and ask them to come down for supper this evening. Then we can discuss it – get their views.'

The copies were ready for distribution by the time Nigel and Sarah arrived. Whilst Ian was pouring glasses of white wine for the girls and beers for himself and Nigel, their two visitors sat reading with incredulity the pages he had handed to them. They gave simultaneous gasps of astonishment and disbelief. Nigel spoke first.

'Nasty business! I suppose we should be grateful Evelyn's death means there won't be a murder trial with all the attendant publicity. If word gets out about all this – and I don't doubt it will – we're going to have very little peace once the tabloids get hold of it. They'll have a field day. I suppose you and I had better pop in and have a bit of a chat with Jill and Keith on our way home. He must be pretty shaken, poor devil! Jill, too, come to that. How would you be feeling, my loved one, if I had been next on the death list?'

'Nigel, don't joke, darling. I know it's your way of dealing with, well, with things like this, but if there'd been even a chance

Evelyn would have wanted to kill you in some ghastly fashion, I just don't know how I could cope with it.'

Nigel drew her closer and planted a noisy kiss on her forehead.

'I do believe you really love me!' he said. 'Anyway, by the sound of it, we were never in danger. We were *against* Keith's plan, not *for* it. Which brings me to Keith's near demise. Did Evelyn say why she wanted him out of the way?'

Sarah regarded him with mock reproach.

'No memory, have you? Think of the last Road Meeting. Think of our newly, self-elected chairman. Think of Keith's announcement that, and I quote: "As chairman I have a casting vote . . .". Ah, now I see you do remember.'

Nigel shook his head, and despite the seriousness of the discussion, a half smile lingered at the corners of his mouth.

'What a hell of a moment that must have been for our Evelyn!' he said. 'Three down and now, with victory in sight, another one to go. I can almost feel sorry for her.'

Despite herself, Sarah, too, smiled.

'Well, I don't!' she said. 'I feel sorry for Keith. It can't have been very pleasant at the bottom of a well wondering if you were about to drown! Cold, too!'

'As will your supper be if we don't go and eat right now,' Migs said.

At any other time, she might have threatened dire consequences if Ian or her two good friends allowed her cooking to be spoilt; but in the circumstances, threat of death seemed just a little too near the bone.

Nineteen

I t was nearly six months before the press decided their readers had lost interest in the Millers Lane murders. For once, the residents were totally united in their desire to keep the reporters out of their homes and gardens and everyone had agreed at an emergency Road Meeting to have a gate installed at the junction of the lane and the main road. Needless to say, Keith shouldered most of the cost although those who could had contributed. The residents, postman, sewage disposal and refuse collectors were given keys. Everyone found it a bit tiresome having to get out of their vehicles to lock and unlock the gate but at least it kept the road private and the press out. There was shortly to be another Road Meeting to discuss the possibility of leaving the gate open in future.

Not everyone suffered from the publicity. Andrew Lavery's literary agent had suggested he quickly produce a new book to be titled *Murder in Killer's Lane*. He'd written it on disc in a month and, with the new digital printing, the book was on sale within two months, the blurb and publicity release referring unashamedly to the fact that he was a resident of Millers Lane where the murders had taken place. It had rocketed into the best-seller lists during which time no other resident in the lane other than the Aymes had spoken to him, resenting as they did the renewed press interest in the locality.

Betty Hollywell decided to remain in Ivy Lodge with her recently widowed sister who had come to live with her. As Evelyn's executor she had plenty to keep her occupied. Moreover, with social services' complete agreement, she 'adopted'

Daphne, who she now looked on as the daughter she'd always wanted and never had. Daphne showed no sign whatever of missing Evelyn or of wanting to return to Rose Cottage. She seemed perfectly content living with Betty, continuing with weekly visits to the day care centre and, when Migs would allow her, pushing the pram up and down the road until Polly, the Peters' new baby girl, was asleep.

Her vocabulary still mainly consisted of nursery rhymes but Betty was teaching her to recite some simple prayers. At their conclusion, she was quite happy to pray for the souls of everyone alive or dead that she knew, including herself, but for some inexplicable reason, she always excluded Evelyn. Betty decided that either Evelyn had been a little too strict with her or else Daphne had somehow picked up vibes from people's condemnation of her sister, however muted they had been. Betty positively glowed with pleasure at the frequent expressions of praise she received for her charitable care of the handicapped woman.

Nevertheless, some of the kudos she might have received went elsewhere. Keith Aymes, who could have been forgiven for resenting Daphne because of her relationship to his intended murderess, had contributed generously to a trust fund he was overseeing for her. Its aim was to pay the fees of an American specialist in brain disorders, her fare to the States, her hospital fees, aftercare, and the inordinately high fees of the Egyptian surgeon who might be called on to operate on her. Meanwhile, Betty told Ellen that an initial visit to the English specialist had thrown up the suspicion that Daphne's escape back to childhood in her adolescence might possibly be reversible.

'Jolly decent of Keith!' was Nigel's comment when Sarah told him this latest lane rumour.

'Doesn't surprise me one bit,' was Ellen's trenchant reply when asked her opinion. 'Mr Aymes is a fine, generous man as Ray will bear me out.'

Ellen was now working almost exclusively for the Aymes and occasionally for Migs. She doted on Dougal who returned her affection and she used every possible excuse for nursing little Polly. She refused to give up any of her time with the little ones to 'do' for the new owners of The Mill House and Rose Cottage, which had been sold to Graham and Tania Lloyd, the new young practice doctor and his wife. The deeds did not, of course, include the quarter acre of the garden which Frank Dodd had sold to Keith.

Coming as the Lloyds did from Scotland, neither the doctor nor his wife had had prior knowledge of the murderous background of the previous owner of the cottage. They had paid a brief visit to it in the presence of a tight-lipped estate agent before putting in an offer and hurrying back to Scotland to sell their flat. They had been shocked when Ellen, delighting in the chance to gossip soon after they had moved in, enlightened them as to Evelyn's grim past. Since they could not afford the time or the money to move again, they had settled down and made the best of it, compensated by the knowledge that they had acquired a very attractive, desirable home at a remarkably low price. The money from the sale of Evelyn's cottage had been put in a second trust for Daphne designed to pay Betty Hollywell a reasonable weekly sum for Daphne's keep.

The Dodds had decided to sell up and retire – or partly so. One of the labourers' cottages on Rogan Farm was becoming vacant and George Baldwin, their neighbouring farmer, offered to sell it to Frank in return for relief milking. Although it had only one room up and one down, it did have a small kitchen and bathroom, and more important to Frank, a half acre of ground at the rear where he would be able to keep some chickens and ducks. Surprising everyone and upsetting his devoted mother, Jack joined the navy, mostly 'to see the rest of the world', Jack told his parents, but privately he liked the idea of 'a girl in every port'. Brenda Baldwin, who had always had a soft spot for Jack, told him he might keep his precious motorbike in one of the farm sheds, and when he came home on leave, he could use their spare room.

Frank then faced the unhappy task of selling his much loved cows, but he recovered after a few weeks when, with the money from the sale of the farm, his stock and the Rose Cottage land, he realized he was at last well and truly out of debt. They even had money in the bank to buy new curtains and carpets ready for their removal in the autumn to Rogan Farm cottage and to pay for a package holiday to Holland next spring where Mary had always wanted to go to see the tulips.

Keith and Jill, ignoring the influx of reporters and sightseers, continued with their plans to modernize the Manor House and renovate it to its former magnificence. They installed under-floor heating in every room; replaced the decrepit old septic tank with the latest Klargester; turned the Brigadier's dressing room into a third bathroom, built a squash court and exercise centre where the old courtyard had been.

Plans were completed for the improvements to Millers Lane and work had begun on digging the trench for the pipes and culvert. So far no one had been inconvenienced by the digging but there had been complaints from residents about the dust the lorries and machines threw up when they were coming and going; as, too, about the difficulty in passing large vehicles on the narrow lane. As Keith said to Jill, 'They can't have it both ways. Once we've widened the lane, there'll be plenty of room to pass!'

The diggers were at work on the third morning after commencement when Keith decided to take a day off work and inspect operations. Following a game of squash with Andrew Lavery and a quick sauna, he walked over to the corner of the lane where the men were working. They had already excavated a trench across the road, removed the hedge bordering what had been Rose Cottage garden and had started on the undergrowth. The digger was, however, at a standstill.

'Problems?' Keith asked the foreman, Bill, who was carrying a rusty old box which was dripping water.

'Morning, Mr Aymes,' he said, laying the heavy box on the ground. 'I was just about to bring this over to you at the house. Sid, Mike and me have all had a go at opening them rusty iron strappings but short of busting the padlocks, the lid won't budge.' He frowned as he stood scratching his head. 'It isn't empty and Sid didn't like to knock it open with the digger in case what's inside is valuable.'

Keith surveyed the small rectangular chest with interest. Not long ago, he'd seen one just like it on the *Antiques Road Show* and had been surprised to hear it would fetch at least over a thousand pounds at auction.

181

'Where was it, Bill?' he enquired as he, too, tried unsuccessfully to break open the lid.

'Bottom of the well, sir!' the foreman answered, unaware that it was not long ago that Keith had nearly drowned in it. 'First thing this morning, we pumped out the water at the bottom – it ran into the stream at the bottom of Siskins like you said. Anyroad, Sid moved in with his digger and along with the bricks and muck out comes this box. Must be pretty strong, sir, for all it's rusted so bad.'

'I doubt there's anything of value in it, but you were quite right not to break it open. Bring it down to my house, Bill. I've a load of tools in my workshop which should do the job.'

The foreman wanted to stay and watch whilst Keith tried a few minutes later to prise open the padlocks with a jemmy, but aware that enough time had been wasted, he sent the man back to work. Which was just as well, he told himself when he'd finally succeeded in his task. The box was obviously extremely old – the kind of container people used when travelling to hot, humid climates where damp and rapacious insects would have penetrated leather or wood and ruined the contents. His grandfather had a similar one which he'd brought back from a posting to East Africa.

As he raised the lid, for the briefest of moments, Keith failed to identify what was contained in the perished rubber sheeting inside. Then with a jolt of surprise mingled with horror, he recognized the unmistakeable skeleton of a tiny child – an infant, partially wrapped in a piece of green oilskin. Following his immediate inclination, he quickly closed the lid and sat down heavily at his workbench while he considered what he had found and what he should now do.

The horrifying murders of Caroline Coleman, Cecil Proctor and the vicar sprang to mind, but he disclaimed them at once as having no relevance. This skeleton must be at least a hundred years old judging by the condition of the tin box in which it had been hidden before being thrown down the well.

Could it be connected somehow to the unlucky Horsborough family? Rose Cottage was originally part of Millers Farm and that had been part of the Horsborough estate. Ellen's stories of the family curse, the hauntings, the ghosts might be relevant after all. One thing was unarguable, the infant was either drowned or hidden after death, and in either case, it must have been murdered. The thought of yet another such discovery in Millers Lane was unbearable, he decided, with all its attendant police, media and morbid members of the public.

Unwilling to consult Jill, yet wishing to talk to someone else about his gruesome find, Keith carried the box up the road to Pear Tree Cottage where he knew Andrew would be in his study working away at his computer. Declining the proffered drink, Keith told his neighbour how the digger driver had unearthed the box, and his discovery of the skeleton. He persuaded Andrew to lift the heavy lid and look at the contents.

Andrew was duly shocked but at the same time immensely interested.

'Can't think why I invent my fictitious horrors when this kind of thing goes on under our noses,' he said. 'Have you told the police?'

Keith shook his head.

'I've come to talk things over with you first, Andrew. The thing is, do you think I *have* to report it? I mean, just think what will erupt if I do so. The lives of every one of us will be made a complete misery all over again and we've only just recovered from the last lot.'

Somewhat to Keith's surprise, Andrew was grinning.

'Come to the wrong person, old fellow! I made the best part of 200 grand from *Murder in Killer's Lane*; and it looks as if I'm going to sell film rights.'

'Good God!' Keith exclaimed. 'We aren't going to have film crews down here, are we?'

Andrew stopped smiling and patted Keith reassuringly on the shoulder.

'Don't worry, I'll make it conditional they don't come near here – that is, if I really can flog the rights. I don't want police and press down here any more than you do. Perdita, that georgeous redhead I was bedding, was too scared to come near the place after the last debacle and went off and found herself another bloke!'

He stopped talking, his expression serious now as he took another look at the tiny skeleton.

'Someone getting rid of an unwanted offspring, I suppose. Couldn't have been old Evelyn's, could it? She was dead against you getting hold of that bit of land.'

Keith looked thoughtful.

'That possibility has crossed my mind. I might pop in when I leave here and ask Betty if there was anything at all amongst Evelyn's papers which could throw some light on this. But with the best will in the world, I simply can't envisage our Miss Bateman having a fling, can you?' He shook his head adding, 'Be honest, Andrew, do you think it would be wrong – immoral, if you like – to simply forget about this? I mean, you and I are the only ones who have seen inside that box. We could shove it on a dump somewhere – bury what's inside, and no one would be any the wiser.'

Andrew crossed the room and went back to sit behind his desk. He picked up a pencil and absent-mindedly began to chew the end.

'I don't think I'd get away with that solution in one of my books,' he said after a minute or two. 'My editor would want all the loose ends tied up. I mean, you and I would be guilty of concealing evidence or something of the sort. The trouble is, we're not dealing with characters in one of my books, are we? This has to have been a murder, don't you agree? What about the real people who were involved last time? Colin, who lost his wife; Betty and Jane Proctor who lost their husbands; the Dodds, even, whose son might have been burnt to death. I suppose that bit of gruesome history would all be dug up again!'

He was silent for a moment or two, then glancing once more at the rusty old box he turned back to look at Keith.

'What say we ask them, Keith? Not the people who've moved in since the murders, but all the others. You could call an emergency meeting and put the question of what we should do to the vote. Wouldn't that be in keeping with the democratic principles our Road Committee enjoys?'

Keith ran his hands through his hair in a gesture of uncertainty.

'You honestly think we'd get everyone to agree? Not very likely, Andrew. Still, we could try, I suppose. Shift the responsibility. Let's go up to the King's Head for a drink,' he suggested. 'We can stop at Ivy Lodge on the way while I have a quick word with Betty. That OK with you?'

Both men were hoping the alcohol would obliterate their shared feelings of anxiety and disquiet.

On his return home Keith motioned his wife into one of the chairs in the drawing room. The many bracelets Jill always wore jangled as she sat down.

She looked extremely glamorous in her newly purchased Betty Barclay trousers and Yves St Laurent shirt, but her face did not sparkle as she said curiously, 'What *is* going on, darling? All this mystery for heaven's sake! It's been going on ever since you went down to the excavations this morning.'

'Too right it has. I've put off telling you but I am about to convene an emergency Road Meeting for tomorrow,' Keith replied, 'so I want to forewarn you.'

'Forewarn me!' Jill echoed uneasily. It was very seldom she saw Keith in such a sombre mood. He was nearly always good humoured, cheerful, jovial, as well as elated by some new project he had envisaged. Even on that dreadful occasion when Evelyn had tried to kill him, by the following day he was back to normal. 'And why the emergency meeting?' she added.

Whilst Keith related the morning's events, for once Jill remained silent.

'So we've decided to ask everyone else's views,' he concluded. 'I'll run off invites on the computer and get them delivered tonight. I've chewed it over with Andrew and he agrees with me that it's probably the best thing we can do.'

Horrified by Keith's revelations, Jill made no demur.

Later that same evening Ian read for the second time the letter which the Aymes' Filipino houseman had delivered whilst they were having supper.

Dear Residents,
    Something of the utmost importance has arisen which concerns you and other long-standing residents of Millers

Lane. This matter is extremely urgent and I have therefore convened an emergency Road Meeting for tomorrow evening here at the Manor at 7 p.m. If you have already made other plans, may I ask you to postpone them in view of the prime necessity for you to attend the meeting. I cannot emphasize strongly enough that your presence is essential.

Yours, Keith.

'An emergency meeting! Whatever for?' Migs echoed Jill's words as Ian read out the notification.

'Sounds serious!' Ian said as he promised to catch an early train home in order to attend. 'You must co-opt one of the village mums to take care of Dougal and Polly, darling, as presumably Ellen and Ray will be expected to go to the meeting, too.'

Later that evening, Sarah dropped by to speculate with Migs as to the mystery behind Keith's letter.

'I'm intrigued, aren't you, Migs?' she said as she helped her with her evening task of wrapping and boxing the baskets of Cox's apples from the tree in the garden. 'I rang Jill and asked her but she wouldn't say a word, Nigel thinks that the fact that Keith refers specifically to "long-standing residents" means the "emergency" must have something to do with the murders.'

Migs nodded.

'Ian thinks the same. He went to have a look at the roadworks earlier and said they'd excavated the trench as far as Rose Cottage and had obviously been pumping water out of the well as everywhere was soaking wet. The workmen had bulldozed the hedge and that big digger thing was parked just by the well. I wonder if there have been problems with the water table or some such, and Keith is going to ask for bigger contributions from us?'

'I don't think he would bother to consult us if that was the case. I think he'd simply have told the men to get on with the job whatever the cost. What I don't understand is why our presence is "essential" and why he has specified the "long-standing residents" and not that new family who bought the Proctors' place or the Lloyds in Rose Cottage. After all, they must be suffering with the machines digging at the end of their garden. I suppose we'll just have to wait and see!'

The following evening Jill Aymes prepared her large conservatory for the evening's Road Meeting. With its comfortable basket chairs and bamboo tables, this new addition to the house was the most convenient room for such an occasion, besides which, it had only recently been decorated and furnished and despite the gravity of the occasion she was anxious to show it off. Everything was in perfect order, she thought as suddenly the telephone rang. She picked up her cordless and a moment later handed it to Keith.

'For you, darling. It's Betty Hollywell! She won't say what she wants – only that she must talk to you!' she whispered, covering the mouthpiece so Betty couldn't hear her. Keith took the phone.

Curious to know what Betty could possibly want to talk to her husband about, Jill stood watching him as he listened attentively to the voice on the other end of the line. The muscles of his face tightened suddenly and she heard the sharp intake of his breath.

'I'll come and pick it up right away, if that's not inconvenient,' he said. 'I'll be with you in two minutes, Betty. OK?'

Before Jill could ask him what Betty had discovered, Keith had pulled on a jersey and was on his way down the drive to Ivy Lodge.

Twenty

O nly now, an hour before the meeting was to convene, did Keith tell his wife about the contents of the iron box. Jill was deeply shocked.

'So that's what all the mysterious goings-on have been about!' she said. Not only had Keith disappeared the previous day on a prolonged visit to Andrew Lavery but then there'd been the phone call from Betty, Keith's rush from the house to collect something from her, and his refusing to reveal what it was. All day, he'd been closeted in his study, making photocopies was all he was prepared to tell her at lunch.

Now, he thought as he uncorked the red wine and put a bottle of white in an ice bucket to cool before the lane residents arrived, a good strong drink or two might be badly needed.

'I don't think I should discuss this new problem with you, darling. If everyone hears developments together, nobody can say afterwards that I'd put you under undue pressure when I call for a vote. Be patient a bit longer, honey. You'll know it all soon enough.'

As usual, Migs and Ian sat in a small group with Nigel and Sarah. Having left her sister to look after Daphne whilst she was at the meeting, Betty Hollywell sat beside Mary and Frank Dodd. Andrew Lavery, Colin Coleman and Jill sat in another group whilst Ellen and Ray sat side by side near the window. Having made sure everyone had a glass in their hand, Keith stood up at one end of the room and opened the meeting.

'I know you've all been wondering what this is about,' he said, 'and I'm afraid what I have to tell you is not very pleasant, to say the least. However, I've given the matter a great deal of thought

188

and realize that you have as much right as I to know all the facts before a decision is made as to what must be done.'

He proceeded to describe how his workmen had unearthed the iron box at the bottom of the newly dismantled well in Rose Cottage garden; how he had removed it to his workshop simply in order to find a suitable implement with which to open it, and to his horror, discovered the skeleton of a baby inside. There were audible gasps from everyone in the room. Husbands took their wives hands. Only Betty Hollywell did not look surprised.

'I expect, like me, you are now wondering who murdered this child – as surely it was murdered seeing the grave it was given. Like me, you have all had to live through the last ghastly year when three murders were committed by Evelyn Bateman under our very noses. Perhaps, like me, you have all at one time or another felt guilt for those murders, wondering if there might have been some way you could have prevented them. Like me, you have undoubtedly reached the conclusion that Evelyn Bateman must have been insane to have carried out such evil deeds for so paltry a motive – namely, to preserve her precious piece of garden. Only insanity seemed to fit the case. Now, however, there is a more fitting missing piece to the puzzle. Jill, darling, would you hand these round? There should be a copy for everyone. If you would all be good enough to read your copy silently, we will then follow up with the discussion for which I asked you all to come here tonight.'

The photocopies were of a letter, handwritten in beautiful italic script; the creased pages of the original letter were clearly showing, indicating the number of times it had been read and refolded. It was dated 10th April, 1952 and was addressed to Evelyn.

My dear child,
I cannot begin to tell you what an overwhelming relief it was to me to receive your last letter. I do not have to tell you that I was beside myself with worry as to how I was going to keep Daphne's condition from your father.
As you know, he has set his heart upon his promotion

from Deputy Head here to the vacant post of Headmaster of Kingsland College. It has been a difficult time for him on the short list as he is waiting for their governors' decision. I thank God that Daphne's situation can no longer jeopardize the outcome. I honestly believe that were he rejected for such a reason, he would never recover from the disgrace.

Thanks be to God that can no longer happen; nor, indeed, need the taint of scandal threaten your precious job. I cannot bear to think that after all your hard work, you might have faced dismissal merely by being so closely related to disgrace – and for that to have happened when none of this was your fault just when Mr Headington-Lock had spoken of your promotion.

No, my dear, such a dreadful outcome is now mercifully behind us and nothing need be said to your father other than that poor Daphne has been recuperating from a bout of influenza under your care at Rose Cottage. Not a day goes by when he doesn't demand she returns home – and I trust now she may do so as soon as she has recovered her strength.

I can find it in my heart to forgive Daphne since at the tender age of fifteen, she was probably too innocent to realize how that dreadful French boy she met last summer would take advantage of her. We shall never holiday in Cornwall again. Now Daphne can return to her studies next term. Please tell her that I shall not be angry with her when she comes home. I think the least said now will be the best for everyone.

I cannot thank you enough, my dear daughter, for providing a place of concealment for Daphne and for arranging for the baby to be safely adopted. Now, mercifully, we can put the whole unfortunate affair behind us. I am mindful of Daphne's impossible desire to keep the child and trust she will soon recover her health and spirits.

Thank you, dearest Evelyn, for your constant love and support and may God bless you and keep you safe.

From Your Loving Mother.

For several minutes, no one spoke. Then Sarah asked, 'Was that letter in the tin box, Keith? Surely after so long it would have disintegrated?'

It was Betty Hollywell, not Keith, who replied.

'I found it in Evelyn's desk when I cleared it after she died,' she said. 'It was amongst a bundle of letters marked "Mother" which I was reluctant to open until Keith asked me to do so.'

'But surely—'

'I told Betty she *must* go through every one of Evelyn's papers in the hope of finding a clue as to what was in the box.' Keith broke in. 'We couldn't ask Evelyn's permission to open her personal letters, and Daphne – well, you all know her state of mind. I thought, you see – and rightly as it has turned out – that there might be an explanation for what was clearly another murder – infanticide, I think it's called.'

'So the baby was Daphne's and Evelyn *killed* it?' Migs said in a shocked voice.

'We must suppose so. It's most unlikely that there were two babies and one was adopted and this one was put in the well. One imagines Evelyn must have made sure it didn't survive after the birth and quietly disposed of it, otherwise why should she have told her mother that it was adopted? I don't suppose she imagined the well would ever be emptied, let alone demolished.'

'But why not let the baby be adopted?' Sarah asked.

'Daphne was only fifteen – very much a minor,' Betty said quietly. 'A legal adoption would have required papers to be signed, quite probably by her parents. One must remember, fifty years ago society was a great deal stricter where morality was concerned. Illegitimate children were tainted with a disgrace that lasted their lifetime, and unmarried mothers were more often than not disowned by their families as well as society. If Daphne's baby had lived, the consequences for Evelyn as well as for Daphne would have been dire, and it's highly unlikely their father would ever have been given the headmastership of a big public school if it became known his daughter had given birth to an illegitimate baby.'

Betty Hollywell's voice was surprisingly clear, as she continued.

'I can well believe that Evelyn, too, might not have been given the chance to work for so prestigeous a barrister. As for Evelyn's parents, when I once complained to her that I thought Robert had been too harsh with one of his erring parishioners, she told me I did not know the meaning of the word; that her father had been a strict Victorian puritan for whom there was only right and wrong, no grey where excuses might be allowed, and that his punishments for even minor misdeeds were extreme.'

'So Evelyn killed Daphne's baby! And Daphne . . . ?'

Migs did not complete the question for she had already guessed the answer – the fifteen-year-old girl, desperate to keep her child, on being told it had died, had had a mental breakdown from which she had never recovered.

'According to Dr Grainger with whom I discussed Daphne last year,' Betty said, 'her medical records showed that she'd been placed in a mental institution at the age of sixteen which tallies with the facts we now know. Poor Daphne remained in the institution until 1999. As you know it was closed down and Evelyn gave her a home.'

Keith took the floor once more.

'We now come to the point of this meeting,' he said as everyone present turned to look at him. 'Its purpose is not just to inform you of these extraordinary discoveries but to ask you all to consider what we should do about them. We have two alternatives. We can report what we know to the police with all the known repercussions; or we can find an appropriate place to lay Daphne's baby to rest, destroy her mother's letter to Evelyn, and forget we found anything in that rusty old box.'

There were audible gasps as he paused. Appreciating how shocked everyone was, he turned to his wife.

'Jill will now go and make some coffee while you are all thinking what you consider we should do. I expect you appreciate that it must be voted by each of you if the decision is not to report this. If that were to be your joint wish, there can be no second vote nor change of heart. I myself will abide by what you all want.'

Ian took Migs' hand and held it tightly in his own. Nigel bent down to whisper something in Sarah's ear. Frank and Mary were conversing quietly together. Colin seemed to be having an argument with Andrew who kept shaking his head. After Jill returned and handed round cups of coffee to those who wanted it, Keith stood up again and lifted his hand for silence.

'Does anyone wish to make a comment?' he asked. 'I think it's very important we endeavour to reach agreement if we can.'

His face flushed, Colin stood up and looked round the gathering.

'I'm finding it hard to believe we are sitting here calmly listening to all this!' he said. 'What can have possessed you, Keith, even to think up this secrecy lark? It's certainly illegal. Frankly, I'm astonished to say the very least.'

To everyone's surprise, it was Andrew Lavery who now took the floor.

'I do realize how shocked you are, Colin. We all are. And I'm sure everyone here appreciates that Evelyn was never properly punished for the murders she committed, which included your late wife. But to keep silent now about this other murder we think Evelyn committed all those years ago is not to protect her; cannot benefit her, nor, as far as I can see from that letter, was it – or any of the other murders – done for her sake. She was protecting Daphne, her father and her mother. Obviously she was trying to stop Keith's plan for underground pipes and the culvert because she realized the well would have to be demolished and the box would be found. You will recall how hard we all found it to believe she had killed three people simply to preserve her bit of garden. Those poor souls she murdered were all voting for Keith's plan. She killed them not because she wanted them dead but to keep her sister's secret safe.'

For a moment, no one spoke. Andrew sat down. Colin sat silent now looking thoughtful.

Nigel said suddenly, 'One does tend to forget how old Evelyn was. Eighty-something, wasn't it? She belonged to a generation not far removed from the Victorians and respectability was everything. I imagine she was very frightened by the possibility of the past coming to light after so long. Maybe that fear was indeed a punishment of sorts for her, Colin?'

'I agree with Nigel!' Sarah spoke up. 'I think Evelyn must have been terribly afraid, not just of discovery in this life, but of what must happen to her in eternal life. She was a very regular church goer, you know, and I have heard her talk of hell and damnation as if she knew for certain they existed.'

To everyone's surprise, it was now Mary Dodd who spoke up.

'She did that!' she said. 'She once told our Jack that if he took the name of his God in vain many more times, Satan would claim him for hell fire sure as his name was Jack Dodd!'

There was yet another strained silence before Keith spoke again.

'I don't think we should consider Evelyn at this point. It is our lives that will be so adversely affected now if we call in Inspector Govern and start the wheels of the law grinding, as they most surely will. We have just been through months of pretty hellish interference from the media. Do we want to go through that again? I know you have decided to sell up, Colin, so you won't be affected as we will. Maybe you would care to abstain and allow the rest of us to reach a decision? Purely in your own interest, would your chances of a good sale not be much the better without any further slurs on the name of Millers Lane?'

Betty Hollywell stood up unexpectedly and in a voice that shook, she said, 'For Daphne's sake, I do beg you all to agree to a quiet burial for her poor baby. None of what has happened is her fault and although I know she is not an unhappy person, she has not been able to fulfil her real potential as have all of us. What Evelyn did, dreadful as it was, was to protect her. Shouldn't we as Christians do the same? I know Robert would wish it, and there is nothing whatever to be gained by anyone, ourselves or any other living person, by revealing the existence of this box and its contents. Wouldn't we all be kinder, nicer people if we pretended Keith had never opened it?'

This time, no one broke the silence until Keith asked for a show of hands. Colin abstained. Everyone else voted for Daphne's baby to be buried quietly and completely privately amongst the bluebells in Millers Wood.

In Ian and Migs' garden, the sun was shining with unseasonal warmth for October. Dougal in a patched pair of dungarees was playing happily in the sand pit. Polly was nearby in her playpen, which Ian had carried out on to the grass. Daphne was sprawled on a rug beside the baby singing one of her interminable nursery rhymes. Nigel and Sarah sat on opposite sides of the garden table, Paul and Susie Lloyd between them, Ian and Migs at either end. They had just finished a simple but enjoyable lunch at which they had drunk copious quantities of the Bordeaux wine Nigel had brought back from a day trip to France. Talk turned to the renovations the Lloyds were making to Rose Cottage.

'As soon as my new cooker arrives and I can actually produce a decent meal, you must all come round for supper,' Susie said. 'That is, if I can prise Paul out of the surgery for long enough to join in.'

'Susie accuses me of being a workaholic!' the young doctor said. 'Actually, I'm keeping well out of the way of the plumber, the carpenter, the painter – you name it! Not that they seem to do much work – it's all gossip. Seems our predecessor left a grizzly legacy.' Seeing the sudden exchange of looks amongst the others at the table, he added, 'Tales of poisons and drowning and arson – not to mention heart attacks and insanity and the curse of the Horsborough family. The men's stories are never ending.'

Susie sighed.

'I have to say, if we'd known one half of it before we'd put in our offer for the house, we'd have withdrawn it instantly!'

'Do you regret coming here then?' Migs asked. Susie smiled.

'Well, not really, although it is a bit spooky at times. If we didn't have such very nice neighbours, maybe we would be regretting it.'

'Flattery will get you nowhere – only a refill of your empty glass,' Ian said as he poured out the wine.

'All the same, did you never wish yourselves somewhere else when the murders were happening?' Susie asked Migs.

'I certainly did!' Ian broke in. 'I was worried out of my mind working away in London never knowing what might have happened to Migs and the kids until I got home at night. I'd have moved like a flash if Migs had agreed but she loves the cottage and – well, she was adamant. "Move? Over my dead body!" she said every time I suggested it.'

There was a sudden silence as Ian's voice died away. Everyone, including Migs, was thinking how simple it would have been for poor mad Evelyn to have despatched her had she voted differently.

'It's no laughing matter, folks!' Ian said as he caught Nigel's eye.

'Agreed, old chap, but "over my dead body" is such a platitude, isn't it?'

'It'll be over yours in a minute, Nigel!' Ian retorted, and as he threw a mock punch at his friend, everyone started to laugh.